SCONES AND SCOFFLAWS

SCONES AND SCOFFLAWS

A Cape May Cozy Mystery

JANE GORMAN

To Phyllis,
Thanks for your
love of cozies!
Jane Gorman

Blue Eagle Press

Paperback ISBN 978-0-9991100-4-1

❀ Created with Vellum

For my sister

1

Anna McGregor put her hands on her hips, narrowed her eyes and stared down her nemesis. She felt her pulse racing, her muscles tightening. To be fair, this wasn't exactly the kind of life-or-death situation she'd imagined being in when she became an anthropologist. But she wasn't an anthropologist anymore. To her, now, this met the criteria of life or death.

She could hear Luke in the attached bedroom and knew he could do this without her. But she was already asking too much of him as it was. She could at least take the first steps to make it easier for him. She had to find a way to shift this worn, dirty bathroom vanity.

She'd helped out with the repairs in other rooms in the old house, making whatever improvements she could on her own. The rooms on the second floor were now perfect. She just needed to get these last few rooms on the third floor finished without disturbing the visitors who'd be moving in later that day. This Bed & Breakfast was all she had going for her right now, and if this failed... well, it didn't bear thinking about.

She'd already removed all the screws she could find that had been holding the wretched cabinet in place, but it must have been glued as well. She put down the box of light bulbs she held, went back into the bedroom and grabbed the crowbar Luke had been using to pry the old molding off the wall. With the crowbar tucked behind the cabinet, she pushed. The wooden unit shifted, but still clung tightly to the wall.

She wasn't giving up that easily.

She readjusted the crowbar to get better leverage and pushed again, harder this time, letting out an unladylike grunt. She paused, blew out a breath, and pushed again, her normally unlined face screwed up in a scowl of determination.

This house was *not* going to get the better of her, she told herself. No. Way. Now push!

She put all her weight behind one last push and felt the unit shift, then lean forward. She stepped back in relief. Right into the ladder she'd left leaning against the other wall. The ladder on which she'd balanced the box of lightbulbs that needed to go into the new unit. The box of lightbulbs that was now toppling over and falling toward the floor.

She leapt forward, snaking her hand out, and caught the box just before it hit.

"Good catch!"

"Luke, I didn't see you there." She steadied herself and grinned. "Looks like all those years of high school field hockey paid off — I still have those goalie reflexes!" She tossed the box of bulbs to Luke.

He caught them easily and flipped the box into the air with a wicked grin. Seeing her face, he held them up as if in surrender and placed them gently on the toilet. "Sorry, you have your goalie reflexes, I still have my running back skills. I'll take over from here, if you'd like."

"Thanks." Anna looked around the room. "How much

noise is all this going to make? My first guests are checking in at three."

Luke shrugged as he eyed the scene. "You know as well as I do, there's going to be noise. But I can work on it during the day, when folks are out."

Anna wiped her hands down her jeans, realizing just how dirty she'd become. Gray and white dust from the splintered wood molding she'd pulled from the bedroom covered her clothes and long ponytail, while splatters of beige paint still stuck in places to her skin, making her look like she actually had the freckles she was so happy to have avoided inheriting from her father.

"I guess I should go get cleaned up. I'm a mess."

"You look good to me," Luke said, then quickly turned his gaze away from her.

She patted him on the back as she squeezed past him, trying not to notice his broad shoulders and heavily muscled arms, and trotted down the hall to the narrow back stairs.

Her own room was on the fourth floor, along with another for family and friends. She'd made sure to finish the second room in a cheery, playful style, as the first family member who'd be using it was a young cousin from Ireland scheduled to visit that summer. A boy named Eoin. Or Oien. Or something like that.

She wasn't sure about taking care of an eight-year-old — that would certainly require some effort — but she was looking forward to meeting him for the first time. And at least his visit wasn't until June. She needed to focus all her attention now on the paying guests.

A quick shower got rid of the dirt and paint and brought her hair back to its natural fiery red instead of dust-enveloped gray. She dithered a bit over what to wear. She wanted to look professional but at the same time comfortable and welcoming. She finally settled on a pair of dark blue skinny jeans that showed off her legs but could still pass muster as business casual. A forest-green button-down shirt of soft flannel and a pair of tan loafers finished the look. She eyed her high-heeled ankle boots wistfully, but knew the flats would be a lot more practical. Plus, at five foot eight she was already tall enough. She didn't want to be towering over her clients.

She made her way back down to the ground floor, stopping to look into each of the rooms that had been booked for that evening. She needed everything to be perfect.

Fresh pink roses in the Rose Room radiated a scent that brought back cheerful memories of Great Aunt Louise. Her rose garden had been the pride of the town — and the envy of a few of her neighbors. Anna had kept Great Aunt Louise firmly in the front of her mind when she'd matched the floral wallpaper and fluffy bed cover to the soft blooms. Tears still came to her eyes when she pictured Aunt Louise, a gardening apron covering her cotton dress, gloves protecting her hands, pulling the few weeds that dared sprout in her beds, deadheading spent blooms and mixing fertilizer into the soil.

Anna had never let Aunt Louise's work ethic get in her way as she and her friends took advantage of the large yard and its proximity to the ocean, but now, looking back, she realized how impressed she had always been by her successful aunt. It was Great Aunt Louise's love for life that had inspired Anna to pursue studies that would help other people. And it was Great Aunt Louise's passion for travel, a passion she'd passed on to Anna through long evenings sharing tales about foreign lands and interesting people, that had ultimately led her to medical anthropology.

Anna straightened the rose-colored curtains and caught the glint of sunlight on the ocean, just visible at an angle from this room. She'd put the work ethic she'd inherited from Great Aunt Louise — along with this house — to great effect in this room. The bed was a brass four-poster Anna had rubbed and buffed back to its former glory. The shining brass matched the wall sconces and the fixtures in the adjoining bathroom. Even there, roses colored the towels, bath rugs and flower-petal lampshade that hung from the ceiling, casting a warm glow over the claw-foot tub big enough for two.

In the Blue Room across the hall, a blue and white ceramic jug and bowl stood pride of place on the wooden mantel, surrounded by a wall of tiles perfectly matching the design on the jug. It added one of the many touches of elegance to the room. Not that this old Cape May Victorian mansion needed much help. In this room, Anna had highlighted the history of the house, said to have welcomed guests as famous as Oscar Wilde and Benjamin Harrison. The fixtures and furnishings brought the late nineteenth century to life, with a Craftsman-style cherrywood bed frame and rocking chair coupled with piles of quilts and throw pillows in glorious shades of blue and gray.

She let her eyes linger on a wall-mounted display of a nineteenth century rug she'd collected during her anthropological fieldwork in Puebla, Mexico. The bright blues woven in patterns throughout the textile matched the room perfectly, and she loved to see this symbol of Mexican culture made during the same time period this room celebrated. She also knew how some of her former colleagues would react if they saw this cultural artifact being used as decor in a room designed for tourists. Anthropologists were not always fans of tourism, particularly when it threatened the fragile ecosystem of indigenous villages or risked objectifying the very tools people used to conduct their day-to-day lives. She'd shared that distrust at one time, when she visited the small villages in Puebla and saw the poverty in which her research subjects — her friends — lived.

Over time, though, she also saw the income they made by

weaving more blankets, firing more clay pots, and selling them by the side of the road to passing tourists. Those extra dollars sometimes made the difference between a meal on the table or going hungry at night. Between having access to the medicine they needed or letting pain get worse. She also knew how much the tourists themselves benefited from the exchange. Travel — visiting foreign places, meeting different people — was eye-opening. She would always encourage it. No, she would never denigrate a trade that brought in much-needed money. In fact, she was proud to be part of the tourism industry now. Kind of. Usually.

She was still frowning as she entered the Ocean Room. It had the best view of the ocean, a clear sight line between other houses to the water two blocks away. She intentionally decorated this room with a beach theme, but she'd gone too far, hadn't she? From the pale turquoise walls to the Berber carpet to the thick duvet colored in a rainbow of pinks and blues, the room screamed beach. She was aiming for relaxing and bright, not cheap and kitschy. A B&B in Cape May should be elegant, refined. She reached out, thinking to remove one particularly common-looking painting of a seagull over the bed, then pulled her hand back. The colors complemented the duvet so perfectly. And that bedcover needed all the help it could get.

Stop fretting, Anna, she chided herself. It doesn't need to be perfect, just good. The house needs to be clean and comfortable. She closed her eyes, took a few deep breaths and let her shoulders relax, releasing the tension she was holding.

Banging from the third-floor bathroom brought the tension right back. She glanced at her watch. She still had another hour before the first guests were due to arrive. Better to let Luke get as much as possible done in that time.

Downstairs in the entrance hall, she stopped and turned

around slowly, looking for anything she'd forgotten, any detail she'd missed. She'd been fighting with this house for three months now. Some days she'd been sure the house was winning — the days when work to repair a small drip revealed a bigger leak, or when tearing down old wallpaper revealed holes in the plaster, or when her foot broke through a worn-out stair on the way up to the fourth floor. Those were the bad days.

But she'd had good days, too. And today was definitely going to be a good day. She would make sure of that. She hadn't abandoned her old life, her old dreams and goals, to move to Cape May just to be a failure. Not that she'd really had all that much choice.

Uh-uh. She shook her head, closing her eyes again.

Take a breath Anna. You got this.

2

Luke had finished installing the new molding in the bathroom and was back in the bedroom, touching up a wall. Anna watched from the doorway, too worried about tracking dust and paint to enter the room. This was going to be the Royal Room, and Luke had outdone himself with the deep-red walls, detailed trim around the marble fireplace and antique decorative lamps on the chandelier.

Anna watched as he reached up to dab paint just below the molding, his muscles moving under the thin white T-shirt he wore. He was a good-looking man, she could admit that. Only a few years older than her, with his own business and a quick sense of humor. His boyish grin, which broke out whenever he thought of something amusing, only added to the appeal of his pale green eyes, his square jaw routinely covered in a five o'clock shadow. But she wasn't looking for a man in her life, not anymore.

"It looks great, Luke, it really does."

Luke looked over and grinned. "Thanks." He glanced appraisingly around the room. "You know, I think it does."

He placed the brush he was holding into the paint tray on the floor and wiped his hands on a cloth. "So, you're running the place on your own, right?"

Anna nodded warily, anticipating some sort of criticism for taking on a task like this, with no real experience and insufficient funds. She'd heard enough of that from her family and friends. Clearly, they had no idea how hard she'd worked while doing her research in Philadelphia and Puebla or how much she'd scraped and saved to stretch out her funding.

"Does that mean you won't have a lot of free time?"

Luke's question caught her off guard. "Free time? Oh. Well, sure ... I hope so." She wasn't used to the idea of having free time. And where was he going with this, anyway?

"Good," was all he said.

The bell over the front door jingled, loud enough to be heard throughout the house. Anna grinned wickedly and rubbed her hands to together.

"Ah, my first victim." She laughed, but suspected Luke could tell how nervous she really was.

She ran down the stairs to find a lone gentleman standing in the entrance hall, a small suitcase by his side.

"Welcome to Climbing Rose Cottage. You must be Mr. Hedley?" Anna asked, since Hedley was the only person who'd booked a room for one.

"George, yes, that's me."

George Hedley wore a long raincoat more appropriate for a rainy day in the city than a day on the beach, even at this time of year. He moved his hands, first stuffing them in the pockets of his coat, then running them through his thinning brown hair, then using one to scratch the other. He shifted his weight as he stood there. Even his eyes didn't stay still, flitting around from the room in which he found himself, to Anna, back to the room.

This man clearly needed a vacation, Anna thought. Well, he'd come to the right place.

"Okay, let's get you checked in, then we'll get you settled into your room."

The decor in the Ocean Room, which George had booked, still rankled Anna. He didn't seem to mind, simply dropping his case on the floor by the bed and looking around mildly. She stepped to the window, pointing out the ocean view, but he didn't express any interest. Maybe it made sense he wouldn't be interested in the beach in April.

"Now, it's just you this week, right?" she confirmed.

He nodded. "Yes... yes, I suppose so."

"Suppose?" She asked. "I mean, you don't know?"

"Oh ... well, I guess you never know."

"You might have guests?" Now she was getting concerned.

"No, no." He raised both hands in a defensive gesture and Anna noticed they looked raw and itchy. "Nothing like that. Just my wife might decide to join me, that's all."

"You're here on business, right?"

"Yes, I am." He looked glum as he said it, then tried on a smile. "But it is beautiful here."

Anna laughed. "It is, yes. And your wife is welcome to join you. But please let me know if she does, I do need to know how many people are staying here."

"Of course." He tucked one hand inside his coat, reaching around to the side of his body.

Anna tensed, then realized he was simply scratching.

"Are you all right?" She asked. "Are you... do you need anything?" She tried to keep her voice light but couldn't hide her concern. Was it rude to ask your first guest if he had some sort of communicable disease?

"No, no," George mumbled as he removed his coat and tossed it onto the bed. "It's just winter eczema." He scratched some more as he spoke. "Get it every year. Usually clears up by now." He glanced at Anna then looked away quickly. "I have lotion for it. It's fine."

The jingling of the doorbell pulled her away from George's scintillating presence and she ran back downstairs to find the Gormleys waiting. An elderly couple, they were in Cape May celebrating their fortieth wedding anniversary. Anna watched as they held hands even while signing the hotel register and sighed, wondering if she would ever feel that safe with a man again.

She pushed sad memories away and helped get the Gormleys settled into the Rose Room.

"I hope you enjoy your time in Cape May," she babbled as she placed one suitcase on the folding luggage rack, the other on the bed. "There's so much to do in town, even at this time of year."

"Yes, of course." Mrs. Gormley clasped her hands in front of her rotund form.

"We're familiar with the town," Mr. Gormley added, looking around the room as he spoke. He walked over to the vase on the desk and touched the flowers.

Was he checking if they were real? Anna realized she'd raised her eyebrows and immediately changed her expression to a friendly smile.

"You've been here before? Do you live near here?"

"In New York, dear." Mrs. Gormley, who hadn't moved from her position near the window since they entered the room, answered. "State, of course, not city."

"Wouldn't live there," Mr. Gormley said gruffly. "Now, you serve breakfast?"

She was in the process of repeating the hours when breakfast would be served when she heard the bell one more time. She took a minute more to mention a few places they might want to see in Cape May, then ran back downstairs to see who had come in. She expected her third set of guests, but the entrance hall was empty. Frowning, she peered into the lounge. Also empty. She walked back through the dining room into the kitchen and from there into the mud room at the back of the house.

Luke stood over a large farmhouse sink, washing out brushes and paint trays. He glanced over as she entered and acknowledged her with a quick nod but kept his focus on his cleaning.

"Did a guest wander through here?" she asked.

He shook his head. "That would be some wander, if they did. Why would you think that?"

"I thought I heard the bell, but there's no one here."

"Are you sure? It's a big house." He straightened up to look at her, water dripping from the brushes he held, and winked. "Or maybe it's a ghost. You know all these old mansions are haunted, don't you?"

She rolled her eyes and let out a loud sigh. "Oh no, not the old ghost stories again. Though"—she held up a finger —"I fully intend to take advantage of that when Halloween rolls around."

She laughed and shook her head as she returned to the lounge, waiting for her last set of guests. She probably would have to get used to a few "ghosts," running this big old house by herself.

3

Her final guests, a young couple visiting Cape May to make their wedding plans, had been picky. Maryanne thought the house would be right on the ocean, not just with an ocean view. Jim didn't realize the B&B didn't offer room service. They both thought the Blue Room would be... well... bluer.

Anna did her best to smile at each of the complaints and provide the best response she could. She even went so far as to offer to bring them tea to their room while they unpacked. They grudgingly accepted — but only if she could serve them Earl Grey.

Hopefully a few days in Cape May would relax them and cheer them up. On the other hand, a few days arguing over wedding details could just make them worse.

Oh fudge, she thought, as she sat in the lounge writing up her shopping list. Today was supposed to be a good day. She smiled and added fudge to her list.

Eventually, everyone was unpacked, settled in as best they could be, and off to see what this historic Jersey shore town had to offer.

Anna knew that happened to be a lot, for all ages and interests. The Gormleys announced their intention of taking advantage of what was left of the afternoon by walking along the famous Washington Mall, the main shopping street at the center of town. George Hedley mumbled something about seeing a friend as he slipped out, avoiding eye contact. The young couple were the last to leave but finally they, too, dropped by the lounge to let Anna know she could clean up their dirty tea cups now as they were heading out to meetings at a few local hotels.

Nice hotels, Maryanne stressed, glancing around the lounge. Anna took the hint, but not the bait, simply smiling and wishing them luck in their quest.

She made her way back upstairs to the rooms, back to what would become a daily routine for her, she knew. This wasn't an easy job she'd taken on. Her parents were sure that at twenty-six she was too young for this much responsibility. Shows what they know, she thought as she climbed her twentieth flight of stairs that day — this was definitely a young woman's work.

Perhaps she'd turn down the beds, that might be a nice touch. She also came prepared with small jars of roasted nuts and half bottles of wine to leave in each room to welcome the guests back when they returned that evening.

She visited each of her booked rooms, turning down the sheets, artfully placing the nuts and wine, checking the bathrooms to make sure each had plenty of the toiletries she provided. She left the Ocean Room for last.

It had been a tough afternoon, she kept telling herself. She'd been so excited that morning, looking forward to her first day. And she'd handled everything well, even the grumbles and complaints. But she now recognized that she'd been running on adrenaline, and it was draining. Fast.

She was exhausted, grumpy and worried. What if the

young couple left her a bad review? That could ruin her business before it even started. Even worse, what if creepy George turned out to be some kind of pervert? What on earth convinced her it was a good idea to open her home to strangers, when she was all by herself?

Anna paused as she walked into the Ocean Room and let out a breath. Almost done. She took three steps toward the bed, tripped over George's small suitcase, which was sticking out from under the bed, and went flying forward, ending up sprawled out on the multihued duvet. She raised her head to see the half bottle of wine roll to the edge of the bed then fall to the floor with a gentle plonk.

Phew! At least it hadn't broken.

She rolled over and pushed herself off the bed, then rubbed her hands together. What was all over her hands? Nuts!

She spun around to see that while the wine had landed safely, the same could not be said of the jar of nuts. The lid must have come loose during flight. Walnuts, cashews and peanuts were sprinkled generously over the bed.

Anna shut her eyes to hold back the tears building up. Get a grip, she told herself. Drawing on her last reservoir of strength, she scooped up the soiled bed linens and tossed them into the hamper in the hall closet. She grabbed the other bedding set she'd purchased for this room and remade the bed, making sure no remnants of nuts hid under the mattress or on the floor.

Standing back to check her work, Anna realized that with the change in bedding, a further change in decor was required. She removed the pastel painting of the seagull then filled the gap on the wall by moving the photograph of old Cape May over the bed. The colors and style worked so much better with the sand-colored duvet.

It hadn't been intentional, but she actually felt better

about the room now. This wasn't the first time she'd fallen into a good idea. Her research in Mexico had been launched when she'd literally tripped over an unusual potted plant in a Philadelphia kitchen garden. Learning how Mexican-American families used the plant in a variety of remedies led to her interest in tracing the migration of medicinal practices. Yep, even accidents could work out for the best.

Luke had left while she was dealing with the guests. Back downstairs, Anna noted with appreciation that he'd left the mudroom spotless. If Luke could be that much of a perfectionist, then so could she.

She added a few more items to her shopping list before heading out. She would still offer the breakfast she had advertised: eggs, toast, jam, muffins. But she was going to add one more item, something all the guests would remember.

She tucked her shopping bags into her purse and pulled the front door locked behind her. No one had ever complained about her famous blueberry-almond scones. No one had ever figured out her secret ingredient, either.

Anna grinned to herself. They were going to be killer.

4

Thick crumbs of blueberry-almond scone lay scattered on the plate and across the table in front of George Hedley. A cup of coffee to the right of his plate had overturned and the white lace tablecloth was stained brown, a few drips trailing down the cloth toward the floor.

He hadn't eaten his scrambled eggs and clumps of yellow were everywhere — strewn about the table, on the floor around him and clinging to his forehead where it lay flat on his plate.

Anna noticed all of this as soon as she entered the dining room to check on her first guest. Her hand shook violently as she dropped the bread basket she carried onto a sideboard. "Mr. Hedley? George!"

She ran to him, putting a hand on his back and shaking him. Should she try a Heimlich maneuver? When she realized he wasn't moving, wasn't even breathing, she held two fingers against his neck. Nothing.

She stepped back. Took a few breaths.

George Hedley was dead. In her dining room. The first

guest she'd ever served breakfast to had died at the breakfast table. What had she done?

She took another step back, trying not to panic, thinking. Sadly, this wasn't the first time she'd encountered death. Her work with poor and impoverished communities had exposed her to so much. She had to stay in control and think straight.

She must have told him the scones had nuts in them, hadn't she? Could this be an extreme allergic reaction?

She rushed back to the still figure and shoved her hands into all the pockets she could find. He wore a suit with a white button-down shirt, his raincoat draped over the chair next to him, so there were a lot of pockets to go through. She grimaced a bit when confronted with his front trouser pockets but pushed ahead determinedly, ignoring the surprisingly cinnamon-y scent of his aftershave.

If he had such a strong allergy, he'd have an EpiPen nearby, that much she knew. But her search of his pockets revealed only a ballpoint pen, some business cards, an unused matchbook with a dark red and black image on it and some soggy tissues. Ew. She dropped those directly onto the floor.

She stayed where she was, squatting next to George. She felt herself shaking again and tried to focus.

She'd been in the kitchen since five that morning, on the spot ready to greet George with fresh-baked bread and scones when he showed up for breakfast promptly at seven.

She'd been in and out of the dining room since then. She couldn't have left him alone for more than five minutes at any one time. Should she have been more attentive, more concerned about his well-being? Maybe he was already ill and she hadn't even noticed. She tried to think back to when he'd first entered the dining room. Acting weird, as he always did, not making eye contact, rubbing his hands together nervously. Did she remember a little sweat on his top lip or on his forehead? She wrinkled her own forehead, trying to remember, but couldn't.

The way the crumbles of scone were spread around the table, it looked like he had choked. Surely she would have heard something if he'd been choking, wouldn't she? She pictured the coffee grinder, fruit juicer and mixer she'd used that morning and admitted to herself that the kitchen was not the quietest place in the house.

But it was where she'd find her phone. Anna jumped up and made for the kitchen.

An ear-shattering screech caused her to spin on the spot, turning back to the dining room. Maryanne stood in the far doorway, screaming for all she was worth. Anna ran over to her, putting an arm around her shoulders.

"Maryanne, it's okay, calm down. Let's go into the lounge."

"Okay?" Maryanne stopped to take a few sobbing breaths. "Okay? This is not okay! Is he.... Is he okay?"

Anna felt herself grinning fanatically at Maryanne's choice of words. She was beginning to panic. "I don't know, I need to call an ambulance. Please, can you go into the lounge?"

Jim's heavy steps as he ran down the stairs preceded his entrance into the dining room. Anna braced herself for another onslaught, not sure how much more she could take before she started screaming, too.

Jim took one look around and said, "How can I help?"

Anna gave him a grateful look. "Please, take Maryanne into the lounge. I need to call an ambulance."

As the two left the room, she approached George one more time. She really didn't want to do this, but knew she had to. Slowly, reluctantly, she put out her hand, resting it against his cheek. He already felt cold to her.

She grabbed her cell phone from the kitchen and called 9-1-1.

5

Anna watched with growing dismay as the police took over her house. They'd arrived at the same time as the ambulance, and though the medics hadn't stuck around, the police did. In fact, they grew in number.

The first officer to arrive followed the medics in as Anna directed them to the dining room. He stopped at the doorway and watched as they confirmed that George was, indeed, dead. She stood behind the officer, trying to peer around him to see what the medics were doing. He glanced down at her, then stepped aside.

"You can look if you want to, but I'd suggest you wait in the other room. This can't be pleasant for you." He stood with his feet planted, hands resting on his police duty belt as he spoke, but his tone was gentle and the furrows of his brow showed concern rather than anger.

"I'll wait in the lounge, then." She backed away, keeping her eyes on the black uniform that once again blocked her view of the dining room.

As the medics started leaving, more police officers arrived. A team of them traipsed through the lounge carrying metal boxes filled with whatever equipment they were using, then stuck yellow tape across the dining room and kitchen doors.

Steps on the stairs reminded her that she still had some living guests. She looked through the lounge's open doorway to see the Gormleys standing, open-mouthed, at the bottom of the stairs, watching the parade of uniformed and plain-clothes men and women moving back and forth across the hall.

"Mr. and Mrs. Gormley." Anna ran over to them. "I'm so sorry. There's been... it's...." She looked around but could see no way to explain this. "It's a tragic accident," she finally finished.

"My dear, what is going on?" Mrs. Gormley asked in a quavering voice as she reached over to grab her husband's hand.

He wrapped one arm around her shoulders, grabbing her small hands with his other. "These are police." He said in his gravelly voice. He looked around. "Tell us what happened."

Anna swallowed, ran her hands through her hair then along her jeans. Truly, she had no idea what had happened. "It's one of the guests. He... he was hurt, I think."

"You think?" Mr. Gormley repeated, frowning.

"Yes. It's Mr. Hedley. He..." Anna put both hands on her face and looked up at the Gormleys.

She looked stunned, shaking ever so slightly. He, on the other hand, had narrowed his eyes and she could see Mrs. Gormley's skin turning white where her husband was squeezing her hands. "George Hedley?" he asked.

Anna opened her mouth to reply but was interrupted by a strong voice.

"Ms. McGregor?"

She tore her eyes from the Gormleys to look at the tall, thin man who'd addressed her. Dark eyes watched her from a pinched face. His brown suit was well cut and should have fit him perfectly, but a notebook and pen protruded from one pocket and he'd stuffed something else bulky into another, throwing off the balance of the suit. His green-striped tie added to the sense that he wasn't a man who spent much time worrying about his appearance.

"I'm Detective Jerome Walsh. I'm going to need to ask you a few questions." He led her back into the lounge and gestured toward her sofa, which she sank into gratefully.

Then immediately jumped up. "The Gormleys. I have to help them. They must be scared."

"You don't need to worry about that, we'll talk to the Gormleys." He nodded to someone standing behind Anna, and as the man moved out to the entrance hall, Anna realized it was the uniformed officer who'd been first on the scene. Who'd offered her a sense of comfort. "Patrolman Burley will fill them in and take care of them."

Anna nodded and sank back down.

"Now"—Detective Walsh pulled the notebook from his pocket and consulted it—"you're fairly new here in town, aren't you?"

Anna nodded again, then stopped, feeling a fool. "Yes." She spoke firmly, clasping her hands tightly in her lap. "Yes, I moved in officially about three months ago."

"And where did you live before then?"

"Philadelphia. I was... I was a student there." She gave the detective the name of the university where she'd been studying and he wrote it down.

"So what made you buy an old Cape May Victorian mansion?" Walsh asked. He spoke in a casual manner, as if just having a conversation with a friend. The feeling was ruined when he added, "Seems an odd choice for someone your age."

Anna raised one shoulder in acknowledgment of the statement. "Yes. Very. So I've been told. It wasn't entirely my choice. I inherited the house, you see. By surprise."

"A surprise inheritance?" Walsh looked skeptical. "That doesn't happen very often."

"No, I guess not. But it happened to me. My Great Aunt Louise died and in her will she left this house to me."

"Louise Gannet?" Walsh asked. When Anna nodded, he added, "Sure, I remember her. She was a hoot, that lady. We all miss her. I didn't know much about her family life, but she was a leader in the community here." He paused, thinking. When he spoke again, he returned to his friendly tone of voice. "So your Great Aunt Louise dies and leaves you Climbing Rose Cottage. Then you open for business and your first guest dies."

Anna stared down at her hands and felt the tears welling up in her eyes. Aunt Louise would not be happy with the mess Anna was making of this.

"Why did you reopen the B&B? Louise had closed for business years ago," Walsh pressed. His voice remained friendly but Anna heard the firmness in it. He expected her to answer. As if she could.

"I know," Anna said. "She had to stop running it when she got too old. But it used to be quite successful. I remember coming here when I was a kid, seeing her dealing with the guests. Everyone always seemed so happy here..." She blinked away more tears. "I had some great memories of this place. I thought I could recreate that."

Anna shook her head and lowered her eyes again.

Walsh waited a moment, then said softly, "Tell me about George Hedley."

Anna took a deep breath and shrugged. "I don't know him. He checked in yesterday. He said he was in town for work. Oh, he has a wife. He said she might be joining him."

Walsh nodded, taking notes. "We'll be in touch with her,

too, of course. Do you know what business he was in?"

Anna shook her head again. "I don't." She sniffled, realizing she was about to cry. "I don't know anything about him. I don't know how this happened. I don't know..."

She felt a comforting hand on her shoulder and looked up to see Patrolman Burley leaning toward her. "Can I bring you some water? Or a cup of tea?"

She nodded, thanking him, then took a few deep breaths, trying to regain control. When Patrolman Burley returned with her tea, she was already feeling a little better.

"What's going to happen next?" she asked, looking back and forth between the two men. She turned her head to see police officers criss-crossing the hall, a loose end of yellow police tape visible from where she sat. "Is my dining room..." She faltered and took a breath. "Is my dining room a crime scene?"

"As far as I'm concerned, the whole house is a crime scene," Walsh replied.

"What?" Anna sat up in surprise.

Walsh scowled at her. "We have to treat every suspicious death as a crime until we know otherwise. It's standard procedure. We don't know how George Hedley died. The medics say he didn't choke, but that's all they could tell. It might have been natural, might have been accident. Then again, might have been something else entirely." He nodded toward Patrolman Burley. "Burley did the right thing securing the dining room and kitchen, but it's not enough. I don't plan to let anything slip through my fingers. If something in this house caused his death, we're going to find it."

Anna's eyebrows shot up. "Not enough? You're not going to arrest me, are you?"

"We're going to need to search the whole house," Walsh replied, ignoring her question. "Do we have your permission?"

"Of course." At least she wasn't being arrested for accidentally killing George. But what could they possibly be searching for? If he didn't choke, how did he die?

"We'll go through his room next, once we're done down here. Can you tell me which room it is?"

"Second door on the right, on the second floor," she answered glumly. "How long will my house be..." she trailed off, not sure what she was asking.

Patrolman Burley answered her. "This might take a while, Ms. McGregor." His eyes flicked briefly to Detective Walsh. "Detective Walsh is rigorous. Your other guests are going to have to find somewhere else to stay."

Anna inhaled sharply as Detective Walsh nodded his approval. "I have to close?"

"A man has died here, Ms. McGregor. In unusual circumstances." Detective Walsh's voice was firm. "You don't want to just continue with business as usual, do you?"

"No, of course not." Now Anna felt guilty for even thinking about her business as her first guest lay dead in the other room.

At that moment, George Hedley left the premises, carried out through the lounge on a stretcher covered in black plastic. She gulped as she watched the officers or technicians or whatever they were, carry him away.

"No, of course not," she repeated.

The Gormleys were the first to leave. They'd started packing and calling other B&Bs before being told they had to. They were lucky it was off-season. They found another place easily. Anna waved them off, then returned to find Jim escorting a still distraught Maryanne down the stairs.

What she had seen that morning had clearly affected her. Her typical sneer was replaced by lines of worry and fear that streaked across her forehead and around her eyes, eyes that were red and swollen from crying. Jim tore his attention away from his fiancée briefly to ask Anna where they should go.

"Oh. I don't know. I could make some calls for you, if you'd like," she offered.

"Thank you, yes. Maryanne's never found a dead person before. I don't know how she's going to get over this."

"Let me help you into the lounge," Patrolman Burley came to Jim's aid. "We can wait there while Anna — Ms. McGregor — finds you a new place to stay."

"Of course. Thank you."

Anna watched the gentle officer escort the couple into her lounge, making sounds of consolation and support. He was pretty good at his job, she thought. Assuming his job mostly entailed comforting distraught victims.

She pulled her cell phone from her pocket. She knew a few other B&B owners she could call. They'd be happy to take the couple. She was more worried about her future guests — and if she'd have any.

ANNA STOOD ON THE FRONT PORCH WATCHING JIM AND Maryanne leave. Would she ever have guests again, she wondered? Who would stay in a Bed and Breakfast where someone had died? As she let her mind wallow in depressing thoughts, she noticed she wasn't alone.

A slip of a boy with round, wide eyes and skinny legs stood in the front yard watching the proceedings intently. He pulled out a tattered notebook and a stub of pencil and started writing.

Glancing behind her, Anna realized the boy could see straight into the hall and lounge, where police officers were setting up equipment, dusting for fingerprints, and doing whatever else it was the police did to investigate a death.

When she turned back to the front yard, a man she didn't know stood next to the boy.

"Ms. McGregor, is it?"

Emotionally drained by the events of the morning, Anna didn't have the presence of mind to hide her surprise at hearing the thick Irish accent issuing from the Black man in front of her.

"Ah, my appearance surprises you. I can see from your expression," he added as she tried to shake her head.

"I'm so sorry. Of course, there are African-Americans in Ireland too."

His eyebrows shot up. "I shouldn't think so! Perhaps those who've moved there. But there's nothing American about me, I can assure you."

Anna thumped her hand against her face. "I'm so sorry. I'm saying... I'm thinking all the wrong things. I do apologize. As you can see"—she waved her hands around her—"it's been quite a morning here. Now, sir. Can I help you?"

"Sir? You do not know me, then? Not expecting me, eh?"

"Um. No, should I have been?"

"I'd been told you'd be expecting me, I was. I bring your cousin, Eoin."

The boy looked up when he heard his name. Seeing both adults looking at him, he clasped his hands behind his back and stood to attention, a look somewhat diminished by the heavy wrinkles that creased his shorts. He wore a woolen vest over his button-down, short-sleeve shirt, and ends of the shirt stuck out in places where it had become untucked. His bright red hair curled around his ears and over his wire-framed glasses. The perfectly round lenses of the glasses made his eyes look even bigger as he stepped closer and looked up at Anna, smiling shyly.

"Hello Cousin Anna." His voice came out in a whisper.

"Ha! Look at him whispering. That lad can talk the black off an iron kettle." The man laughed. "I had an earful throughout our drive down from New York."

"Eoin?" Anna finally found her voice. "My cousin Eoin, from Ireland?" She pronounced the name like the English name Owen, as she had been told by her father when he'd first arranged the visit.

"Eoin." The boy responded in a high-pitched voice, pronouncing it more like "Oween."

"Oween," Anna replied.

"Eoin," he repeated in his high voice, shaking his head.

"Eoin," the man said.

"Oweeen." Anna tried to lengthen the name.

Man and boy both shook their heads.

"Look, lass, I'll be off then. Sorry to have found you in such dire straits," he added, looking inside the house to the scene of investigation. "But I have a tight schedule. You'll be fine here with your cousin, lad."

He turned to leave.

"Wait," Anna called out, stopping him in his tracks. "I wasn't expecting Eoin"—she noticed the boy looking up at her and shaking his head, but she forged on without trying her pronunciation again—"until June."

The man's eyebrows raised again. "I can't help you with that, miss. Your own family made the arrangements with me. It seems likely they would have shared the same information with you, don't you think?"

Eoin nodded vigorously. He ran over to the man and said something Anna couldn't hear.

"The lad says they emailed you." He nodded once. "Right, I'm off. Have a wonderful summer, Eoin." He raised a hand in a farewell wave as he passed out through the front gate.

Anna stared after him then turned her stare onto the boy in front of her. He pulled his lips into a shy smile, pushed his glasses up on his face with one finger, and blinked rapidly at her.

6

Anna looked down at the boy in her front hall, her hands on her hips. He tilted his head up to look back at her, a worried expression on his face, his lips squeezed together so tightly they were turning white. She'd just finished a call with her mother that had mostly explained what Eoin was doing there early. And how she'd failed to get the message.

"I did know you were coming, of course, Eoin —" she started.

"Eoin," he said, his voice coming out as a nervous squeak.

"Right, Oween." She held up a hand to forestall the correction she knew he was about to make. "I just didn't expect you until June, that's all. Don't worry," she added quickly as she saw the tears pooling in his eyes. "I'm all ready for you. Come on, ignore these men and women, let me take you up to your room."

She grabbed his small suitcase in one hand, took his hand in her other, and led him up the three flights of stairs to their rooms. She showed him around the cheerful space, explaining the various toiletries she had for him in the bathroom, stowing his few items of clothes and books in the room's closet.

Even as she tried to chat lightly, she could hear the noise of the officers searching her house, gradually making their way up, level by level. She couldn't stay here. She couldn't keep Eoin here while this was going on.

"Come on," she said, smiling brightly. "Do you want to go out for a walk?"

Eoin nodded solemnly and Anna noticed he grabbed his small notebook and pencil as he left the room. She picked up one of his cardigans, draping it over his shoulders as they went downstairs, and considered her options. She could go to the coffee shop on Washington Mall. She'd spent plenty of afternoons there before, working, chatting with friends and neighbors.

Today, the idea of facing all the questions her neighbors were sure to ask — not to mention the risk of further spreading the news that a man had died in Climbing Rose Cottage — turned her feet toward the library and the computers available there. Maybe she could focus enough to work on some of her ongoing marketing efforts.

The unobtrusive, one-level building that held the local branch of the Cape May County Library was not usually a hotbed of activity, so Anna was surprised to see a cluster of teenage girls gathered around the reference desk. Felicia Keane, the librarian, huddled close with them, directing their attention to various books and passages within them. She looked up to catch Anna's eye and gave her a sharp nod that encompassed the group in front of her. She might be a while.

"Ms. Keane, what about the eighteenth century?" One of the girls asked, recalling Felicia's attention to her in the process. The girl, who stood a few inches taller than the others, shook her head as she asked, causing the beads fastened to the ends of her many long braids to bounce against each other. Other girls in the group looked up at her and nodded their agreement.

"Ah, well that would be in this book." Felicia reached behind her and pulled out another volume.

Baffled as to what they could be researching, Anna moved past them toward the computers against the back wall. Marketing, that's what she was here for, she reminded herself.

The reminder didn't help. The comfortable nook set back into the window opposite the reference desk looked too cozy to pass up, particularly with the shelf of popular books leading the way.

Taking Eoin's hand once again, Anna led the way to the chairs by the window. "Do you like to read, Eoin?"

He nodded, his rounded eyes scanning the shelves as they passed. She slowed her pace, letting him examine each shelf until he saw one full of books for young readers. He squatted in front of the shelf — unnecessarily, Anna thought, since the position brought his eyes below where they needed to be and he had to look up to read the titles — then pulled one down with both hands.

He'd chosen a book about the history of Cape May. Perfect! She grabbed a romance novel and settled into the lounge chair in the window. With Eoin curled up in the chair next to her, she prepared to spend some time in the hills of Scotland. She glanced once more at the girls. They had broken into two groups of three, sitting around a large table with pads of paper stacked around them. They were each writing furiously, taking notes from whatever volumes they had gathered. One small girl pushed her glasses back up her face periodically as she bent over the books, her thick, straight hair falling into her eyes. Another chewed on her lip as she focused on her work. An interesting group, for sure.

She snuggled deeper into the chair and opened her book.

Within minutes, she was lost in the castles and clans of the highlands.

"Anna!" Felicia's whisper was loud, almost violent, and Anna jumped, dropping the book onto her lap.

"What?"

Felicia laughed silently, one hand over her mouth. "I've been standing here for almost a minute trying to get your attention." She perched on the padded windowsill next to Anna and put a hand on Anna's leg. "How are you, dear? You seemed upset when you came in. And who is your friend?"

"This," Anna gestured to the sleeping boy, who had curled into a ball wrapped around his book, "is my cousin from Ireland. Well, technically he's the son of my Dad's cousin."

"How nice for you." Felicia kept her voice to a whisper to avoid waking the child. "How long is he staying?"

Anna pursed her lips. "I'm not really sure. To be honest, I wasn't expecting him for a couple more months. I think he's staying through the summer."

"That's a lot of work for you, Anna." Felicia let her concern show on her face. "Is that why you looked upset when you came in?"

Anna wasn't surprised Felicia had noticed. Felicia's friendly disposition and obvious willingness to help others was coupled with the sharp eyes and mind of a librarian. She was a woman who knew what to look for and where to look.

"Felicia, a man is dead." Anna kept her voice low, but that still didn't take the tragedy out of the words. "In Climbing Rose Cottage."

Felicia's eyes widened and her eyebrows went up, deepening the lines that already covered her forehead. Her browned skin reflected the years she'd spent living in the sun and wind of the Jersey shore town.

"What happened? Are you all right?" She leaned even closer to Anna.

"I'm fine, thank you. And I don't know what happened. The police are at the house now, trying to figure it out."

"The police? So someone was"—Felicia glanced up at the girls still gathered around their table—"killed?" She dropped her voice so low she practically mouthed the word.

Anna nodded.

"Who was there, was it Evan Burley?" Felicia asked.

Anna leaned forward. "Yes, he was there. Do you know him?"

"Of course." Felicia raised one shoulder in a shrug. "A very nice young man. I'm glad he's involved. For you, I mean." She turned her appraising eyes back onto Anna. "What else can you tell me? Who died?"

Anna told Felicia about George Hedley, about the scone, about finding the body. She shivered a bit as she spoke, but it felt so good to let it out, to tell someone friendly. Someone who didn't suspect her of poisoning her own guest.

"You think he was poisoned?" Felicia asked when Anna had finished her story. "But you said the police didn't know how he died?"

"Oh. I don't know." Anna considered it. "I guess I just assumed it. But why?" She asked herself as much as Felicia.

Felicia watched her, waiting, running one hand over her gray hair, cut into a no-nonsense style that matched her personality.

Anna thought back through everything she'd experienced that morning. The shock of seeing George, emptying his pockets, feeling for a pulse. "The smell," she finally said, looking back at Felicia, who nodded her encouragement.

"What did you smell?" Felicia asked.

Anna shook her head. "I'm not sure. It was out of place. I need to think about that."

A noise from the next chair turned both women's attention to the uncurling boy. He stretched and yawned, more of his shirt coming untucked in the process. As he settled into an upright position, he looked back and forth between the two women, the light glinting off his glasses as he did so.

"Eoin, this is Ms. Felicia Keane, the librarian. Felicia, this is my cousin, Eoin."

"Eoin," he corrected her in his high-pitched voice.

"Eoin," Felicia responded. She must have said it correctly because Eoin beamed with delight.

"Hmm." Anna frowned. "Felicia, tell me, who are those girls? I'm intrigued."

Felicia laughed silently again. "They're much like you, Anna. Our next generation of geniuses."

Anna put up a hand to wave away the compliment and smiled. "How so?"

"They're on the high school debate team." She jutted her chin toward the girls. "They come here every Wednesday, gathering the facts they need to form their arguments. Each week it's a different topic, but they don't know in advance what the topic will be, so they have to study everything."

"Everything?" Anna asked skeptically. "That's a pretty big order."

Felicia raised one eyebrow. "All current events and hot topics are on the table. Last month the debate was about whether marijuana should be legalized. Before that, they debated transgender restrooms. It really could be anything."

Eoin leaned forward in his chair, staring at the group of girls, clearly as impressed as Anna was.

"Wow," Anna said. "Do they get to choose a side?"

"Nope. And they get very little time to prepare. That's part of the challenge. They get the statement, oh, for example..." Felicia held up a hand and spoke in a monotone, "Resolved, that marijuana should be legalized." She dropped her hand and shrugged. "They get a set period of time, less than an hour, then they have to argue either for or against the topic."

"I'm good at studying, but at least I know my topic."

"It's an amazing club, I'm telling you. Students have to learn about all current events and controversial topics. They carry these note cards around with them, you wouldn't believe." Felicia laughed but her laughter was tinged with pride. "Today they researched... let me think... women's rights and maritime laws."

"Impressive." Anna looked back at the girls with new admiration. "Imagine having to be ready to present a compelling argument on anything." She folded her hands over her book. "Sounds fabulous, being able to lose yourself in research."

"You miss your research?" Felicia asked.

"I do." Anna smiled sadly at her. "I miss my lab and my work with the community. I miss the challenges and anticipation of solving a puzzle."

"If you go back into it, Anna, what would happen to Climbing Rose Cottage?" Felicia asked softly. "You've put so much into getting it up and running again."

Anna took a deep breath. "I know. And I don't know. But after today, I'm not sure the cottage will really be up and running after all."

7

The police had indeed been thorough in their treatment of her house. She tried to be charitable, recognizing their job was vitally important. However George had died, she needed to know. His family needed to know. And that meant the police had to investigate.

The intrusiveness of their investigation, however, was beyond anything she'd anticipated.

The police had turned out every cabinet, shelf, nook and cranny in her kitchen. They'd clearly gone through the lounge and dining room and gray powder covered surfaces on the table, chairs and cutlery drawer. They'd gone through the Ocean Room, as she'd expected, but she was unsettled when she entered her own room to find it in disarray from a search.

Well, she thought, they could at least have put her bras back in the drawer neatly! She suddenly had an image of Patrolman Burley going through her underwear drawer and blushed like a schoolgirl. Then giggled.

She was losing it again.

Dropping her underwear, she walked down the hall and tapped on Eoin's door. "Eoin, are you okay in there?"

She pushed the door open and peered in. The room was empty and she could hear water running in the adjoining bathroom. Should she be helping him? Could eight-year-olds wash themselves? She really had no idea how to care for this child. She was going to have to pump her mother for more information. She pulled the door shut and waited outside the room.

Finally, the sound of running water stopped. She waited a few more minutes, then heard Eoin's light footsteps crossing the room. She tapped on the door again.

"Come in." Instead of calling it out, Eoin had whispered the words.

Eoin stood by the bed, the towel in his hand dragging on the floor. He must have showered, because his hair still dripped, leaving wet patches running down his pajamas. Teddy-bear pajamas, Anna noted with a smile. She crossed the room to Eoin and gave him a big hug. "Hey there, do you feel better after washing up?"

He nodded but didn't answer. She took the towel from him and hung it up in the bathroom, taking the opportunity to straighten the soap dish and shampoo bottle he'd left tipped over on the edge of the shower.

Back in the bedroom, Anna folded back the sheets as Eoin climbed in, yawning again.

"I don't know what time you usually go to bed, but you must be so tired after your flight."

Eoin nodded, and Anna thought she saw his top lip tremble.

She leaned forward and enveloped him in another hug. "I'm so glad you're here Eoin. We are going to have fun together, aren't we?" To her relief, he hugged her back. She felt his little head pushing against her chest and smiled.

She left him curled up in the bed, the blankets pulled right up over his ears. She let out a breath as she pulled the door closed. What a day.

Back in her room, she picked up the phone and called the only person she wanted to talk to at this point.

"Hey girl!" Sammy answered in her usual, cheerful manner. "How's the dough rising?"

Anna had long since got used to Sammy's bizarre ways of asking how she was doing, each building on Sammy's undying devotion to the bakery she owned in West Wildwood, the next town up the Jersey shore.

"Sammy, it's bad." Anna felt her voice tremble and swallowed hard. "Someone died."

"What? What are you talking about?"

"It'll be on the news soon, I'm sure. One of my guests. Here, at Climbing Rose Cottage. He died."

"Oh, Anna, how terrible." Anna heard the sound of a metal mixing bowl hitting the counter, the sudden silencing of a mixer that had been running in the background. "What happened?"

"I don't know. That is, the police are looking into it."

"The police?" Anna heard a stool scrape on the floor and knew Sammy had just stood. "It wasn't a natural death, not an old man dying in his bed or something like that?"

Anna shook her head, then added, "he died in the dining room. While eating my scones."

Sammy was silent. Which was not common with Sammy. In all the years she'd known her — which was all her years — Sammy had always had something to say. Her best friend since before they could walk, Sammy had shaped Anna's opinions of the town they'd grown up in, the movies they both loved, the sports they both enjoyed. Anna had done her share of influencing Sammy, too. After all, Sammy had followed Anna's advice to pursue her passion in baking.

"Sammy, are you there?" Anna asked.

Sammy cleared her throat. "I am, sorry. Anna..." Sammy's voice was hushed, serious. "Do they think your scones killed him?"

"What?" Now it was Anna's turn to jump up. "I sincerely hope not. I mean, they didn't say..."

"Oh honey, I wish I could come over but I have a wedding I'm working on. I simply have to get this done today. Can I come by tomorrow?"

"Of course, yes. Thank you, I'd love the company."

"And are you going to be okay staying there in that house by yourself tonight?"

Anna shook her head. "It's worse than that, Sammy. I'm not alone."

"I don't get it. Who's there?"

"Remember I told you my cousin Eoin was coming to spend the summer with me?"

"Sure. He's coming in June, right?"

"Right. That's what I thought. Turns out there was a change of plans. He arrived today."

"Today? The day a man dies in your house?" Sammy practically screamed the words. "How did you not know he was coming?"

Anna let out a laugh. "Because I didn't call my Mom. It was a sudden change in plans. My Dad's cousins emailed me, but their messages went to my spam folder. My Mom called me, but I didn't call her back because I was so stressed out about opening Climbing Rose Cottage and I thought she was just going to harangue me again about being too young to take this on."

"Oh, honey. What are you going to do? Are you both going to stay there?"

"What else can we do? This is my house. And he's my cousin." She thought of the small boy asleep in the next room and smiled. "He's adorable, Sammy, I can't wait for you to meet him."

"I can't wait, either. And Anna, I know you're determined, but it's all right to need help sometimes." Sammy's voice was soft, caring. "I'll see you tomorrow."

Anna walked aimlessly around her house, picking up a book here, straightening a pillow there. The totality of the work that would be required to put the house back into shape overwhelmed her. It was easier to think about small things right now. She could wait until tomorrow to deal with the bigger messes.

After an hour of straightening up, Anna felt better. At least the lounge and front hall were presentable. She could tackle the kitchen and guest rooms tomorrow. Now, to do something about her own room. Her eyes slid toward the doorway at the back of the hall as she headed to the stairs. Had the police searched Aunt Louise's rooms, too? Were they now as torn up as the rest of the house?

A lump caught in her throat as she thought of her Great Aunt Louise, the indignity of strangers digging through her private things. Things Anna hadn't even been able to face herself yet.

She swallowed hard, took a deep breath, and kept moving up the stairs. At the top, she paused to look down one more time, checking the front door was locked, all the lights downstairs turned off, then turned toward the back stairs up to her own room. A deep, shuddering creak passed through the house and Anna froze. What was that?

She stood as she had frozen, one foot in the air, afraid to move. But she heard nothing more, saw nothing unusual around her. She laughed out loud to break the silence and resumed walking. Just the house settling. Old houses were always making noise. She was halfway up the back stairs when she heard another noise. This one was higher pitched, more screeching than creaking, but softer and harder to hear. And was followed by a definite *thump*.

Now, she could admit to herself, she was scared. Had someone broken into the house? What kind of burglar would break into a crime scene?

Oh. She froze again. Didn't they say the criminal always returned to the scene of the crime?

She shook her head again. She didn't even know that George had been killed. There was no reason to suspect a killer had broken into her home.

She grabbed the field hockey stick from her closet and headed back downstairs. She needed to prove to herself there was no one in the house.

Unless George himself was back, to finish his breakfast. Anna tried to laugh at the ridiculous thought, but her laugh came out as a high-pitched squeak. Not the brave front she was trying to put on.

"Is anyone there?" she called out. Her voice sounded as weak as her laugh. She coughed and tried again. "Is anyone there?" she shouted as she made her way back downstairs.

The doorway that led to Aunt Louise's room was dark. She continued to the lounge, holding the hockey stick out in front of her. Not the best weapon, she knew, but all she had right now.

She tiptoed into the lounge, sticking her head in and looking quickly left and right before entering the room. Nothing moved. No more creaks or whines. She paced slowly around the room, her breath gradually returning to normal.

"It was just the house settling." She spoke out loud, trying to convince herself. "There's no one else here." Her foot hit something hard that slid across the room when she kicked it.

She screamed and jumped back, hitting the switch for the overhead lamp. Light flooded the room and she spun around. "Who's there? What's going on?"

Her eye fell on a book lying on the floor about three feet from the bookcase. Of course, that's what she had kicked. A book.

She bent down to retrieve it, carrying it back over to the bookshelf. All the books had been disturbed by the police search. She'd organized most of them, putting them back into order and pushing them safely onto the bookshelf, but she hadn't done a thorough job, she knew that. This one must have been balanced precariously on the edge of the shelf. And must have slipped off.

That's it, she told herself. Nothing to be scared of. She dimmed the lights, deciding to leave them on low just for tonight, and headed back upstairs. Nothing to be scared of, she repeated to herself. Just an old house settling. Just a book that wasn't secure falling off a bookshelf. Nothing to be scared of.

8

Anna did not sleep well that night. She hadn't really expected to.

Up early after her restless night, she faced the prospect of dealing with the mess in her kitchen. She was in the middle of scrubbing down her counters, a fresh pot of coffee brewing, when the bell over the door jingled. She didn't go immediately, taking a minute to remove her kitchen gloves and wipe her hands. As she stepped toward the kitchen door, Patrolman Burley stuck his head through it.

"Good morning, thought I might find you in here."

"Oh, Patrolman Burley. Hi. I mean, um, good morning. I'm just..." she lifted her arms then let them fall in a gesture of despair. "I'm not sure what I'm doing."

"Seems like you've got quite a mess on your hands." He glanced around the kitchen. "Sorry about that."

"I am allowed to be cleaning up in here, aren't I?"

He smiled. "Yes, you are. And please, call me Evan."

She felt the tension in her shoulders relax, the edges of her mouth turn up. "Evan, of course."

The deep brown of his eyes reminded her of the Scottish hero she'd been reading about yesterday. It would be nice not to have to go chasing around the dark house in the middle of the night with a field hockey stick.

"I'm sorry you have to deal with this. I have a few minutes, I could help." Something in her expression caused him to take a step back. "Or not, if you prefer to do it yourself."

"Why did you tear apart my kitchen like this?"

"It wasn't just me. We had a team going through the whole house."

"I noticed that," she responded, feeling her cheeks grow hot.

"The thing is, Anna — may I sit?" He gestured toward the marble-topped bar that ran opposite the sink.

"Of course. Sure. Would you like some coffee?"

He waited until she'd poured his cup, then continued. "The thing is, Anna, one of your guests died in unusual circumstances and we need to find out what happened to him."

"Wait. What do you mean, what happened to him?"

"I mean, we need to know what killed him." Evan said, still looking directly at her. "Or who."

Anna gulped and looked down at the coffee pot still in her hands. She turned her back on Evan to replace it on the burner and realized her hands were shaking. She took a few breaths.

"So you think he was murdered?" she asked once she felt sure her voice would sound normal.

Evan shook his head, taking another sip of his coffee. "Well, this *is* a police investigation. But it's too soon to say if it was an accidental death or intentional. We still need to determine the exact cause of death. That's why we searched the house. We were looking for anything that might have been used."

Anna dropped onto the stool next to Evan. "Murdered. I mean, murder. That can't be a common thing in Cape May."

"It's not. Detective Walsh is running the investigation for now, but it won't be long before this attracts attention from the higher-ups. We need to get to the truth, and fast. Walsh has some experience with this sort of thing, so..." He toyed with his mug and Anna realized there was more. The worst was yet to come.

"So?"

"So we have to consider the possibility that you may have been responsible."

"Me?" Anna heard the shriek in her voice and shut her lips tight.

Evan seemed focused on his coffee, giving Anna the time she needed to take a few breaths.

She tried again. "Me? Why would I kill my own guests?"

Evan raised his hands in what was probably meant to be a calming gesture. "Not on purpose, I'm sure. But we don't yet know what killed him. We need to consider all options."

"I see. So I'm a suspect. In a murder investigation."

"Don't overreact. Suspect is too strong a word. What if something in this house killed him — either an allergy, or something poisonous you didn't realize he might encounter."

Anna shook her head, flabbergasted. "I'm a trained scientist. I know what's poisonous and what's not. There's nothing here that could—"

"Okay, okay. Look, you're simply a person of interest at this point, that's all."

Anna's brain spun through possibilities. "Who else is a 'person of interest?'" Her voice betrayed her skepticism of the term.

"I can't talk to you about the investigation. As much as I trust you, you must understand that."

She examined his face, trying to figure out how to handle this. His nose was wide and lopsided, as if he'd been in a fight once. His mouth curled up on the sides. But somehow the unevenness of it all made him look honest. Trustworthy.

"Why?" she asked.

"Why what?"

"Why do you trust me?" Evan's gaze held hers and she gripped her mug more tightly. "I mean, we don't know each other."

"That's not entirely true. You and I may not be close, but I knew your Aunt Louise. I know other people in town who know you. And I'm a good judge of character. You have an honest face."

Anna raised a skeptical eyebrow. "Well, if he was killed, there must be other suspects. Other people who actually knew George, maybe someone who worked with him, or his friends. Just through my own research I know how extensive one individual's network can be. I worked on a medical analysis of a man who—"

"I know. We know." Evan cut her off. "Look, I respect your perspective, but it's not the same. This is police work, not academic research. It's what we do. I'm sorry to be the bearer of bad news." Evan put down his mug and stood. "My offer to help clean up in here still stands, if you change your mind. And please don't misunderstand what I've said."

Anna opened her mouth to object to his dismissal of her research when a squeak from the door drew both of their attention. Eoin's head poked through the doorway, his big eyes moving as he stared around the room. With a nod, he stepped through and into the kitchen.

Shooting a questioning look at Anna, Evan said, "Hello. I don't believe we've met yet."

"Evan, this is my cousin Eoin. He's come to stay with me for the summer," Anna explained.

"Eoin," Eoin piped up, predictably.

"Oween." Anna tried again.

Eoin looked at the floor, shaking his head.

"Well, Eoin, it's a pleasure to meet you." Evan put out a hand and the Eoin grabbed it, shaking it vigorously. His eyes grew even wider as he looked up at the large, uniformed man.

"You're a copper?" He asked, in the strongest voice Anna had heard him use yet.

Evan laughed. "I am. Though I've never actually been called that before."

Eoin's smile split his face and he pulled out his worn notebook and started scribbling in it. He made his way to the table without looking up from his book and hopped onto a chair while still writing. Evan raised his eyebrows at Anna and gestured at the boy. Anna shrugged and shook her head.

"You probably want something to eat, don't you?" She turned to dig through her cupboards. "Let's see, what do you like? Pancakes? Sausages? Muffins?"

Eoin put the notebook on the table, folded his hands, and looked at Anna expectantly.

"Eoin, shouldn't you be in school at this time of year?" Evan asked.

Eoin nodded, pushing his glasses up his nose as they slipped. "My school burned down."

Anna dropped the bag of flour she was holding onto the counter. "What? You didn't tell me that."

Eoin shrugged and toyed with the edge of his notebook. "There was a fire."

Evan moved closer to him and knelt in front of him. "What happened?"

"We couldn't go to school anymore. Mum and Da' said they would teach me at home, but when the man came to set the standards, he said I'd already finished all the lessons for my year." He glanced up at Anna out of the corner of his eye, and she saw a grin spreading across his face.

"You'd already done all the lessons? So you don't have to learn anymore?" Evan repeated, throwing his own questioning look at Anna.

"I like to read," Eoin said as if that answered everything.

"Uh-huh." Evan stood. "I'll leave you two to it. Eoin, I'm sure I'll be seeing more of you. Anna, you might need to do a little research into that story."

"No kidding," Anna replied under her voice.

Evan took a couple of steps toward the door, then turned back. "I also came by to let you know that Mrs. Hedley, George's widow, will be by later this morning. She wants to pick up his belongings."

"Oh no, I don't think I could face her," Anna said.

"You don't have to be here if you don't want to be. I could be here, or arrange for someone else?" Evan looked down at her, his hands resting on his belt. "Would that be better?"

Anna thought about her options and felt miserable either way. Either she faced the widow of the man who'd just died while eating her scones, or she ran and hid like a scared child. She could tell Evan the truth. Tell him about her fears last night, her late night hunt through the house with a field hockey stick. It would have been nice to have someone else around then, particularly someone as big and comforting as Evan.

Or she could be strong. She could be the woman she wanted to be.

"No." She looked up to see Evan watching her closely. "No, I'll be here. In fact, I'll go pack up his things. That's all right, isn't it?"

"Sure." Evan smiled. "Good luck."

ANNA STOOD IN THE MIDDLE OF THE OCEAN ROOM. POOR Mr. Hedley hadn't really brought a lot of things with him. He was only staying for four nights, to be fair. The closet held two white shirts and a tie. Presumably he'd only brought one suit, the one he'd died in. A pair of sneakers had been tossed against the chest of drawers, either by George or the police who'd searched his room, suggesting he had some more casual clothes in the chest of drawers.

Looking around the bare space, Anna was struck by the difference between this room and the Gormleys' room. When they left in a hurry, they'd been carrying not only their two suitcases, but extra shopping bags overflowing with bright beach clothes, shoes, hats and toys that must have been intended as gifts for young friends or relatives. Their room had been a mess, too, thanks to the efforts of the Cape May police. But underlying that mess had been a sense of joyful abandon. Even after only one night in the room, they'd opened all the small bottles of toiletries Anna had provided, made use of all the towels. They'd even taken advantage of the bubble bath, as she'd found the empty bottle lying on its side next to the oversized tub.

George's room, by contrast, felt sterile. Drawers gaped open, the closet doors stood ajar, but there were so few items inside them the police hadn't had to search very hard.

Moving to the bathroom, she saw that George hadn't used any of the toiletries she provided, choosing instead to rely on travel-size containers he'd brought with him. The mirror was streaked where he had run his hand across it, wiping away the steam that would have accumulated during a hot shower. Sighing, she opened the toiletry bag that stood on the vanity. One by one, she picked up the small bottles, carefully wiping everything off before putting it in the toiletry bag.

She paused with a used tube of toothpaste in her hand. Certainly no one would want that. She tossed it into the trash can along with a soap wrapper, then went back to her careful packing. None of the bottles were labeled, each one the kind you could buy in a drug store to fill from larger containers. Very practical. Very neat. She packed bottles she assumed were shampoo, body wash, shaving cream, aftershave. It was highly unlikely Mrs. Hedley would want any of these, but it didn't seem fair to throw them all away.

One plastic tub seemed empty. Unscrewing the top, Anna saw that it had contained a lotion of some sort. She thought of his itching hands and figured he'd been using this cream to soothe his eczema. It was cinnamon scented — the smell immediately brought her back to that horrifying moment in the dining room, digging through George's pockets — but she thought she caught a whiff of a fishy scent, too. She tossed it in the trash, then carried the toiletry bag back into the room.

George's small suitcase had been tucked away behind the bed. Anna opened it up on the folding luggage rack. She pulled each item from the closet, carefully packing them, then added in the pair of sneakers.

She paused before tackling the drawers, but if the police could go through her intimates, she could pack up George's. In a second drawer she found some more informal wear — jeans and collared T-shirts — which she folded just as carefully.

She grabbed some papers from the desk, noting the name and logo of a company named Varico with a West Cape May address. She stacked the papers neatly and placed them in the suitcase on top of the clothes.

Making sure everything was well protected, she closed the suitcase, took one more look around the room, and carried the bag downstairs.

That had, quite possibly, been the saddest thing she'd ever

had to do. Even her despair at the death of Aunt Louise had been tempered with the knowledge that Louise had led a long and happy life.

But George? Certainly not a long life, and Anna wasn't all too sure he'd been particularly happy, either.

9

Anna settled into the lounge, the small suitcase standing on its own, isolated, across the room, waiting for Catherine Hedley. As she stared at the case, she thought about what it contained: the last things George Hedley saw or touched. How awful.

She tried to look away, to look around the room or out the window instead. At least she'd provided him some beauty in his last days. Hopefully he found the Ocean Room peaceful. This attempt to raise her spirits failed miserably when she realized one of his last views had been of that horrible pastel seagull painting.

She shuddered and stared once more at the bag. Who had he been, really, she wondered? She knew so little about this man who had died in her dining room. Who the police think she might have accidentally killed. He'd seemed odd, no doubt, creepy even. But she shouldn't judge him by his appearance. Maybe he was simply shy. Awkward. Uncomfortable around other people.

She'd known plenty of people like that. Scientists who went into academics because they were more comfortable interacting with a microscope and specimen than other human beings. Or men and women who kept illnesses hidden from friends and family because they were embarrassed or afraid of the treatment. Or couldn't afford it, a situation she'd come across far too often in her own fieldwork. She'd met all kinds of people and had found something to respect and admire in everyone.

She felt the tears well up in her eyes again and pulled out her phone to distract herself. Skimming through her emails didn't help, as bill after bill popped up on her screen. Water, heating, electricity, gas, insurance... the list went on. She'd been counting on this week's income to pay most of those. Not only was she not getting that income now, she was out the money and time she'd put into groceries and preparations for those guests. She tried to swallow down the feeling of despair that rose within her.

This was not healthy, she finally told herself. Mrs. Hedley could still be a couple of hours away, since she was coming down from Trenton.

Anna marched back upstairs and launched herself into the arduous process of stripping the linens in all the rooms. She focused on her work, trying to ignore the voice in her head telling her this was a waste of time. Why clean rooms that no one would ever want to stay in again?

She shook her head and worked harder, wiping down every surface in each room as she finished stripping the beds. She scrubbed showers, tubs and toilets, dusted under beds. As she worked, she started to feel better. As if she could scrub away this horrible launch of her B&B and start fresh. She needed new guests, she needed a new start.

She stopped to stick her head out the front door periodically to check on Eoin. He sat in one of the Adirondack chairs on her front porch, his feet kicking at the air far above the ground. He'd finished the book he'd picked up at the library yesterday and was now engrossed in another history of the area.

When she'd finished every other room, Anna dragged herself to the Ocean Room. Realizing it would be futile to try to ignore what had happened, she let herself indulge in her grief, tears slipping from her eyes as she bent over the toilet. A man was dead. It was right to grieve. Even if she didn't know the man.

For the first time, she realized she felt regret for not having known George better. That was good, she told herself, better to think of him as someone who could have been a friend instead of someone who could have been a pervert.

She found herself breathing a little heavier as she heaved the laundry basket filled with towels and sheets down two flights of stairs leading to the large washer and dryer in the basement. At least with chores like this she wouldn't have to worry about joining a gym!

Two hours later, she was sweating and sore. She'd lost count of how many times she'd been up and down the stairs or bent over the washer digging the clean linens out of the back of the machine, heaving them into the dryer, ironing and folding. The steam from the iron had left her long, red hair in ringlets around her face and she felt the sweat gathering on her brow and the back of her neck.

She let out a sigh and grabbed the last basket of clean sheets and towels, heaving it onto her hip and starting the trek upstairs. She was halfway up the main stairs to the second floor when the front doorbell jingled.

Anna turned on the steps, laundry basket still balanced on her hip, to see who'd come in.

The woman in the foyer stood perfectly still, looking as if she'd been standing there for hours instead of seconds. She stood with her legs pressed tightly together, her brown skirt just covering her knees, her feet in plain, thick-soled shoes.

She wore a short raincoat tied tightly at her narrow waist. Her hands were clasped around a triangular purse that she held in front of her body like a shield, her knuckles turning white with the pressure.

For a moment, the woman seemed frozen, but Anna soon realized that even as she stood perfectly still, tears streamed down her face.

Anna shook herself out of the daze she was in and trotted back down the stairs, dropping the laundry basket on the floor at the foot of the steps. The woman started, as if noticing Anna for the first time.

"Mrs. Hedley?" Anna ventured, offering a hand.

The woman ignored the hand but nodded, a slight movement but at least it was something.

"I'm Anna McGregor. Please, come in." She gestured toward the lounge and Mrs. Hedley's eyes followed the gesture.

For a moment longer, neither woman moved. Anna felt herself fidgeting, shifting her weight from foot to foot, glancing around the room and into the lounge where she could see the edge of George's suitcase as it sat next to the door.

"Mrs. Hedley?" Anna finally spoke again, this time putting her hand on Mrs. Hedley's shoulder in a friendly gesture. "I'm so sorry for your loss."

Mrs. Hedley jerked away and turned her head to look Anna full in the face. Anna wished she hadn't. The anger she directed at Anna was so strong, she took a step backwards and raised a hand in defense. Mrs. Hedley's eyes almost glowed with hatred and the skin on her neck turned a dark shade of pink.

When Mrs. Hedley spoke, it came out in a low, angry hiss. "How dare you?"

10

Catherine Hedley sat primly on the edge of the deep sofa. Anna had finally managed to move the petite but extraordinarily powerful woman into the lounge. Anna perched on a chair opposite, waiting for Mrs. Hedley to say something else. Anything. To explain her earlier outburst.

"Can I offer you a cup of tea?" Anna asked. "I have Earl Grey, English Breakfast, or maybe an herbal—"

"No," Mrs. Hedley cut her off. "Thank you." She continued to clutch her purse tightly in front of her, her feet flat on the ground, her knees pressed closely together. "I'm sorry for my reaction just now. I'm... well, in shock, I suppose." More tears rolled down her cheeks and she brushed them away with one hand, the other still clutching her purse. "This has been very difficult for me."

"I understand," Anna nodded. "Please, take as long as you need."

Mrs. Hedley pulled a tissue out of her purse and dabbed at her nose and eyes. "I didn't expect this..." Mrs. Hedley took a deep shuddering breath.

"No, of course not, how could you? Perhaps... would you like to tell me about George? I didn't get to know him very well."

Mrs. Hedley's back straightened, though Anna was surprised it could straighten more than it already was, and she stuffed the used tissue back into her purse and snapped it shut. "I will handle my loss on my own terms, thank you. I won't stay. I will simply collect my husband's possessions and leave."

Anna gestured toward the suitcase. "It's all in there, I packed everything up."

Mrs. Hedley's eyebrows shot up and she turned in her chair to look toward the suitcase, then returned her glare to Anna. Her anger hadn't faded, it seemed, simply moved temporarily into the background. "You did what? How could you?"

"Mrs. Hedley... I don't understand..." Anna was at a loss for words.

Mrs. Hedley stood in one fluid movement. She turned as if to leave the lounge, then looked back toward Anna. "Show me to his room."

Anna jumped up and lead the way upstairs, still at a complete loss to understand the widow's anger. She knew that anger was one of the stages of grief, but she'd never seen someone express it like this before. She stole a peek at the woman behind her but could reach no conclusions with so little evidence.

"Here it is, the Ocean Room." Anna allowed Mrs. Hedley to enter first.

"It's been cleaned." Mrs. Hedley said.

"Yes, the police finished with their search of the room and said I could clean it. But as I said, I packed up all of your husband's things very carefully."

Mrs. Hedley walked over to the window, then to the bathroom. She rested one hand on the doorjamb and leaned into it. For a moment, Anna thought maybe the woman had been overcome by her grief, but when she spun around her rage had only increased.

"How dare you?" She repeated. "First you kill my husband, then you pack up any evidence. I... I ..." Mrs. Hedley started to sputter, her face turning deep red, her lips pursed. "I will tell the police about this."

"But the police said I could," Anna repeated, feeling her own anger growing in defensiveness and trying to keep it down. "I got permission from them before I did anything. And Mrs. Hedley, please, I did not kill your husband. How could you think such a thing?"

Mrs. Hedley took a step toward Anna and Anna inadvertently took a step back. "He died because he was here. If he wasn't here, he wouldn't have died."

"But you can't possibly know that," Anna exclaimed. "We don't even know how he died yet."

"I know perfectly well that if he was at home with me, I would have been keeping an eye on him."

Anna had no trouble believing that. Suddenly, George Hedley's nervousness made a lot more sense.

"I would have been the one feeding him," Mrs. Hedley went on. "He would be eating a healthy breakfast, not some fattening pastry. I would make sure he was doing everything properly. If he choked, I would have taken care of him."

Anna tried to imagine the petite Mrs. Hedley wrapping her arms around her much larger husband, trying to squeeze. Oddly, the image worked. Mrs. Hedley was clearly stronger than she looked.

"Mrs. Hedley"—Anna stood up tall and looked down at the other woman—"I did not kill your husband. I had nothing to do with his death. And you have no way of knowing if he would have died regardless of where he was. I do not appreciate your accusations."

"Humph." Mrs. Hedley took another step toward Anna, her eyes narrowing. "I don't really care what you appreciate. My husband is dead. I blame you. And I'm not leaving until the police arrest you for what you've done."

"Ahem. Ladies?"

Both women jumped and turned toward the sound of Luke's voice. Anna must not have heard the doorbell over the blood pounding in her ears as she fought her rising anger.

"Is there any way I can help?" He asked the question lightly, but Anna could see how tense he was, prepared for anything.

"Luke, we're okay, thank you. Aren't we, Mrs. Hedley?" Anna asked the other woman.

"Who are you, the accomplice?" Mrs. Hedley asked rudely.

"I'm the handyman," said Luke, keeping his voice cool and calm. He leaned casually against the wall, but Anna could see the tension in his arms and legs. He was ready to move. "I do work around the house. I heard you two arguing and thought I could help."

Anna held up a hand, angry at herself for how relieved she felt to see Luke. She did not need a man to step in and save her. Not from the minute Mrs. Hedley.

"I believe Mrs. Hedley was just leaving." She raised an eyebrow toward Mrs. Hedley. "To visit with the police, apparently."

Mrs. Hedley's lips turned down into a tight frown, pulling the skin of her face into an angry mask. "Indeed I will."

She nodded once and stalked out of the room, Luke stepping aside to let her pass.

Anna ran after her, watching as Mrs. Hedley fled silently down the stairs, popped into the lounge to grab George's suitcase, then left the front door swinging open behind her as she left.

Anna ran down, slammed the front door shut, locked it and leaned back against it, her breath coming in short, raspy bursts.

Luke called down from the top of the stairs. "Glad I was here."

Anna glared up at him. "How dare you?"

11

Luke stared down at Anna, his mouth gaping. "How dare I? What the..." He shook his head in confusion. "I just helped you get out of a tricky situation."

Anna stomped up the stairs toward him. "I didn't need your help. I didn't ask for your help."

Luke put both hands up and backed into the upstairs landing. "I have no idea what you're worked up about. I thought I was helping."

Anna pursed her lips, her chin jutting out, and tried to breathe calmly. She shut her eyes and nodded. "I know you did," she said, once she'd regained control. "But I was dealing with a guest. I don't expect you to jump in when I'm working."

"A guest?" Luke laughed. "She wasn't your guest, Anna. And from what I heard, she was accusing you of murder."

"Ugh." Anna rolled her eyes. "I know she was. And it was upsetting. This whole thing is upsetting. But I need to manage this business on my own, without your help. Even when dealing with difficult situations."

Luke shook his head, his eyes still wide with confusion. "You're being..." his voice trailed off.

"What?" Anna felt her anger rise again. "What am I being? Emotional? Childish? Acting like a woman?"

"Okay, I've had enough. Sorry I tried to help. I won't do it again." Luke threw up his hands and stormed to the back stairs. Anna heard him pounding up to the third floor.

She put both hands on the banister and leaned forward, her head dropping between her shoulders. She let out a shuddering breath.

She shouldn't have attacked Luke like that. She knew it. She was angry at Mrs. Hedley and she took it out on Luke. But she hadn't asked for his help. She hadn't asked for anyone's help.

She also hadn't asked for her first guest to die at her breakfast table.

She let herself laugh out loud at the absurdity of the situation, then straightened up. Looking down the stairs she saw the full laundry basket still sitting where she'd dropped it. It seemed so long ago.

She stomped back down the stairs, grunting as she heaved up the basket and made her way back to the guest rooms. She was a small business owner now; she had to be strong. She had to be independent. She had to be able to take care of herself. Luke would just need to accept that.

12

An hour later, the banging coming from the third-floor bathroom had subsided. Anna was no expert, but she was pretty sure painting the bathroom didn't actually require Luke to attack the walls with that much aggression. Hopefully, he'd calmed down a bit now.

She certainly had.

An hour spent making beds then revisiting her budget, her marketing plan and her bank account, had forced her to calm down and think rationally. And to realize just how lucky she was to have found Luke. She'd looked into other contractors and knew how much Luke was undercharging her for the work he was doing. She couldn't have gotten this far without him.

She found him in the bathroom, on his knees setting out the new tiles for the floor. He hadn't heard her approaching so she tapped lightly on the door frame, peeking in while Eoin waited in the bedroom.

He looked up and she felt a pang of sorrow when he didn't flash the quick smile she'd become used to.

"Luke, I'm really sorry."

He frowned, shrugged, put the tile he was holding down into place and stood. "Thanks, I appreciate that." He'd accepted her apology, but he was acting different. More distant.

"There's someone I want you to meet," she said. She stepped into the bathroom and waved Eoin over. He stopped in the doorway and his forehead furrowed as he looked at Luke.

"Hello. You have new guests already?" Luke asked.

"Oh no, this is my cousin from Ireland. He's come to stay with me for the summer. Eoin, this is Luke. Luke, this is Eoin."

Anna didn't even blink when she heard the small voice pipe up, "Eoin."

"Oween?" Luke asked and Anna felt guilty for being relieved she wasn't the only one who couldn't pronounce Eoin.

"What are you doing?" Eoin asked, his eyes fixed firmly on the floor.

Luke kneeled down next to him. "I'm placing tile. See, it's like a puzzle."

Eoin kneeled down, too, his head only two feet above the floor. He peered at the tiles and nodded. "I see. How do you get them to stay?"

Anna laughed and felt herself relax as Luke launched into an explanation of grout and how tiling worked. Eoin listened intently to every word. Anna got the impression that as of tomorrow, Eoin would be able to tile a bathroom all on his own.

"Thank you for teaching me that," Eoin said once the lesson had ended. He put out a hand and Luke shook it firmly.

"My pleasure young man. You're a good student. Drop by any time you want to see what I'm working on."

Eoin beamed at the compliment, glanced shyly up at Anna, then scurried out of the room.

Anna watched him go with a sad shake of her head. "I don't know why he won't talk to me like that." She let out a breath, then remembered why she'd really come looking for Luke.

"Look, the thing is—"

He cut her off. "You don't owe me an explanation. You hired me to do work around the house, that's all."

"I assume you know what happened here."

"Yeah, I heard. I stopped by yesterday, but the police had the whole place cordoned off. Didn't let me in. Even though I need to be here to get my job done. I guess you're right." He shrugged again. "I'm not that important for this business. It's up to you how you want to manage things."

"No, that's not it at all." Anna sank onto the side of the tub, letting her hands hang down between her knees. "Please, let me explain. I feel really bad."

Luke glanced over at her and Anna saw a spark of light in his eyes that reassured her. "The thing is, I just got out of a long relationship. To say it ended badly is an understatement."

"I'm sorry to hear that." Luke's voice made it clear he really meant it and Anna's spirits lifted. Then he continued, "But that doesn't explain why you reacted the way you did, just from my trying to help."

"I know." She chewed on her lip, looking around the room, thinking about how she could explain this to someone who wasn't there, who didn't understand. "He stole my work."

"He stole it?" Luke looked confused. "Like, he stole something you made?"

"No." Anna shook her head. "My research. He used my research and took credit for it."

Luke leaned back against the doorjamb, watching her. "What kind of research did you do?"

"Medical anthropology," Anna said. "I'm getting my PhD. I'm pretty darn close, actually. Just have to finish my dissertation. But when he took credit for my work... I guess I kind of flipped out."

Now Luke was grinning. "You? Flip out? Nah."

Anna laughed at the sarcasm in his tone. She deserved that. "What can I say? I got really angry and said some things I shouldn't. First to him—"

"Sounds like he deserved having some things said to him."

"Yes," she said tentatively. "But then I said some things in anger to the other faculty at the school. Not only did he publish my research as his own, but they believed him when he denied it."

Luke's forehead furrowed as he thought. Anna could almost see his mind working behind his green eyes. "Didn't you have any way to prove it? To prove that you'd done the work, I mean? I gotta admit, I don't know what kind of research a medical anthropologist does."

"Yeah." Anna nodded. "Kind of. They formed a board to look into the charge and I gave them all of my data, notes and preliminary work. I do research with households in Mexico and in the U.S. about their diet, where they get their food, their medical care, things like that. Making connections between cultural traditions and medicine in Philadelphia and Puebla."

"You're a nutritionist?"

"No." Anna grinned. "It's a little different. I work to explain the causes of poor health in communities, studying how diet and education and medical care and even child care fit together to create medical outcomes. I'm particularly interested in informal networks of health providers, home remedies and indigenous recipes that have been passed down through generations. It all connects as culture, and makes some people healthy and some people unhealthy."

"You work with people to find out if something in their community or in their lifestyle is hurting them."

"Exactly. I worked with Mexican communities in Philadelphia, tracing the spread of ideas and beliefs as they follow migration patterns. If something is helping them or hurting them, I figure out where that thing fits in, who has control over it, and how to work toward healthier communities." Of course, there are some things people can't control, she thought, like if there's a crazy poisoner running around. She blinked and looked back up at Luke. "I gave them all my notes." She balled her hands up into fists as she felt her anger rising again. "Honestly, though, they shouldn't have needed them."

"And you told them that. Not in a kind way, I'm guessing."

Anna took a deep breath. "They didn't appreciate it. Told me I needed to take some time to cool off. They made him take time, too. But in his case, they're just calling it a sabbatical. For me... I don't really know what it means."

"So you came to Cape May?" Luke raised his eyebrows. "Not the reaction I would have expected." He laughed as he spoke, keeping his tone light.

Anna laughed with him. "Okay, when you say it out loud it sounds kind of extreme. But remember, Aunt Louise had just died and left me this house. It all kind of happened at the same time."

Luke nodded, wiping his hands on his jeans. "I get it."

"Really?" Anna asked skeptically.

Luke half smiled and nodded, looking around the room. "Look, I build things. I don't do research," he winked as he spoke. "But I make things. And I know how I would feel if someone took credit for my work. I'd be pissed off."

Anna grinned as she stood. "Thank you. I really appreciate you understanding."

"But"—Luke held up a work-roughened hand—"that doesn't mean I would never work with anyone else again. 'Cause that"—he smiled to take the sting out his words—"would be a little crazy."

"Hmm." Anna sank back down onto the tub, looking at the floor. "I don't know. I was just so excited to have this B&B. To be my own boss. To do something for myself. *By* myself. You know?" She looked up at him hopefully.

"Of course I know. Trust me, I get it, I run my own business, too, remember?"

She nodded.

"But you hired me to do things you couldn't do on your own, right? And when you need an electrician, you'll hire an electrician. Hell, when you needed the cops, you called the cops."

Anna felt herself flinch.

"Sorry, bad example," Luke said. "But you get my point. This isn't about you. I work with a lot of small business owners in Cape May. Just because this is your business doesn't mean you have to do everything yourself, on your own."

She sighed. "You're right."

"And Anna"—he leaned forward so he could look her in the eye and she felt herself flush at his closeness, at his earthy scent of sweat and wood shavings—"it doesn't get easier. You're gonna get attached to this place. To what you do. It's your baby, right? But you gotta remember it's a business. It's not personal."

Anna thought about the effort, the tears, even occasionally the blood she'd put into the house so far and shook her head. "No way. How could I not take this place personally? I mean, I have to, for the amount of work I put into it."

"I get that. But that's how it works. Just look at Richard Gormley."

"What?" Anna looked up at Luke, surprised. "Mr. Gormley who was here?"

Luke nodded. "Yep. He started a business down here, ended up being pretty successful. But he got bought out. Just a few years ago. I remember how upset he was, because I was doing some work on their house."

"I didn't realize they live in Cape May," Anna said, confused why the elderly couple would have stayed at Climbing Rose Cottage if they had a house in town.

"They don't anymore, obviously. They moved to upstate New York to live with their daughter. But they like to come and visit now and then. I know he still misses the place, he misses his business. But look how happy they are. He made the right choice when he sold Varico."

"Varico?" Anna asked, a thought jiggling about in her head.

Luke nodded. "His business. He didn't want to sell it, but he did, and it was the right thing to do. Now they're retired, happy, and with plenty of money to live on and enjoy their old age."

Anna laughed. "I'm hardly at retirement age, Luke."

"Okay, I know. I'm getting ahead of myself. I'm just saying, it's business. Don't take things so personally."

She stood again. "You're right, of course. Thank you. Now"—she glanced around—"let's talk about how these tiles get laid out."

13

Anna left Luke to the task of installing the new tile floor and was taking a quick break when the message from Sammy came through. The accompanying text simply said, “I’m coming over.”

She glanced at Eoin as he ran past her into the kitchen. “Help yourself to the lemonade,” she called out as the kitchen door closed behind him.

Anna’s first reaction to Sammy’s message was relief. She looked forward to sharing her fears and worries with her friend. But even as she felt herself relax, her eyes skimmed over the local newspaper article Sammy had forwarded to her.

“... unexplained death ... local B&B owner considered suspect... unsafe.” She looked back up at the headline. “Killer B&B in Cape May?”

She felt the blood drain from her face. Her hand shook and she tossed the phone down onto the chair next to her, then jumped when it rang. She snatched it up.

“Hello?”

“Hello, Ms. McGregor? This is Jonathan French. I need to cancel our reservation for next week.”

Anna tried to keep her voice calm. "Cancel? Of course. Will you be rescheduling your trip? I'm happy to revise your reservation to a later date."

"No, thank you." His voice was crisp, firm. "That won't be necessary."

The line went dead.

Anna slumped down in her chair, holding her head in her hands. How could this be happening? She'd only just opened and she'd worked so hard to get the reservations she had. She couldn't afford to lose any more. And yet she had a feeling the Frenches wouldn't be the last to cancel.

Eoin ran back through the lounge, carrying a large glass of lemonade in both hands. Anna jumped up and took the glass from him. "Let me help you with that. Do you want some cookies?"

Eoin nodded, his eyes wide, but said nothing.

"Cat got your tongue?" Anna said, smiling.

Eoin shook his head no. "Sorry," he whispered, then ran back out to the porch.

In the kitchen, Anna put a few cookies and Eoin's lemonade on a tray and carried it out to him on the front porch. At least he seemed to enjoy just hanging out at home reading. But she was definitely going to have to find some things for him to do this summer. Fun things. Kid things.

Her mind was toying with the idea of children's activities as she crossed back through the front hall when the sound of a tile saw from upstairs brought her back to reality. Her current, customer-free reality. Luke was still at work. Maybe she should let him go? She wouldn't be able to pay him if too many more guests cancelled. She only had six other reservations right now. She'd been hoping to get more quickly, but that didn't seem likely now.

She felt a clawing at the pit of her stomach, a sensation

she remembered far too vividly from the stressful days at graduate school.

No. She stood up and tucked her phone into her pocket. She wasn't giving up yet.

Grabbing safety goggles and a large mallet from the mud room, Anna went outside determined to tackle the next project on her list.

The ramshackle wooden shed stood about thirty feet away from the house in the side yard. At one point it had been painted a bright green with dark green edging, to match the colors of the main house. Now, the colors were faded, the wood worn and splintered. The same fate that awaited the rest of the house if Anna couldn't earn the money to keep it up. She looked up at the house, admiring the colorfully painted gables, the typical Victorian excess of the multifaceted roofs and asymmetry of the bay windows. It was beautiful, in an awkward, colorful, exuberant way. And Anna wanted to keep it that way.

Anna remembered the old shed from her childhood, from the many weekends and summer months she would spend in Cape May with Aunt Louise watching over her. She and Sammy used to hide behind the shed when they played hide-and-seek in the yard. Anna had made the mistake once of hiding inside the shed. Only once.

She could still remember the fear in Aunt Louise's eyes when she came running out of the house to grab Anna and pull her out of the shed. As a child, she couldn't understand what Aunt Louise had been so upset about. Why shouldn't she try to find a hiding spot among the heavy spades, sharp rakes and rusty saws? Now, years later, she still felt guilty for scaring poor Aunt Louise so much, even if it hadn't been intentional.

She put a hand on the rotting wood and felt it give beneath her touch. Back then, the shed had been unsafe because of what it held. Today, it was unsafe all on its own, even standing empty.

Anna grabbed the mallet in both hands, pulled her arms back and swung with all her strength. The heavy head of the tool sank easily into the old wood, leaving a wide, splintered hole.

Anna took a step back and looked at what she'd done. She grinned. And took another swing. Then another.

She felt the sweat pouring down her face as she attacked the old shed, but she didn't care. With each swing, she felt her tensions lighten. This — she grunted — was for Mrs. Hedley. She took aim and swung again. *Grunt*. That one's for whoever wrote that horrible article. She rubbed a hand over her face and felt the sawdust building up on it. She must look a mess. She didn't care.

Another swing — another heavy grunt — she heard the loud *crack* of an internal beam breaking in half and the wall collapsed inward. She kept swinging, attacking each of the walls, breaking them down into splintered wood.

Each cracking sound, each splintered piece of wood made her feel stronger, safer. She laughed to herself and it felt good. She let the head of the mallet fall to the ground and laughed again.

Still smiling, she turned to look around the house, then froze, the mallet still in her hand, her vision blurred by the sawdust that had accumulated on her goggles.

Mrs. James and Mrs. Santiago stood at her gate, watching her, their mouths agape. Anna didn't know them well but had met them once or twice around town. She raised a hand to offer a friendly wave, but both women frowned.

Mrs. James leaned close to Mrs. Santiago and whispered something, then both women shook their heads and scurried away.

Oh fudge.

Now her neighbors not only thought she was an accidental murderer but a violent one as well. With Mrs. Santiago and Mrs. James involved, the news would spread through the close-knit community of the Our Lady Star of the Sea parish like wildfire.

If she were going to have any chance of saving her business, the police needed to come up with the real reason George Hedley died, and soon.

ꕤ 14 ꕤ

Anna raised her head when she heard the creak of the wooden gate, wondering what else could possibly happen today.

"Oh, Anna." Sammy ran up the flagstone path and sat next to Anna on the porch step, wrapping her arms around her friend. "Look at you! What happened?"

Anna grinned and leaned into her friend. "Nothing, really. I was just working on the shed."

Sammy leaned forward to look around the side of the house, where the old shed lay in splinters and dust. "I see that. Looks like you won that round." She held Anna at arm's length and examined her. "At least I think so. You look a mess."

Anna could only imagine what she looked like. She'd simply dropped onto the porch step after her nosy neighbors had run off. She could still feel the sweat drying on the back of her neck and knew she was covered head to toe in dirt, sweat and sawdust. Unlike her friend who was, as always, perfectly dressed and made up. Anyone seeing Sammy now, her embroidered peasant shirt hanging loose over stylish jeans and high-heeled ankle boots, her silky blond hair catching the light, would never realize this was the same woman who could be found at 5 a.m. every morning covered in flour and whipping up bread, cakes and muffins in the sweltering heat of her bakery kitchen. Now, her baby blue eyes glistened at the sight of her best friend clearly in despair.

Anna picked up the mallet from where it had fallen next to her. "Who knew running a B&B was such dirty work?"

"Come on, let's get you cleaned up." Sammy helped Anna up and walked behind her to her room on the fourth floor. On the way, Sammy peeked into the Royal Room. "I see you still have the luscious Luke working for you?" She wiggled her eyebrows as she spoke.

Anna gave her friend a sideways look. "I'm not going to justify that with a response."

Sammy threw her hands up in despair. "But why not?" She asked, carrying on a conversation they'd had many times before. "You can see as well as I can he's gorgeous. And he clearly likes you."

"And he works for me." Anna opened her closet door and stood staring at her clothes. Nothing looked right. "How unprofessional would that be, to get involved with someone I hired?"

Sammy walked over and nudged her friend gently out of the way. "Don't get dirt all over your clothes. Go get washed up. I'll find something for you to wear."

Anna left Sammy digging through her closet with relief as she stepped into her bathroom. She spent longer than she should have simply standing under the hot water, letting the uplifting scent of her Eucalyptus body wash clear her mind and raise her spirits. When she was clean and comfortably wrapped in a fluffy bath sheet, she reentered her room. Sammy had laid out a pair of jeans, sweater and silk scarf.

Anna was dressed and sitting at her vanity when Sammy reappeared carrying a steaming mug.

"Here, I made you some peppermint tea." Sammy placed the mug at Anna's side and flopped down onto the bed. "Now tell me about it."

Anna paused for a moment, not sure where to start. "George died at the table," she started, then stopped. "But you know that. The police think, I mean, his wife thinks, and maybe I did, I don't know... I didn't kill him, did I, Sammy?"

"Of course you didn't. Now, start again, and this time tell me everything."

So Anna did, from the moment George arrived at Climbing Rose Cottage to the moment Mrs. James and Mrs. Santiago whispered about her in the street. She explained about packing up George's room and how furious that had made Mrs. Hedley, how guests were already cancelling and how she just didn't know how much longer she'd be able to keep pretending to run a B&B if she didn't have any guests.

"Oh Sammy, I really need the truth to come out about how George died," she ended, looking down into her now empty mug. "And heaven help me, I hate to say this...."

She looked up at her friend, who nodded encouragingly. "Say what?"

Anna frowned as she felt tears come to her eyes. "It's just, I almost hope his death wasn't accidental. Because if it was, then that means something here, something I did, killed him."

Sammy jumped up from the bed. "That's a ridiculous thing to say. For all you know, he had a heart attack. There's no way you can be blamed for that."

"Mrs. Hedley is convinced that if he'd been back at home under her eagle eyes, she would have saved him."

"Well that's just nonsense and you know it. Come on." She grabbed Anna's arm and pulled her up. "We're going out.

You clearly need a break. First the death, then your cousin. Speaking of, where is he?"

Anna followed Sammy back downstairs and out to the porch, where Eoin was tucked into a chair around the corner, reading. He looked up at the sound of their steps, his expression vague. As soon as he saw Sammy, he smiled. Just like a man, Anna thought. Even as an eight-year-old.

"Eoin, this is my best friend, Ms. Sammy Shields. Sammy, this is my cousin Eoin."

"Eoin," he corrected her, as Anna had come to expect, but this time his voice had a dreamy quality to it. His eyes were fixed on Sammy.

Sammy laughed. "Right. I won't even try. It's so nice to meet you. I understand you're here for the whole summer?"

She grabbed another chair and pulled it up next to his.

Eoin practically glowed. "I am," he said in his high pitched voice, his Irish accent adding a trill to his words. "I'm excited to see Cape May. I've been reading about the town, about the history and... em... geography. Now I get to spend even more time here with me Cousin Anna."

He then launched into an explanation of how he had been scheduled to visit in June, but his school burned down, but he'd already passed all his tests, so his parents sent him earlier than expected and Cousin Anna hadn't received any of the messages warning her. He didn't seem to stop to take a breath.

Sammy laughed again, but Anna simply stared. "Why don't you talk to me like that?"

Eoin turned his face toward her, but kept his eyes case down. "Sorry," he whispered.

"Shh." Sammy put an arm around him. "Come on, we're taking Cousin Anna out to have some fun. And I guess you're going to come with us. You can't stay here alone."

"I don't know, Sammy. I'm not really up for much," Anna said.

"Let's do the wine and cheese thing, we always like that. We could go to that winery in North Cape May. They have a fire pit, that's always fun."

Anna stopped and snapped her fingers. "Wine and cheese. Yes! I knew I remembered that name from somewhere. It's near the cheese shop."

Sammy, who had already stepped off the porch, turned back to Anna. "Okay, what's that look for? What name? What are you thinking?"

"Nothing, nothing," Anna reassured her. "It's a great idea. But let's go to the other one, the winery in West Cape May. That's near the cheese shop we like anyway. Remember? We used to go there all the time."

"All right, that sounds good." Sammy looked at Anna with suspicion clearly painted on her face. "But why do I suspect there's more going on here than just wine and cheese?"

15

Anna leaned forward over the glass case, her eyes scanning the rows of options. Brie... blue... Camembert... Manchego... Stilton... this was her favorite cheese shop for a reason.

She felt Eoin at her side and looked down at him. He'd clasped his hands together in front of him and was leaning forward so his nose almost touched the glass case. His eyes moved back and forth in amazement over the array of cheeses. He looked up at her and grinned, then turned his attention back to the cheese.

"What do you think?" She turned to Sammy, but Sammy had just stuffed one of the free samples into her mouth. "Sorry, bad timing! I'm leaning toward something with a stronger flavor, maybe a Stilton?"

Sammy shrugged as she chewed. "Why not that and a brie, mix it up a bit."

"Perhaps with one of our fig jams?" Manny, the shop owner, offered. "They go very well with the brie, in particular."

"Thanks Manny, you're a genius." Anna smiled at her

friend. "This way we can pair them with a bottle of white and a bottle of red."

"How are things going for you Anna?" Manny asked as he wrapped up their selections. "I understand you've been having some trouble."

"You could say that," Anna responded without making eye contact.

"Oh no, don't go there." Sammy, who'd just passed one of the samples to Eoin, jumped into the conversation. "The whole point of this afternoon is to get our minds off what happened. Yes, Manny, it was bad. A man died in Anna's house. But it wasn't her fault. You know that," she chided the man, who looked hurt.

"Of course it wasn't. I would never think that," he said. "Anna, please, I'm so sorry."

Anna waved a hand. "It's okay, Manny, I know you were asking because you care. This is a big deal, though. I don't think I'll just be able to take a few afternoons off and get over it." She looked at Sammy. "Sammy, no one's ever going to forget that someone died at Climbing Rose Cottage. Never."

"Maybe not, but they will get past it. People must die at hotels all the time."

"Well, a Cape May B&B is hardly just a hotel," Manny chimed in. "I don't think that's a fair comparison."

"Manny's right. I need to get this case wrapped up. Fast."

"Case?" Manny asked, clearly confused. "Did you want a case of something?" He looked around his shop.

"No, sorry, it's nothing." Anna laughed. "This is all. Thanks Manny," she added as she grabbed Eoin and guided him out the door.

"Okay, now what?" Sammy asked, and Anna could tell from her tone that she was worried.

"Look." Anna pointed across the street.

"What am I looking at?" Sammy asked as her eyes

scanned the single-story row of shops and offices that filled the block. "What?"

"There." Anna pointed to the office on the end. Only a small sign over the door indicated the name of the business, Varico. It didn't look as if they were trying to attract customers.

"What about it?" Sammy asked, still confused.

"That's the business. The one where George Hedley worked and that Richard Gormley sold a few years ago."

"And...?" Sammy dragged out the word, her confusion turning to concern. She shifted her weight onto one leg, put a hand on her hip and stared at Anna.

Eoin stood between the women, silent, his owl eyes moving back and forth between them as they spoke.

"And we need to find out what it is. And why it's connected to both of my guests. The living one and the dead one. Don't you think it's weird, the connection between the two guests?"

"Not necessarily." Sammy maintained her pose but shook her head at her friend. "It's a small town, after all. People are connected."

"Come on." Anna reached for her friend's hand. "Let's go find out."

"Oh no." Sammy shook her head and backed away. "No, no, no. Why would we possibly go there. Anna, you need to relax. You're not thinking straight."

"Sammy, the only way I will ever be able to move beyond this is when the truth comes out. If someone did kill George, I need to know."

"Don't you mean the police need to know?" Sammy asked, but had already started following Anna.

"Hey, Luke was just telling me that everyone needs to accept help now and then. So, the same thing must apply to the police, too, right?"

16

The office's reception area looked out onto the parking lot and across the street toward the cheese shop, so the young man sitting behind the desk must have seen them pointing, arguing and eventually coming over. The front wall was comprised entirely of windows, including the glass door that offered more resistance than she'd expected. Sammy had had to help pull, in fact, making their entry into the office less than elegant.

By the time the three of them were standing in the small space, the young man had stopped whatever he'd been doing and sat there watching them. "May I help you?" he asked with surprise. Apparently they didn't get many drop-in visitors.

Anna looked around frantically, trying to get any sense at all of what this office was. She saw no posters or flyers, no brochures or even posted rules that would give her a clue. Sammy didn't seem to be doing any better, as she simply took a step back and pushed Anna forward.

"Yes, hi," she started nervously. "I'm here because of George Hedley."

"George." The young man's face fell, his head tipping to one side as his eyes moved to something on the edge of his desk. Perhaps a picture, Anna thought. She felt a pang of regret for having barged in like this. But she was here now, no point turning back.

"I'm so sorry for your loss," she said, meaning every word.

"Are you friends of his?" the young man asked.

Anna took a breath. "Sort of... well, that is to say, I didn't know him very well. But I thought..." she cut herself off, not quite sure where to go with this.

"We're hoping you have some information about the funeral," Sammy jumped in and Anna shot her a grateful look. "We didn't see anything posted."

"Oh, right." the young man stood and reached across to a shelf behind him. "Sure. Actually"—his brow puckered as he looked back at them—"Actually, it says right here." He held out a copy of *The Cape May Standard*.

Anna took it, grimacing with embarrassment. "Right, sorry, I should have noticed that."

"So what is this place?" Sammy asked, looking around the sparse office then back at the young man. "What do you do here?"

The man's eyes narrowed. "What do we do? I thought you said you were friends of George?"

"I said I didn't know him well," Anna pointed out. "And only on a social basis."

"Social?" Now the young man looked entirely unconvinced. "Look, I don't know who you are—"

Whatever he was about to say was cut off. A man walked into the reception area from a back room, talking as he entered. "Charles, I need those 2017 reports, the ones with—"

This time it was Charles' turn to cut him off. "Mr. Murphy, these women are here asking about Mr. Hedley."

Mr. Murphy looked up, noticing Anna and Sammy for the first time. "Oh. Asking about what?" He shook his head as he pulled his glasses off his face. "I'm sorry, who are you?"

He glanced back and forth between the two women, his eyes dark in a chiseled face. He wore a white button-down shirt, open at the neck, and sported a short mop of curly hair that had once been brown but was now tinged with gray.

Anna put a hand out and approached the man. "Mr. Murphy, my name is Anna McGregor. I knew George very briefly, and I was simply hoping to learn a little bit more about him."

"And about his funeral arrangements," Sammy added, giving Anna a meaningful glance.

"Right, that too." Anna said.

"I see." He looked over at Charles who just raised his eyebrows and shrugged. "Come through, then."

Anna, Sammy and Eoin followed him back to his office, which was no more decorative than the front room. A row of worn metal filing cabinets lined one wall. A lone desk sat facing them. No chairs were provided for visitors.

"Please, sorry," Mr. Murphy mumbled as he pulled open a closet door and produced three folding chairs, lifting them easily with one hand. "I don't usually have clients here." He came toward them to set up the chairs so they were facing the desk. As he moved, his shirt strained at times against the muscles of his shoulders and back, suggesting a man who worked at maintaining his physique. He moved back behind his desk and took a seat, inviting them to do the same.

"And what is it that you do here, Mr. Murphy?"

"Please, call me Paul," he responded. "Well, we're import/export. You must know that, if you know George. George and I are — were — partners."

Anna tried not to show her surprise. "What do you import and export?" she asked.

Paul raised both hands and gave an expansive gesture. "Whatever is needed. Mostly furniture, works of art, things that are ordered by stores locally."

"Locally here in Cape May?" Anna asked.

"Makes sense," Sammy said.

"Here or in Trenton, where our other offices are." As he spoke, Paul's brows lowered and his eyes narrowed. "I keep telling you about myself, but I still don't know who you are."

"Mr. Murphy... Paul." Anna leaned forward in her seat. "As I said, my name is Anna McGregor, and this is my friend Sammy Shields and my cousin Eoin."

"Eoin," Eoin piped up on cue to correct her pronunciation.

Anna glared at him and continued. "I own Climbing Rose Cottage, the B&B where George... where George was staying. Here in Cape May."

"Oh, I see." Paul's chair scraped against the tiled floor as he pushed himself back, away from the desk. "But why are you here? I don't understand."

"I have to admit, I'm not entirely sure myself." Anna smiled at him, trying to put him at ease. "I wish I had known George better. I just feel terrible about what happened, and I'm trying to get a sense of who he was. What he was like. You know?"

"No, I don't." Paul shook his head slowly. "I don't understand at all. A man dies in your home and you come here asking questions about him."

"We're very sorry to bother you," Sammy said. "I told Anna she shouldn't be here. But you must understand, she's very upset. I'm sure you are, too, losing your partner like this."

"Humph." Paul let out a low laugh. "We weren't friends, not really, just business partners."

"But he did come down here for work, off and on, right?" Anna asked. "When I spoke to him, he seemed to suggest that."

"He did, indeed." Paul leaned back in his chair and the overhead fluorescent lights cast shadows below his taught cheekbones and square chin, making him look almost ghoulish. "Frankly, more than he needed to. Our paperwork is all done on the cloud, our storage units are here and in Trenton. If we need to meet, either just the two of us or with clients, we almost always do it over the phone or video conferencing. I don't know why he came down here so often."

Picturing the grim face of Mrs. Hedley, Anna suspected she might understand. She thought some more about what she knew about the company. "I also know Richard Gormley," she said.

"You do?" Paul sounded genuinely surprised.

Anna nodded. "Yes, he's been a guest at my B&B as well."

"My, my, my, what a small world." Paul's words were lighthearted but Anna noticed that his eyes had once again narrowed and his hands gripped the edge of his desk.

Eoin seemed to respond in kind, leaning forward and gripping the edge of his chair.

"I'm not very familiar with how you ended up taking over Mr. Gormley's business, Paul," Anna said. "Did you simply buy it from him?"

"Something like that." Paul spoke through tight lips, his head barely moving. "It was a long time ago."

"But I understand Mr. Gormley didn't really want to sell, isn't that true?"

Paul stood. "As I said, it was a long time ago. George and I weren't even partners yet then, so I fail to see how it could be of interest to you. You have the information you came for now, yes?"

Anna and Sammy shared a glance as they stood. "Yes, thank you. But isn't there—"

"There's nothing more I can say," Paul said firmly. He walked across the office and opened the door. The interview was over.

17

Anna and Sammy both burst out talking as soon as they'd stepped out of the Varico offices.

"What do you think that was about?" Anna asked.

"He was definitely nervous about something," Sammy said at the same time.

Both women laughed, then Anna continued. "Definitely. But what?"

"His whole attitude changed as soon as you mentioned Richard Gormley, didn't it?"

"Hello Anna, I'm surprised to see you here. What brings you to these offices?"

They spun around in surprise to see Evan Burley behind them. They had turned their backs on him when they'd exited, and in their excitement about their interview with Paul Murphy hadn't even noticed him standing there. Eoin, on the other hand, was already looking up at him, his eyes opened wide and a broad smile on his face.

Evan smiled back at the boy and put his hand out. Eoin

grabbed it, moving to stand closer to the officer, his expression one of pure pleasure.

"Patrolman Burley... Evan..." Anna stumbled over her words. "Hi. Yes, me too. I mean, I'm surprised to see you here..." she paused, having completely run out of words.

Sammy stuck a hand out toward Evan and offered her brightest smile. "Sammy Shields. I'm a friend of Anna's. Nice to meet you."

"Right, sorry, Sammy, this is Patrolman Evan Burley. He came to the house when... well, when George died. He was very kind to me." She smiled at Evan, hoping he'd forget the question he'd asked.

He didn't. "I'm glad I could help. Sammy, it's very nice to meet you. So tell me, why are you ladies here?" He glanced down at Eoin. "And what are you doing, young man?"

Eoin looked at Anna, then looked back at the ground and said nothing.

"Here?" Anna looked around. "Oh, well we came to buy some cheese." She helpfully held up the bag she still carried from the cheese shop. Across the street. She winced at her own brazenness.

"Right," Sammy chimed in, looking up at Evan through her lashes. "We're taking the afternoon off. Getting some cheese and visiting a winery. Doing some wine tasting, you know?"

"Uh-huh." Evan replied, looking across the street to the cheese shop, then back at them. He raised an eyebrow in a clear question and waited. Anna had to suppress a laugh when Eoin, still holding tightly onto his hero's hand, mimicked the expression.

"Right, why are we here, you mean." Anna nodded, looking at the ground.

Sammy chewed on her lip and looked down the street to examine the cars she saw there.

"Look, the truth is... I wanted to... that is...." Anna looked up at Evan.

"It was me," Sammy spoke up. "I run a bakery. In West Wildwood. Best cakes around," she added helpfully. "If you're ever looking for a bakery, it's the Wild West Bakery."

"Good to know, thank you. Why did you need to come here?" Evan asked.

"Well, we were at the cheese shop," Sammy said slowly, clearly trying to think fast. "And I saw the sign and remembered hearing about this company. Varico." She gestured at the sign above the door. "And thought, maybe I could get some work done."

"On your afternoon off," Evan said.

"Exactly." Sammy nodded. "You know how it is. When you run a small business, you're never really off."

"No, I guess not."

Anna realized she was grinning like a mad woman and bit her lip.

"May I ask what your business is with Varico?" Evan asked.

"Just shipping some orders," Sammy answered, her eyes open wide. Not blinking.

Anna giggled and Evan looked at her. He managed to pull his hand free of Eoin's.

"Look, ladies. I'm not sure what to make of this. A man has died and we're still trying to figure out what happened. I suggest you stay away from his businesses, from his family..." he looked pointedly at Anna and she realized with a gulp that Mrs. Hedley must have followed through on her threat to go the police with her accusations.

"You can't believe Mrs. Hedley, Evan. You know I didn't kill George."

"I do, I know." He put a strong, comforting hand on her arm. "But I think it's best for everyone, including you, if you just keep your distance from this for a while. And you, too, I'm afraid." He turned to Sammy. "I understand you have a business to run, but I'm sure there are other companies you can work with. At least for now."

"Right, of course." Sammy nodded seriously. "Turns out they weren't able to provide what I need anyway."

Even as Sammy spoke, Anna realized that as soon as Evan spoke to Paul Murphy, he'd expose their lie. Oh fudge.

"Evan," she said, "would you like to join us at the winery? We have plenty of cheese." She held the bag up again.

Evan laughed. "That's a tempting offer, thanks." He glanced at his watch. "I'm still on duty, I'm afraid, for another hour."

Anna felt Sammy nudge her elbow but refused to look at her friend.

"It's just that, well, I want to explain. Really, I mean." She glanced at Sammy, who was looking at her like she was insane.

"So you haven't really explained so far?" Evan gave them a look faking surprise.

"Oh," Sammy said, looking down.

"Look, Anna, Sammy." Evan looked at them both kindly. "I don't think you killed anyone, Anna, but you are still a suspect. You need to understand that. Don't go running around trying to get to know George better, or trying to make yourself feel better. I know this is hard for you, I really do. But this is still a police investigation."

"I just thought I could help," Anna mumbled, looking at the ground.

"I'm sorry, what was that?" Evan asked.

"Look, you should know that Paul Murphy got all squirrelly as soon as we mentioned Richard Gormley," Sammy explained.

"And he's being cagey about George, too." Anna added. "There's something he's not saying."

They both looked up at Evan hopefully. He took a step back, looked out over the parking lot for a moment, then back at Anna. "I can't make this any clearer, Anna. You must not get involved in a police investigation. If Detective Walsh found out you were talking to people who are involved — not just talking to, but asking them specifically about George..." He let out a breath as he shook his head. "I won't tell him. This time. But you need to stop."

Anna bit her lip and frowned. "Fine. We'll just go enjoy our wine and cheese. Come on Eoin."

She grabbed Eoin's hand and dragged him back across the street, fuming. When she'd seat-belted the boy into the car, still parked in front of the cheese shop, she glanced back and saw Evan standing there, watching them.

"That was rough," Sammy said. "And why did you invite him to join us? I mean, he is cute and all..." Sammy looked out her window to watch Evan as they drove past.

Anna shook her head. "He makes me so mad. First he says he trusts me, he acts like he wants to help me. Then he tells me I'm a suspect." She banged her hand against the dashboard. "Ugh!"

"Okay, okay, calm down. He's just doing his job."

"Exactly!" Anna felt her anger growing and took a few deep breaths. "He is just doing his job. He wants to help me. And by going to Varico and talking to Paul Murphy, I just made myself look even more suspicious."

18

"So why do you think Paul Murphy reacted the way he did when you brought up Richard Gormley's name?" Sammy asked as she popped a cube of cheese into her mouth.

"Hmm," Anna said, thinking. She took a sip of Chardonnay. "Luke said Richard didn't want to sell his business. It sounded like he was forced to."

"How can someone be forced to sell?" Sammy asked. "No way I'd sell my bakery to someone else."

"Well, what if you were ready to retire?"

Sammy screwed her face up in disgust. "I'll never retire. I love my work."

Anna laughed and looked around the winery. They sat in a room off the main tasting floor. Windows lining one wall opened up onto the vineyards beyond to provide a gentle, peaceful backdrop. Definitely what they needed for the conversation they were having.

Eoin perched on one of the tall stools at the table, one leg dangling in the air, the other folded in half with his foot on the seat of the stool. He sipped his lemonade as his round eyes took in everything around him.

Plenty of other people had had the same idea and the tables scattered around the room were mostly full. The winery had a good setup here. Visitors entered through the gift shop first, then on to the tasting room. Once they'd found a wine they loved, they could buy a bottle, grab some snacks if they hadn't brought their own, then settle down at a table to enjoy themselves while admiring the beauty of the vineyard.

"So let's just say Richard really didn't want to sell. Somehow George forced him to." Anna considered this, then shook her head. "But that brings us back to the same questions. How'd he force him to sell? And since Richard did sell, what does that have to do with George being dead?"

Sammy shrugged. "Maybe Richard killed him. Out of revenge. For stealing his business."

Anna took another sip of wine, considering this. "Makes sense, actually. He must have really hated George."

"Or Paul Murphy, don't forget him." Sammy raised a finger as she spoke.

"He was not a nice man," Eoin said, nodding. "He seemed angry."

"He did get angry when we mentioned Richard, didn't he?" Anna patted Eoin's arm. "Or maybe things weren't going well with the business. You hear about business partners falling out. Maybe he really wanted George out of the way."

"Maybe." Sammy chewed on another chunk of cheese. "But how? And think about it, Richard had plenty of opportunity." Sammy's voice rose with excitement as she warmed to her idea. "He was right there. He could have poisoned George."

A few faces turned in their direction and Anna shushed her, laughing. "Keep your voice down."

"Sorry. But think about it. Who else was in the house when George died?"

Anna pictured her other guests. One thought of the terror on Maryanne's face when she'd seen George, was enough to know that she and Jim were not involved. And she knew she hadn't done it.

"You're right. The Gormleys were the only other people in the house."

"Ooh." Sammy laughed again. "Maybe Mrs. Gormley did it, to get revenge for her husband."

Now both women were laughing, the thought of elderly Mrs. Gormley sneaking around the house poisoning people too much to bear.

"Ladies."

They both jumped with surprise at the interruption.

"Felicia." Anna smiled at the librarian. "What are you doing here?"

"Doing here?" She looked around and laughed. "Even librarians get to enjoy themselves sometimes, Anna. Eoin, good to see you again. Hi." She put a hand out toward Sammy. "Felicia Keane. I was a friend of Louise Gannet."

"Oh gosh, I'm sorry. Felicia, this is my best friend Sammy."

"Nice to meet you," Sammy said as she shook Felicia's hand. "I loved Aunt Louise almost as much as Anna did. She was always kind to me when I came down to visit."

The older woman acknowledged the memory with a nod, then looked over their table. "I see you're well supplied." She picked up the bottle of wine and examined it. "Good choice. Their Chardonnay is their best wine, in my opinion. Though, Eoin, I think you made a very wise decision with the lemonade."

The boy grinned and took another sip, then reach into his pocket to pull out his notebook and pencil. He sat poised, his eyes moving back and forth between the women, as if ready to take notes at a meeting.

"So"—Felicia replaced the bottle on the table and leaned in, looking at each young woman in turn—"you're here talking about who murdered George Hedley."

Sammy's eyes widened in surprise and Anna put a hand over her mouth.

"Oh no," Anna said, "were we really being that loud?"

Felicia laughed. "Indeed you were. And remember, it's not just the other guests here who might be listening. The staff have ears, too, you know."

Anna looked over at the counter near the door. Two young men in winery shirts were talking together in low voices. One of them looked over at Anna, then quickly looked away. Anna gulped.

"Oh fudge. What if they tell Richard Gormley we've been talking about him."

"Exactly," Felicia replied. "It's not a good business practice for a B&B owner to gossip about her guests."

"Okay, but you know that people already think Anna was somehow responsible for George's death, right?" Sammy jumped in. "Let's keep this in perspective. It's not a good business practice for B&B owners to let their guests die, either."

Anna shook her head and slumped lower in her chair. "You're not helping, Sammy."

"It's all right." Felicia leaned closer in. "Now, tell me why you're talking about Richard Gormley and George Hedley's death."

Anna shrugged, embarrassed now that they had been. "We were just trying to figure out if Richard might have ... somehow... for some reason..." She noticed that Eoin was writing furiously. She leaned closer to him, hoping to see what he was writing, but as she moved he pulled the book closer to himself. Humph.

"You think Richard Gormley might have killed George Hedley?" Felicia whispered, looking around the room as she said it. "Why would he do that?"

Sammy leaned forward conspiratorially. "Think about it. Richard didn't want to sell his business to George, everyone knows that. So maybe he just got so angry about it and killed him."

"He was in the house at the time," Anna added.

Felicia frowned as she looked back and forth between them, then nodded. "I understand. You need to get people to stop thinking you were responsible for George's death. And to do that, you need to find out who really was responsible. Why you don't trust the police to figure that out, I have no idea."

"It's not that—" Anna said.

"No, it's just—" Sammy said at the same time.

Felicia held up a hand to cut them off. "Okay, okay. Well, you'll need a lot more than just the suggestions that Richard Gormley might have been angry and had opportunity if you want to convince the police to look at him as a suspect."

"True," Anna said glumly as Sammy nodded. Then Anna brightened. "And what about Paul Murphy, George's business partner? Do you know him?"

"A bit." Felicia nodded. "He's worked in town for a few years now." She stared out the windows at the vines beyond. "I suppose I could ask around about him, see what I can find out."

Anna grinned. "You're the best, Felicia."

"And what do we do?" Sammy asked, the excitement back in her voice.

Anna chewed on her lip, thinking. "I'm not sure. But we definitely need to learn more about George Hedley."

Sammy nodded. "I'll look him up online. There's always crazy amounts of information available about people."

Anna sat back in her chair, wondering if she could finally relax for the first time in what felt like ages. "You two are the best, thank you."

"You'll get through this Anna." Felicia patted her shoulder. "I promise. Cheer up."

19

Friday morning, Anna woke to a day that looked as depressed as she was. She lingered in bed, watching the barely budding trees outside her window moving in the wind. A quick rain shower tapped against the glass then drifted on. She shivered and pulled her blanket up over her shoulders. Maybe she should just stay in bed today.

Everything had seemed so positive yesterday in the winery, but now that she'd had time to think about it, she knew she was fooling herself. What could she and Sammy really find that the police couldn't?

She closed her eyes, listening to the wind and rain. A memory flashed through her mind. Another morning much like this. But on that morning, she wasn't alone. She had cuddled up next to Steve, resting her head on his shoulder. He'd wrapped an arm around her, keeping her warm. They'd stayed in bed late that morning, chatting about life, talking about their plans for the future. Academics was a tough career. She knew she had to be willing to move around the country, to take jobs at universities when they were offered to her. And he'd have to move around, too. There was no guarantee they'd always be working in the same town.

At the time, it had made her sad to think about that. She didn't like the idea of being on her own. She loved the feeling of him next to her. He made her feel loved, made her feel safe.

She opened her eyes and sat up. He hadn't kept her safe, had he? It had all been an illusion. In the end, he'd been the very one who hurt her.

She jumped out of bed, determined to do something useful today.

She prepared a simple breakfast — no point in wasting money on anything fancy — but Eoin seemed to enjoy his cereal. A few quick calls settled the boy's plan for the morning. The Cape May Center for Community Arts had a youth program that would be perfect for him. He didn't seem overjoyed at the prospect, simply blinking up at her with his big eyes.

"One day, Eoin—"

"Eoin."

"— you are going to feel comfortable enough around me to chat with me the way you seem to do with everyone else. And then you can tell me what you really want to do." She smiled at him as he finished off his cereal, then helped him get settled in the lounge with one of his books.

She brought a cup of tea out to her desk in the lounge and got to work. Her focus right now needed to be on getting more guests, not on investigating George's death. Guests who weren't afraid to stay here. She couldn't hide the fact that someone had died here, Anna knew that. It was in the newspapers, it was hardly a secret. But the news would pass, she was sure. Other events would catch people's attention. Other events, good or bad, would make headlines. She needed to move on.

Anna started with her social media presence, spending hours lining up a series of posts and videos that she scheduled through a service. Keeping in line with the general theme of Cape May, she posted images of Victorian women in fancy dresses, beautiful old photographs of the Cape May historic houses, and of course a few funny cat videos. Just for the laugh. She interspersed notices about her room availability and prices, including one post focusing on the importance she placed on safety and cleanliness. Then another cat video, to lighten the mood.

After social media came emails, her newsletter, then the various websites that promoted hotels and inns, updating her information and responding to their requests for updated information.

She sat back and stretched the kinks out of her shoulders and arms. Scheduling these posts was all well and good, but she'd have to keep a close eye on her phone so that she could reply to any comments the posts received. She hated how much time she had to spend on marketing, but it really wasn't optional.

And it couldn't all be done online, either.

Her mind was on her ads and marketing efforts as she grabbed her rain hat from the hall closet and a wool sweater that could withstand the slight drizzle that had started up, but the movement she saw out of the corner of her eye brought her back to the immediate present with a start. Had she really just seen something, or was her mind playing tricks on her?

She dropped her hat onto a chair and moved toward the still darkened doorway that led to Aunt Louise's rooms. Anna had not yet ventured into these rooms, despite being in the house for three months. They held too many memories, too many tears. She knew she needed to get in there and start going through Aunt Louise's things.

She could picture the rooms perfectly, memories from her many visits throughout her life still vivid in her mind. They were full of mementos Aunt Louise had picked up over the years, everything from fine art to local tchotchkes. Whenever Aunt Louise had had the time, she'd traveled the world. She'd picked up wooden boxes and jade statues, lace and tapestries, scarves and jewelry. It was a haphazard collection, but at the same time, Aunt Louise kept her private rooms pristine, a place for everything and everything in its place. Just like the rest of her life.

So what, then, had made Anna think she'd seen a movement?

She tiptoed closer to the doorway, then scoffed. Why was she tiptoeing? She intentionally stepped louder as she approached the doorway, then stuck her hand around the corner to flip on the overhead light.

Nothing moved. The short hall was empty, bar the two portraits hanging on the wall of Aunt Louise's mother — Anna's grandmother — and someone Anna didn't know. Two doors led off the hall, one straight ahead, the other to the right. Anna knew that straight ahead lay Aunt Louise's bedroom; to the right, her private sitting room. It was a good setup. It allowed Aunt Louise private space while still keeping her nearby in case she was needed by the guests.

One day soon, Anna was going to have to open those doors. Revisit her memories of her favorite Aunt. Go through her belongings, sort through what could be kept and what needed to be given away. Probably clean up the mess left by the police when they searched. Anna grimaced at that thought.

One day soon, but not today. She wasn't ready yet. Not until she could be confident that she would be successful in running the business Aunt Louise had built. She had some more work to do first.

She flipped the light back off. It was time to get to work and to get Eoin to the community center.

20

Eoin safely, if somewhat morosely, enrolled in the creativity lab, Anna wrapped her wool sweater more tightly around herself and headed out to Washington Mall with the flyers and brochures she'd had printed up for Climbing Rose Cottage. The main street in the town, it had been pedestrianized years earlier and housed lines of shops and restaurants on either side with pretty gazebos, benches and flowerpots along the center. The stores along this street offered something for everyone, including works by local artists, creative clothing boutiques, toy stores, kitchen goods and, of course, fudge.

Crowds of visitors thronged the street, despite the weather. A few folks fought with umbrellas that weren't strong enough to withstand the wind, but most were wrapped in coats and hats. Even the gray skies couldn't hide the attraction and beauty of the street — or get in the way of business.

A young woman stood outside a fudge shop, ducking under the awning, holding a tray of samples covered in plastic to protect them from the rain. Anna smiled and nodded as she grabbed a sample. She'd be back later to buy more, no doubt. The restaurants were crowded, guests lingering in the warmth and out of the rain. The stores were busy too, as wet shoppers jogged from one to another, looking over the jewelry, clothing, books, paintings and keepsakes that were on offer.

Anna joined the crowds, moving from one store to the next. She knew most of the shopkeepers by now, having worked this route before. In each store, she asked to talk to the manager, then requested permission to leave her brochures near their registers and post a flyer to their bulletin boards if they had one. Almost all of the managers and owners agreed. It was in their best interest to keep her business running, too. After all, they all shared a dependency on tourism to Cape May to keep their stores afloat.

Finally feeling a little upbeat about the future of her business, Anna pulled open the glass door to Bric-N-Brac. The antique-slash-odds-and-ends store located just off the main street and run by Jacob and Emily Ahava, carried everything from top-of-the-line antique chairs to a kite in the shape of a pirate.

"Hi Jacob, how are you doing?" Anna asked as she entered, seeing the owner working behind the register. "And how's Emily?"

"We're doing well," Jacob answered, his nordic accent still recognizable despite their many years in the country. "I hear you've been having some problems, though." He frowned down his nose at her.

Anna took a breath. "Yes, of course you've heard. It's a tragedy."

Jacob nodded then turned as his wife came in from a back entrance. "Anna, how nice to see you." She smiled, but the smile seemed somehow cold to Anna, not her customary effusive greeting.

She figured she should just get down to business. "I'm here to see if I can leave some of my new brochures with you." When neither of them responded, she added, "For your customers to pick up?"

Emily took one of the brochures and looked it over. "Very nice." She handed it back without agreeing to let Anna display them.

"Is something wrong?" Anna finally asked.

The couple shared an expression, then Jacob frowned at her again. "I have heard, from some friends, that you have been saying things about Richard Gormley."

"Oh." Anna's hand flew to cover her mouth to hide her surprise. And her guilt. She nodded. "I see. I mean, I understand. But no, it's not that..." she petered out, not sure how to defend herself against an accusation that was true.

"He is a good man, Anna," Jacob continued. "A strong man. He was a good neighbor. I don't like to hear bad rumors about him."

"No, of course not." Anna shook her head. "I'm so sorry. You're right, I was talking about him. But not to say anything bad, I promise." She crossed her fingers behind her back as she spoke, but it didn't assuage her guilt. "I just wanted to learn more about him. I met him for the first time when he stayed in Climbing Rose Cottage. You know, when..." she paused, once again lost for words.

"When poor George Hedley died," Emily said, nodding. "It was a tragedy, for sure."

"I am surprised you don't know Richard," Jacob added. "He lived in Cape May for many years."

Anna nodded. "I'm surprised, too. Do you know why he moved away?"

Jacob shrugged and frowned. "I suppose it was his time to retire, to pass the baton on to another generation." He glanced at his wife. "Something we have been considering ourselves."

"Oh, I'm sorry to hear that," Anna said.

"He didn't want to retire," Emily chided her husband softly. "He wasn't ready to sell his business."

Anna waited, but Emily only stared at her husband, while Jacob simply looked down at his hands folded on the counter.

"So why do you suppose he sold his business?" Anna finally asked.

"Who can know?" Jacob answered. "Maybe Susan convinced him it was time. His wife," he added when he saw the confusion on Anna's face.

"Maybe George made him a really great offer," Emily chimed in. "They did buy that big house in New York."

Anna glanced around the store, still holding on to the brochures she hoped to place there. "I don't suppose you know Paul Murphy, do you? He runs Richard's business now."

Jacob and Emily both shook their heads. "He lives in Villas," Jacob said, mentioning a town a few miles north on the bay side. "We don't see him down here so much. He works here, that is all."

"I've heard that George partnered with Paul because he knew he'd need someone to deal with clients," Anna said. "I guess he wasn't the most outgoing of people."

Jacob frowned yet again. "We don't know George at all. Just the name, from Richard talking about him."

Emily rolled her eyes. "Oh yes, when he got going." They both laughed.

"You mean, talking like he was angry at George?" Anna asked.

Emily and Jacob both clamped their mouths shut. Jacob put out a hand and took the brochures from Anna. "You can leave these here. But you must stop saying things like that about Richard Gormley."

"Right, sorry." Anna grimaced. She really needed to work on her diplomatic skills if she was going to keep asking questions like this. "Thanks for taking those," she said with a wave as she left the store.

21

The drizzle had picked up and was now definitely rain. Anna could feel cold drops rolling from her hat down into her collar. She shivered and pulled her sweater tighter around her, pulling the collar up. She still had a few more stores to visit before calling it a day.

Coming from Bric-N-Brac, she walked another block on the side street that ran parallel to Washington Mall. She was just turning the corner to head back to the main street when she heard her name.

"Felicia." She smiled at the older woman. "How are you? Did you have a good time last night?"

Felicia put an arm around Anna's shoulder. "I'm fine, but more to the point, how are you? You look like a drowned rat."

Anna laughed but couldn't disagree. That's kind of how she felt.

"Come on." Felicia turned her away from Washington Mall. "You can use a break. Come home with me for a hot cup of tea."

Anna gratefully followed her friend back around the corner then up one more block. Even in this weather, the bright colors of the imposing Victorian houses looked cheerful and warm. Some of these houses were B&Bs, just like hers, but others were private residences. Through the lace curtains Anna could glimpse shining wood floors, sparkling chandeliers and walls lined with art and books.

Felicia led her up the steps to one such house. Its pale blue exterior was trimmed with a brighter blue, a wide covered porch wrapped around from one side of the house to the other. Windows shone brightly in the gray light of the day, looking warm and comforting. Anna shivered one more time as she followed Felicia into the entrance hall then through a door in the back of the hall into the kitchen.

Completely modernized, the kitchen wouldn't have matched the style of the house except that Felicia had somehow made it seem a natural fit. A silver wood-burning stove sat in one corner, putting out a flickering heat that drew Anna toward it. As she stood warming her hands, she glanced around the rest of the kitchen. Sleek metal appliances were balanced with dark walnut cabinets and marbled counters. Overhead lights kept the work surfaces bright but smaller lamps dotted the room, emitting a mellower cast.

Anna hung up her damp sweater and sank into a chair at the table near the fireplace as Felicia bustled about the kitchen preparing tea and cookies.

"So," Felicia said as she carried her tray to the table and joined Anna. "What were you doing wandering around in the rain?"

Anna laughed. "Delivering those." She pointed to the box of brochures. "Asking businesses to display them for their customers. Just in case any want to come back to Cape May sometime."

"Just in case?" Felicia snorted. "Who wouldn't want to come back?"

Anna grinned as she sipped her tea. Then her smile faded.

"People might not want to come back to Climbing Rose Cottage, though. Once they hear about George Hedley."

Felicia nodded. "I know, honey. I'm so sorry. Tell me, you and Sammy seemed pretty excited about doing some research of your own. Have you found anything new?"

"I haven't checked in with Sammy, yet. She was going to see what she could find about George." Anna looked down at the table as she shook her head. "I did find out a little bit more about Richard Gormley, but managed to antagonize people in the process."

"Oh dear, what happened?"

Anna told Felicia about her conversation with the Ahavas. "I thought they weren't even going to help me by taking my brochures," she concluded. "I guess they're just mad at me for poking my nose into other people's business."

Felicia leaned forward to look Anna in the eyes as she smiled kindly. "Well, what did you expect? You *are* poking your nose in."

"Yes, but into *my* business, remember? I'm doing this to save my business, not hurt anyone else."

Felicia raised one hand in a shrug. "True. And if you do help the police find out what really happened to George, you'll be helping more than just your business. You could end up helping the whole town."

"Who's helping the town?" The question came from the doorway and Anna turned in surprise.

"Anna, this is my friend Kathy. Kathy, Anna McGregor. She's Louise Gannet's niece. She runs Climbing Rose Cottage now." Felicia's eyes lit up as she introduced Kathy.

Kathy grabbed a mug and joined them at the table, dropping a slice of lemon into her cup before adding the tea. "Nice to meet you." She grinned at Anna and slid forward in her chair until her legs straddled it, her elbows resting heavily on the table. "Now, how are you helping the town?"

Felicia laughed. "You heard about George Hedley dying."

"Of course." Kathy nodded brusquely and blew on her tea, furrowing the already deep lines around her mouth and crinkling the skin around her eyes. She looked about the same age as Felicia, with similar weather-beaten skin and short hair, though her hair was still chestnut brown as opposed to Felicia's gray.

"Well, Anna is hoping to find some information about how George might have died. To help the police."

"Huh." Kathy replied, but added nothing more.

Felicia shared a look with Kathy and nodded, then turned back to Anna. "Now you do remember what I said about Evan Burley, don't you? You must trust him. He's a good man and a good police officer. He'll do the right thing."

Kathy nodded. "Definitely don't do anything to get in his way, though. He won't appreciate that."

Anna grinned at the idea of big, comforting Evan ever acting angry. "That's hard to picture."

Both older women laughed. "We've known Evan for years, haven't we Kath? He can get annoyed, trust us."

Anna thought about this. She did trust Evan, no question. But he wasn't in charge of the investigation. "How about the detective in charge, Detective Walsh. Do you know anything about him?"

Felicia wrinkled her forehead and shook her head. "Not me, Kath?"

Kathy nodded as she took another sip of tea. "I know him. Sort of. He's in the same rowing club as me, but I wouldn't say we're friends. There were some rumors when he first moved here." She shook her head. "But we're not going to start gossiping about him, are we?"

Felicia grimaced and raised her eyebrows. "My, my. No, I suppose we're not."

Anna ignored the admonition. "What rumors? I mean, I get it's just gossip, but seriously — what?"

Kathy rolled her eyes and took another sip of tea. "I don't know the details and I wouldn't say if I did. Just that something happened in his last position and he moved here to get away from it."

Anna could certainly relate to that. If people were gossiping about her past, they could say exactly the same thing.

"How about Paul Murphy," Anna asked Kathy. "Do you know him?"

Kathy sipped her tea as she thought about it. Finally, she said. "I believe he's related to Vivienne Arnold, isn't he?" She turned to Felicia.

"Oh, that's right. I'd forgotten. Yes, I think they're cousins," she replied.

"Vivienne Arnold?" Anna asked, her curiosity piqued. "Is she any relation to Luke Arnold?"

"That's right, yes." Kathy nodded. "Her son is Luke Arnold."

"Who took over his father's construction company"— Felicia raised an eyebrow at Anna— "and is now working on Climbing Rose Cottage, I heard."

Anna's lips formed a thin straight line. "Word sure does get around in this town."

Felicia smiled and raised her mug in a sort of toast before taking another sip.

The three women sat silently for a moment, drinking tea and munching on cookies, each lost in her own thoughts. Anna ran through what she knew about George Hedley, Richard Gormley, Paul Murphy and even Evan Burley. Their faces swam about in her head until she finally put her tea down and took a deep breath, glancing out the window as she did so.

"The rain has stopped. Finally. Thank you, both, so much for this. I needed it." She grabbed her sweater from the chair by the fire. It was warm and dry and she felt comforted wrapping herself in it once more.

"You're welcome here any time, Anna. Good luck with your endeavors." Felicia waved toward the brochures. "And of course, your other endeavors." She added with a wink.

"But don't do anything to get in the way of the police doing their job," Kathy added sternly.

"Of course not," Anna replied brightly. "But I can still look into things, right? Learn more about the people in this town?"

Felicia came over and gave her a hug, which surprised her. She hugged Felicia back. "Thank you, again. I needed that."

Felicia patted her once more on the back before letting her go. "Satisfy your curiosity if you must, Anna, but don't get yourself into any more trouble with your neighbors than you're already in. You never know when you'll need them on your side."

22

The pause in the drizzle didn't last long. Anna was once again damp and chilly by the time she dragged herself to the last shop on the street. She had posted all her flyers and was almost out of brochures. She pulled the last few from their damp cardboard box, tossed the box into a nearby recycling bin and tucked them under her sweater to keep them dry. With her hands free, she pulled open the door of the shop on the end of the street, one she hadn't had a chance to visit yet in her brief time in Cape May.

The shop was dark but warm, a small electric heater tucked behind the counter coughing out heat. The sign outside said Magic Shop, but the store seemed to offer so much more. She saw figurines of wizards and dragons, board games and puzzles, books and even some foodstuffs. She walked along one bookshelf, browsing the titles. The books ran the gamut. Some offered recipes and histories of natural healing, how to use gems and how to meditate.

Anna picked up a book and flipped through it, curious. She recognized recipes for remedies she'd seen used in some of the communities she'd studied in the city. Remedies passed down through generations and carried across borders as people migrated, looking for better lives for themselves and their children. Farther along the shelf however, the titles turned to darker topics: dark magic, casting spells, even making potions. She laughed to herself, but shuddered nonetheless. Creepy material for such a gray day.

Shelves running along the far wall held piles of dried herbs in plastic bags and a variety of oils in small tubes. She picked up a few to sniff. Home remedies could be harmless, she knew, but they could just as easily be deadly. She wasn't surprised to see vials of CBD oil and liquid nicotine. The more mysterious herbs might attract the interest of a few shoppers, but the real money was no doubt made with these more popular potions.

She returned to the front counter where a young woman with jet-black hair and a nose ring sat playing on her phone.

"Hi, I'm Anna McGregor. I own the Climbing Rose Cottage," Anna started, as always, by introducing herself. "I'm looking for the manager."

The woman glanced up from her phone but kept tapping it as she spoke. "Sure. What I can do for you?"

"You're the manager?" Anna tried not to act surprised, but knew she'd failed.

The woman finally put her phone down and turned to face Anna directly. Anna realized she was quite pretty, her small nose turning up at the end over a round mouth, her dark eyes made even darker by lines of black that circled them then led off to the sides of her face in the style of an Egyptian goddess. "Not quite," she said. "I'm the co-owner."

Anna felt the blood rush to her face in her embarrassment and tried to laugh it off. "I'm so sorry, I shouldn't have assumed. I know how it is when people think I'm too young to run a B&B."

Thankfully, the young woman smiled, too. "No worries, I

get it all the time. And I am *co*-owner, I don't run this place by myself. I work here with my uncle. I'm Brooke."

"Brooke, it's great to meet you. I'm sorry I haven't been in here before now, because now I'm here to ask for your help." Anna launched into an explanation of how she liked to keep brochures advertising Climbing Rose Cottage at the registers of local stores. "I know a lot of your customers are already staying in other hotels, but I also know that once they've spent some time in Cape May, they'll want to come back. And they'll need a place to stay when they do."

"Sure, happy to help." Brooke gestured to a low shelf just below the register, the kind of place where shoppers could browse for impulse items while paying for their main purchase.

Anna thanked her and stepped toward the shelf, seeing a gap where she could just fit her brochures in. She simply had to move that pile of flyers for a club over slightly; there was plenty of room for both.

She leaned toward the flyers and her hand froze. They were emblazoned with a red and black image. An image she recognized immediately.

❧

HER HAND SHOOK AS HER MIND FLEW BACK TO THAT horrific moment. Kneeling down next to George. Digging frantically through his pockets hoping to find the one thing that could save him. Knowing, even as she did it, that it was too late for him.

She could still see, vividly, the items she'd pulled from his pockets and dropped onto the floor. That image — everything from that morning — was imprinted permanently on her brain. Anna's breath came faster as she saw in her mind the matchbook. The matchbook with the deep-red and black image. Lying on her dining room carpet, tossed down with the pens and crumpled tissues.

"Are you okay?" Brooke's voice cut into her thoughts and she spun around, suddenly confused. "Seriously, are you okay?"

Brooke walked out from behind the register, came over and put a hand on Anna's shoulder. "You look like you've seen a ghost."

"Ha!" Anna let out a laugh with the breath she'd been holding. "Nothing that dramatic. But ..." She pointed to the flyer. "What is that an advertisement for?"

Brooke narrowed her eyes. "You could pick one up, you know? And read it?"

"Right, right," Anna replied, but even as she said it she took a step back.

"All right, come over here and sit down," Brooke said, directing Anna to a chair behind the register. "Is that better?" Her words were kind but Anna saw a hint of steel in her eyes. And anger.

"I'm sorry, really. I'm sure it's not good for business to have someone freaking out in your store."

Brooke looked around at the empty store. "What business? But I can see that you're upset about the Pink Passion Club. What's wrong with you? Why do you care what people do with their time?"

"The what?" Anna asked, thoroughly confused. She had no idea what she'd done to upset Brooke and no idea what she was talking about.

Brooke raised a pierced eyebrow. "So you don't know about it?"

"Is that what the flyer is for?" Anna asked, confused.

"Yeah..." Brooke took a step back and looked at Anna. "Are you one of those church-going types?"

"Church-going?" Anna thought guiltily that it had been

far too long since she'd attended church. "Sure, I mean, sometimes. Why?"

Brooke shook her head and walked back to her register. "Forget it. Just ... yeah, that flyer is for the Pink Passion Club. Down off Sunset Boulevard. You may not have noticed it before, it's to the right just after the honey farm."

"Have you been there?"

This time Brooke grinned at her. "You really haven't heard of it?" She laughed. "Yeah, I've been there. They've got a great happy-hour deal, with live music. Can't beat it, right?" She glanced at her watch. "Too bad I'm open until eight tonight."

Anna took a breath and stood up. "Thank you so much for your kindness. Again, I'm sorry I lost it for a minute there. That image on the flyer... it just reminded me of something that scared me. That's all."

"This image?" Brooke asked, holding up the flyer. She frowned as she looked at the picture than back at Anna. "Really? Most people don't even recognize it for what it is."

"Oh. Right." Anna wasn't sure how to answer. She had no idea what it was supposed to be. Only where she had seen it last. "Anyway, thanks again. And for taking my brochures, too. I'll see you around."

Anna could feel Brooke's eyes on her as she left the shop. She kept walking around the corner until she was sure she was out of view, then she leaned back against the brick wall and took another breath.

Whatever that club was, it had some connection to George. She pulled out her phone and dialed.

"Hey Anna, what's baking?"

She smiled when she heard Sammy's friendly greeting. "Not you, I hope." They both laughed at their old joke. "Listen, what are you doing tonight?"

"Tonight?" Sammy paused. "Let's see, sterilizing counters,

closing out the cash register, taking stock. A thrilling Friday night for me."

"Sammy, I just saw something. It's kind of weird."

"I'm listening."

"There was a matchbook. In George's pocket."

"In George's pocket?" Sammy asked incredulously. "When did you go through George's pockets?"

Anna shuddered at the memory, pushing it out of her mind. "Never mind, the point is I saw this matchbook. And I just found out where it's from."

"I thought it was from George's pocket."

"Stop it, you know what I mean," Anna grumbled. "It's from a club. The Pink Passion Club. Have you ever heard of it?"

"Nope," Sammy answered and Anna could hear the frown in her voice. "Why? Is it important?"

"I don't know." Anna slumped back against the wall. "It just brought back memories. Of George... dead."

"Oh, honey, then why are we talking about it? Do you want to get together tonight? I could come over, we could watch a movie. Sound good?"

Anna considered it. That did sound good. Something to take her mind off her problems. To get the image of George, dead at her dining room table, off her mind. She shook her head.

"How about we go out? I just heard about a place that has a great happy hour."

"Mm-hmm," Sammy responded knowingly. "Why do I think you're about to suggest the Pink Passion Club?"

Anna grinned. "Because you know me so well. I'll meet you there."

23

Anna stopped her bike when she reached the gravel parking lot and glanced around. This must be the place, though it had taken her a while to find the sign, hidden as it was under a low-hanging awning.

She was early for her date with Sammy. Finding a babysitter for Eoin had been easier than she'd anticipated. Felicia was full of suggestions of local teenagers eager to offer their services, and it hadn't taken long to find one who was available on such short notice. She allowed herself a pang of remorse as she pictured Eoin's little face looking up at her as she left him with the young man. He clearly wanted to go with her, and she hated the idea of doing anything that might blunt his feelings toward her. They'd already spent two hours apart earlier today. But this was not a place where he could join her.

The salmon-colored, single-story building blended into the neighborhood. It was one of a handful of stores along the street that backed into a residential area. A beauty parlor in a miniature version of a classic Victorian mansion, a honey farm, the Pink Passion club, a wicker store — each stood independently, and each added to the charm and small-town feel of the street.

But this was the only building whose windows were covered from the inside with deep-pink curtains, whose sign was hung as if intentionally to obscure it, and from which emanated the sounds of a Dolly Parton song.

Anna thought about going in, but decided she'd better wait for Sammy. She didn't know anything about this club, and while she didn't think any bar in Cape May could be dangerous, she felt a chill going up her spine as she thought about the events that had brought her here. She stepped back onto the sidewalk and leaned against a low fence, letting her mind roam over what she'd learned so far and how much she still didn't know.

Sammy showed up ten minutes later, jumping out of her car and running over to Anna.

"How did you find this place?" Sammy asked, laughing. "I had never heard of it before. But I mentioned it to one of my employees, and she thought it was hysterical that we were coming here."

"She did? Why?" Anna asked, confused.

Sammy raised an eyebrow. "Let's go in and find out."

"Before we go in"—Anna put a hand on her friend's arm to stop her—"did you get a chance to do some research on George?"

Sammy grimaced and shook her head. "I did, but I didn't come up with much. I thought everybody had an online track record. George must have been the most boring man in the world. The only information I could dig up on him was about his work. And believe me, that is not exciting stuff."

"All right then." Anna straightened her shoulders. "Let's see what we can learn in the Pink Passion Club."

The bouncer at the door scrutinized their IDs, more strictly than necessary, Anna thought. She and Sammy clearly both looked over the age of twenty-one. With a nod, the burly man handed them back their licenses and pushed the wooden door open for them.

The first thing Anna noticed when she stepped inside was the stage at the far end of the room. A stage on which three Dolly Partons danced and sang in unison, belting out a familiar tune. The bright lights focused on the stage drew attention away from the rest of the room, but Anna saw more fabulously costumed people at the tables and standing at the bar — Cher, Marilyn Monroe, Beyoncé and more Dolly Partons.

She and Sammy shared a smile and headed for the bar, feeling distinctly underdressed.

"What can I get you?" The bartender asked over the sound of applause that broke out as the stage performance ended.

"I'm driving," Sammy said. "So a soda for me."

The bartender turned to Anna, who shook her head. "I'm not sure yet."

When he returned with Sammy's soda, Anna leaned over the bar toward the bartender, speaking loudly over the sound of the next performance.

"Do you know George Hedley?" she asked the bartender.

He frowned and shook his head. "Is he one of the performers?" he asked, gesturing toward the stage.

"Oh," Anna answered, surprised by the question. "I don't know."

Sammy just shrugged and sipped her drink.

The bartender's eyes narrowed. "Why are you asking?"

"Well... um..." Anna stammered. "I was a friend of his and I know he was a regular here at Pink Passion." She felt herself blush at the lie — in truth, she had no idea if George had even ever been there or had just picked up the matchbook somewhere.

"Regular customer? Hmm, maybe... no, I'm not sure. Wait, did you say *was*? Not is?"

Anna nodded sadly. "George passed away the other day."

The bartender abruptly pushed himself away from the bar and walked to the far end, where he had an animated conversation with a man in a sexy white dress and blond bombshell wig. He pointed toward Anna and Sammy and both men turned to look at them. Anna sank lower onto her stool.

"We're not very good at this, are we?" she asked Sammy.

"Speak for yourself. I think I'm doing pretty well." Sammy offered Anna a wicked grin. "I'm having fun."

When she looked back, the blonde bombshell was making his — or was it her? — way down the bar toward them. There was no point pretending she hadn't noticed, so she allowed herself to stare as he walked, truly impressed by how gracefully he was able to walk in those heels.

"I'm Jason," he introduced himself in a voice that was decidedly manly. "I understand you're asking about George?"

Anna nodded and Sammy put out a hand. "Love your look," she said. "Let's see, low-cut dress, sexy pout, masses of blond hair — Brigitte Bardot?"

Jason grinned. "Got it in one. And you are?"

"I'm Sammy, and this is my friend Anna. We just have a few questions. I hope you don't mind."

"That depends on what you want to ask. We get some unfortunate questions around here, as you can imagine. Look, I need a drink. Can I get you anything?"

Sammy held up her soda. "Not for me, thanks."

Anna shrugged. "Sure, I guess, whatever you're having."

Jason put his head back and laughed out loud. "Brave girl."

As he leaned over the bar to confer with the bartender, Anna leaned away from him to whisper into Sammy's ear. "We shouldn't be here, should we?"

"Why not?" Sammy hissed back. "This is fun."

"I know, it is." Anna looked around the bar with a smile. "But I mean we shouldn't be prying into George's life like this, should we?"

Sammy raised an eyebrow. "No, we should definitely not be. If he did hang out here, he probably didn't want anyone else to know."

"Particularly not that horrid wife of his." Anna shuddered, picturing once again the tiny woman planted firmly in her entrance hall. The image of Catherine Hedley only reaffirmed Anna's determination.

"Well, it's too bad, but I need to find the truth. We won't go gossiping about George, I promise. I just need to make sure Mrs. Hedley doesn't get away with accusing me of killing him."

She stopped talking when Jason presented her with a pink beverage in a martini glass, a tiny pink umbrella holding a raspberry into the drink. "Here you go," he said, "my favorite cocktail. To all the scofflaws here tonight."

Laughing, Jason took a sip, then raised his glass to Anna, encouraging her to do the same.

Anna lifted the glass to her lips, but before taking a taste she leaned toward Sammy. "I feel as bad about this as you do, but I can't let my business go under before it even starts. I don't have a choice."

She smiled at Jason and took a sip of the cocktail.

24

"Wow, that's good!" Anna didn't hide her surprise. She hadn't expected something quite so tasty, particularly when it looked like it would be far too sweet.

"It's a Scofflaw," Jason said. "A classic cocktail, first made in France." He wiggled his eyebrows. "Perfect for Brigitte Bardot. Come on, let's find somewhere we can talk."

He guided them to a relatively quiet table at the far end of the bar from the stage. Cher had taken the stage, and for a few minutes all three of them sat and enjoyed the over-the-top performance. The atmosphere in the club was easy, relaxed, with members of the audience cheering and singing along. Anna could see why people enjoyed it here.

Finally, she dragged herself back to the reason she was here. "So you knew George Hedley?" she asked Jason.

Jason frowned slightly as he stared down into his drink. "I knew him. I met him here, a few times. I was really sorry to hear about what happened to him."

"I'm sorry, too. I didn't know him that well."

"Clearly." Sammy laughed under her breath.

Anna glared at her. "But it must be hard to lose a friend."

"A friend?" Jason asked, surprised. "Huh. Yeah, I guess we were friends. But..." He raised his head and gestured around the bar. "Look around."

Anna did as he suggested, still seeing the enthusiasm and excitement that she'd noticed earlier.

"It's a great bar, looks like everyone is having fun."

"Exactly. Fun." Jason put down his drink with a bang. "That was George's thing, too. He didn't take this — take us — seriously. This was all just fun to him."

Anna saw the confusion on Sammy's face and knew she was as surprised as she herself was.

Sammy leaned forward over the table toward Jason. "How seriously do you and the other performers take it?"

Jason laughed lightly, easing the mood that had grown suddenly tense. "Look, I have a day job, right? I get paid to keep people safe and alive while they're at the beach."

"You're a lifeguard?" Anna asked.

"Does that surprise you?"

Anna glanced over his tight dress and heavy makeup. "Yeah, kind of." She lowered her head as she grimaced. "Sorry, I guess that's rude."

"This"—Jason gestured to his dress and to his wig—"is my creative outlet. I need this, I thrive on it."

"But it is still for fun, right?" Sammy asked. "I mean, you couldn't do this for a living?" She looked back at the stage with a new understanding. "Does anyone do this for a living?"

Jason looked pained. "It's not about that, not about money. It's about..." he looked around as if hoping to find the words he was seeking floating in the air above them. "It's about pride, self-respect. It's about letting me be me and enjoy myself the way I want to. Not the way anyone else thinks I should." He lowered his head and stared down at the table. "Everyone assumes I think it's fun to go out and drink a keg or so of beer and hit on drunk girls in bikinis. How is that any better than this?" He looked at Anna defiantly.

"It's not," she said quietly. "I think I get it."

"But George didn't?" Sammy asked.

"I thought he did." Jason paused to take a drink. "We met a few times, he was a nice guy. Obviously shy. And nervous." He laughed at some memory that he didn't share. "But once he relaxed, he was fun to hang out with. And he got it. He enjoyed this." Jason waved a hand about vaguely, indicating the room.

"Did he... um..." Anna wasn't sure how to phrase this. "Did he dress up to come out?"

Jason grinned at her. "No. He loved it, loved coming out. But not for that. You could just tell he relaxed as soon as he walked into the bar. But then..." Jason shrugged and took another drink.

"What changed?" Anna pressed him.

"I thought he understood, but he didn't. We were becoming friends. He even said he could offer me investment advice. I guess he has a background in private equity or something. But then last month..." Jason's voice died off again.

"What happened?" Sammy asked, her eyes affixed to Jason as he told his story.

Jason frowned, his eyes downcast, saddened by whatever he was remembering. He lifted one shoulder in a half shrug. "He said some things. He laughed. He made out like this was all just a big joke."

Anna put a hand out and rested it briefly on Jason's arm. "I'm sorry he hurt you. Did you ever see him again?"

"Oh yeah. He was here a few days ago, as if nothing had changed. All happy again." Jason laughed lightly under his breath. "He didn't even know how hurtful he'd been."

"Was that on Tuesday?" Anna asked. "He was here that night?"

Jason leaned back into his chair as he nodded. "That was Tuesday. Okay, look, enough about that. Let's talk about you ladies." His face lightened as he intentionally shifted the mood. "Tell me more about you."

"I bake for a living," Sammy said with a wink, then went on to say more about her business.

As Sammy spoke, Anna thought over what she knew about Varico and how Luke said it had been taken over, even when Richard didn't want to sell it. That was the sort of thing private equity firms did, wasn't it?

She looked over at Sammy, but she was engrossed in a discussion with Jason about his dress, running her hands over the silk and beads. Or perhaps over the muscles below the dress. Anna started when Jason looked over at her with an enticing look in his eye. Was a man dressed as Brigitte Bardot seriously flirting with her? She shook her head and laughed at the absurdity of it.

"So did he ever give you that financial advice? Did you make any money off it?" Anna asked.

"Nah." Jason shook his head. "Like I said, he was never really serious. He suggested it a few times — he brought it up you know, I didn't," Jason added defensively. "But it's probably for the best. I went by his office down here once, and there's definitely something off about that business and his partner."

25

Anna and Sammy squeezed past a crowd near the stage to get to the restroom. Once inside, Anna grabbed Sammy and pulled her over to a corner near the mirror, where they could pretend to be primping while comparing notes.

"Jason mentioned that George was involved in a private equity firm," Anna started. "Aren't they the kind of firm that buys out other companies?"

Sammy grimaced. "I'm not really sure. I think that sounds about right." She stepped forward as a large Marilyn Monroe swept into the bathroom, giggling as she came.

"So maybe there was bad blood between George and Richard?" Anna pressed. "I mean, it would make sense. George bought out Richard's company, against his will."

"Yeah, but he did buy it out, he didn't just take it." Sammy pointed out. "Luke and the Ahavas said that, in the end, Richard was better off. He paid him a lot of money, I guess."

Anna turned to stare at her reflection. Celebrities were crossing in the night behind her, but she ignored them. "Right. But he could still harbor some resentment."

"And what about the fact that George was a regular here, at the Pink Passion?" Sammy asked. "This is not the type of place you'd expect him to spend his time, is it?"

"I know." Anna started chewing on her lip, then saw how ridiculous it looked in the mirror and stopped. "Ordinarily, I wouldn't think that was relevant, but having met his wife, I wonder..."

"Wonder what?" Sammy leaned in toward the mirror to reapply her lipstick.

"Oh, it's nothing."

"Okay then." Sammy turned and grinned at Anna. "What about Jason?"

"What about Jason?" Anna asked, surprised. "You think he was so mad at George he killed him?"

Sammy laughed as she brushed her hair into an even silkier sheen. "That's not what I'm saying. I know he's in a dress and all, but he is a good looking man. And he was definitely making eyes at you."

Anna laughed. "He's dressed as Brigitte Bardot." She shook her head, then thought about it. "He must be in shape, if he's a lifeguard."

"He is, I can vouch for that." Sammy nodded. "Come on, we better get back out there."

Back at the table, Jason was chatting with a woman who leaned low over him as they spoke. Her long dark hair fell over his shoulder and her low-cut dress revealed more than she probably realized. Or perhaps not, Anna thought. The woman laughed as Sammy and Anna approached, a wide smile made even brighter by sparkling red lipstick.

"I'll see you later," she said, patting Jason on the shoulder. He touched her hand as she moved away, nodding briefly at Anna and Sammy.

Anna sat back down at the table feeling shabby and plain

in comparison. Sammy, on the other hand, glittering as she always did, wasted no time asking about the other woman.

"Just a friend." Jason grinned. "For now. We'll see."

He must have caught some kind of look from Anna because he said to her, "Are you surprised?"

Anna felt her face grow red and hoped it didn't show in the dim lights. "I admit, I assumed you were gay."

Jason raised his drink in a mock salute, "You know what happens when you assume. But seriously is that the vibe I'm giving you?"

"Definitely not," Sammy answered for her.

Anna shook her head no.

Jason grinned again. "So how about a drink sometime?" He glanced around. "Not here, somewhere more... traditional?"

Jason had his head turned toward Anna so couldn't see Sammy nodding vigorously behind him. She laughed. "Sure, why not. Here's my card — it's for my B&B, but you can reach me at that number."

"All right boys and girls." Sammy stood. "I have another early morning tomorrow. Come on, Anna, I'll give you a ride home."

Jason held out a hand to Sammy, then pecked Anna on the cheek. She couldn't help but smile. What a strange night. Asked out on a date by Brigitte Bardot! But as unexpected as it was, she was seriously considering it. She was ready for something completely different in her love life.

"So this wasn't a total waste of time, then." Sammy said as they settled into her car. "I'm glad I came here tonight."

"Definitely not a waste of time," Anna agreed. "And I'm glad you came out, too." She felt herself still smiling, and for a moment forgot the real reason they'd been there. Only for a moment. Her smiled faded.

Poor George. Who was he, really? Some kind of private equity evil genius who took over people's businesses against their wishes? Or a stressed-out man looking for a quirky way to relax and have fun?

26

The rain had passed, the low gray clouds blown over, and the ocean waves shimmered under the glittering morning sun. Anna took a deep breath, inhaling the comforting scents of ocean, salt and sand. She shut her eyes, turning her face to the wind and sun. It hadn't taken long to get through her chores that morning. Not having any guests to cook for or clean up after certainly made a difference.

Any guests besides Eoin, that is. She opened her eyes to watch the boy playing tag with the waves, running as close to the water as he dared while they pulled away, then screaming with joy as he ran away when they chased him back up the beach. She'd made a call that morning and got him enrolled in another activity at the Community Center later that afternoon. These were great classes and she was glad she could offer Eoin some kind of educational opportunities. Though he seemed perfectly content to rely on his own readings and his own explorations.

She took one more breath then continued her walk toward the World War II bunker that lay half buried about a mile and a half down the beach. Her eyes scanned the horizon as she walked, where gulls bobbed and weaved on the ocean breeze, calling angrily to each other whenever they felt threatened. She could relate to feeling threatened.

She pulled out her phone yet again, scrolling through emails and messages, hoping for a reservation, even an inquiry about prices. Anything positive she could latch on to. There were no new requests for rooms, but on the plus side, no one had left a negative review and no one else had cancelled yet. Thank goodness for that, at least. She still had six other reservations. The next set of guests were due to arrive on Thursday.

Would this death still be hanging over her then? What if the police never did find out how George had died?

Don't be ridiculous, she chided herself. They'll find out, one way or another. Whether he had a heart attack, an allergic reaction, or really was killed by someone, the police would find out. But then the question remained, would people still blame her — and Climbing Rose Cottage — for his death?

The wind had picked up slightly. She pulled out the scarf she had shoved into her pocket, wrapping it around her neck and tucking her hair in. She needed to think. To figure out what she should do. For her, the beach was the best place to do that.

She stayed as close to the water's edge as she could without getting wet, walking on the hard-packed sand. Dunes rose out of the beach to her right, offering a protective shelter to the bird sanctuary that lay beyond. A few tufts of long grass waved from the top of the dunes.

"Eoin, come look at this." Anna stopped and pointed down to the sand.

Eoin trotted over to her, squatting down to get a closer

look at where she was pointing. Small bubbles were popping all over the wet sand, leaving pinprick size holes.

"Did you know there are clams under there?" Anna asked.

"Clams?" Eoin repeated. "Under the sand?" He looked up at Anna as if she were crazy then turned to stare at the sand again.

"Yep. Look." Anna scooped up a large handful of wet sand. As the sand sifted through her fingers, two tiny clams were left in her palm.

Eoin's mouth opened wide and he gasped with delight. "Those are clams?"

"They are." Anna laughed as she placed them back onto the wet sand and the clams immediately dug their way back under ground. "They're still tiny now, but they burrow under the sand while they grow."

Eoin couldn't take his eyes off the sand. As they continued to walk, he would squat down every ten feet or so, his face so close to the sand she thought he'd inhale a clam or two. Every now and then he'd let out a squeak and raise a hand to show her his catch before dropping it back down.

She loved walking in this kind of weather, even with the wind. She could breathe easy, relax, let the spirit of the sea uplift her. She shut her eyes as she walked, knowing there was no one around, nothing to trip her up or get in her way. Just her, the sand, the sea and the gulls.

Opening her eyes again, she pulled on her dark sunglasses and considered that with her sunglasses and scarf, she finally looked more like she should have done last night at the bar. What an odd experience that had been. She was glad she went, glad to find out about the club and glad to learn a little bit more about George. But where did it leave her? George was still dead. She had found a few reasons why people might have been mad at him, but mad enough to kill him?

Even more important than why George was dead, she

needed to figure out how she was going to move forward. Should she try to dig more into George's death? Was she really helping or only hindering the police? Could she really sit back and let the police do their jobs, knowing that the survival of Climbing Rose Cottage was on the line?

Come on, Anna, she told herself. You're good at analyzing complicated situations. Gather all the evidence you can then figure out how it fits together, what it's telling you. Don't just look at what happened but at what might have caused it.

Waves broke far out from the shoreline, diminishing to nothing more than rolling mounds as they made their way onto the beach. Anna easily side-stepped the incoming surges, keeping her feet dry. Seaweed and driftwood gathered along the water's edge where the waves had abandoned them, drying and bleaching in the sun and the wind. Anna picked up a thick piece of driftwood, wondering if she could think of something artsy to make of it. Sadly, she didn't have that kind of talent. She turned and threw the stick far out into the ocean, watching it plop into a still patch between the waves. A passing gull glanced down, perhaps wondering if a fish had jumped. Another gull, not as easily distracted, had kept its eyes on the real prize and dropped into a sudden dive, swooping down into the water then sailing back up into the air, the silver fish in its beak glinting in the sunlight.

Trawlers shimmered on the horizon, almost too far away to make out. Closer in, a group of sandpipers raced along the beach, running along the path of the waves, pecking at the clams below the surface. Anna laughed at the speed of their tiny legs before the whole group took off into flight, looking for fresh hunting grounds farther along the beach.

Twenty minutes later, the magic of the ocean had done its trick. She felt lighter, more relaxed. She slowed her steps to examine the sand, helping Eoin search for Cape May diamonds.

She knew who she was, she couldn't help that, couldn't change it, anymore than Jason could change who he was and what he wanted. She had a vested interest in how this turned out and she wasn't someone who could simply sit back and let other people make decisions that would have such a dramatic affect on her life, her business.

As much as it felt like prying, like digging through old memories that didn't belong to her, she was doing the right thing by trying to learn more about George and his life.

THE FIGURE COMING TOWARD HER SHIMMERED THROUGH the distance and the light. She blinked and tried not to stare at it. It would come into focus eventually.

They had made it down to the bunker and halfway back. Her legs were tired from the long walk on the sand but she felt good. She needed the exercise. And it's not like she had anything else to do that morning. She'd run into a few neighbors on her walk and a few more tourists she didn't recognize. The beach was mostly deserted, and she was glad for that. She loved it in the off-season, feeling like it was just her and the sky and the sea.

The figure was becoming clearer now, a man walking alone. He wore jeans and a dark blue windbreaker and his brown hair ruffled in the breeze, showing a hint of redness where the sun hit it. His eyes were hidden behind his aviator sunglasses, but Anna knew he was watching her. Just like she was watching him.

Eoin clearly was not tired, despite the long walk. As soon as he recognized the man, he ran toward him, full of youthful energy. Still at a distance, Anna saw them greet each other, then saw Eoin being lifted into the air, his little legs swinging around him. She couldn't help but laugh at the sight.

"Anna," Evan said when he was close enough to be heard. "How are you?"

"Hi Evan," she replied. "Out for a walk?"

"Just taking a break." He grinned as he got closer. He stopped, waiting for her to reach him, then turned and walked along next to her, Eoin trotting along next to him.

"Aren't you on duty?" shc asked.

"I am. But even cops get a lunch break." He took a breath and looked out at the ocean. "Sometimes I need to get up and walk away for a few minutes, you know? To clear my mind."

"I know exactly what you mean."

They walked in silence for a few minutes, each enjoying the sights, sounds and scents of the Jersey shore in spring.

Eventually, she had to ask. "How's the investigation going? Are you any closer to finding out what really happened to George?"

"What really happened? What do you mean?" Evan asked.

"I mean, that I didn't kill him. That he didn't die just because he was staying at Climbing Rose Cottage," Anna said, annoyed that Evan didn't understand how important this was to her.

He stopped walking, grabbing her arm to turn her to face him. "Is that what you think? That you were responsible for his death?"

"Well..." she raised her eyebrows and lifted her arms in despair. "Didn't you say that was a possibility? That I might have accidentally killed him?"

Evan let out a breath, then took his sunglasses off to look her in the eye. "I did say that, yes. And I'm sorry, but it is still a possibility. We don't have the toxicology report back yet. We've ruled out a few things — he didn't choke, he didn't have a heart attack. We do think it was poison. But Anna, even if it was an accident, that doesn't mean you were responsible."

Anna frowned and turned back to her walk, picking up her pace in her anger. Didn't he realize, that's exactly what it meant? He kept up with her easily.

"Are you looking into anything else, besides my murderous B&B?" she asked. "If he was poisoned, then maybe someone intentionally poisoned him."

"We are looking into that, of course."

She refused to look at him, keeping her eyes focused on the distant horizon. They were approaching the main beach now and more tourists were out, walking on the beach, some camped out on beach chairs wearing sweaters or wrapped in towels.

Eoin had shifted his attention from the wet surface to the dry. He stumbled along the beach trying to catch a seagull before shifting his attention to a crab scuttling across the sand. Fortunately, he failed to catch either.

"There are things about George you might not know," Anna said, keeping her voice low. "Have you even thought about why he was here in Cape May?"

"Why he was here? He was here on business."

Anna gave him a withering look, making her disbelief clear with her eyes. "Oh yeah? And what about the Pink Passion Club?" As soon as she said it, she regretted it. It hadn't been her plan to expose George's secret like that. But Evan had gotten her so worked up.

"Tell me about that. What is it?" Evan asked.

"Just a club." Anna shrugged. "George went there a lot, it turns out. He knew some people there. That's all."

"So why are you mentioning it?" Evan asked, confused.

"I don't know. I shouldn't be. I'm sorry I even brought it up."

"Look, Anna, I'm heading up here." Evan gestured toward one of the streets that ran up from the beach, lined with hotels, B&Bs, cafés and stores. "But you have to believe me. I know you didn't kill him."

She was still frowning but she let herself look at him. The concern on his face melted her anger. Mostly. "But you still think it could have been an accident? Something in my house that poisoned him?"

"It could have been an accident, yes. But we don't know it was something in your house, right? We simply don't know. And it's pointless to guess."

Anna looked down at the sand, where a little sand crab scooted away. "Will you tell me when you do know?"

"Anna, I can't really talk to you about the case," Evan cautioned. "But, hey—" He took her hand and looked her in the eye. She swallowed and looked back. "I will tell you as soon as we know you're off the hook. Okay?"

"Thank you Evan. For everything." She watched him make his way up the beach, knowing that as much as she trusted him, she couldn't simply sit back and wait. She turned north again, with a new destination in mind.

27

Instead of heading home, Anna walked a few more blocks up the beach and turned up onto the street that led to the library. She'd been hoping to pop in for a quick chat with Felicia, but even better, she caught Felicia leaving the library.

"Anna, Eoin." Felicia waved. "I've been seeing a lot of you lately."

Eoin smiled brightly at the librarian.

"This isn't actually a coincidence," Anna admitted. "I was looking for you. Do you have a few minutes?"

"Sure." Felicia waved her over. "Walk with me. I only work mornings on Saturday, so I just finished my shift."

Anna and Eoin joined her and the three of them strolled toward the main street, enjoying the scent of spring, the fragile blooms budding in front yards, the trills of songbirds enjoying the warm weather. Felicia took a deep breath and smiled. "I do love this time of year, don't you?"

"Usually." Anna agreed. "This year has been a little stressful."

"Oh, I'm sorry, honey." Felicia tucked Anna's arm under her own. "It's great that you were out yesterday with your brochures. I'm sure that will help. Your house is gorgeous. As soon as people see those pictures, those rooms, they'll be calling by the dozen to make reservations."

Anna laughed at the thought. "I sure hope you're right, Felicia." She narrowed her eyes for a moment. "Tell me, you talk to people in town, what are the other B&B owners saying? Are they getting more calls than usual?"

"Eoin, be careful!" Felicia's call drew Anna's attention to the boy. She hadn't noticed when he'd stopped following them and instead trotted into a neighbor's yard. Now he was on his toes peering into a birdhouse, his hands gripping the edge of the metal base that held the house.

"Eoin, you shouldn't be there," Anna called, running over to him.

"I'm sorry," he whispered, dropping back onto his feet and taking her hand. "I just wanted to see the birds."

"Of course you did, honey. Tell you what, why don't I find a birdhouse for our yard, too?"

Eoin's eyes lit up and he nodded as the two of them returned to where Felicia waited on the sidewalk.

"You're wondering if people are booking elsewhere, afraid to stay with you?" Felicia responded to Anna's earlier question. "I don't know. People are still calling, booking rooms. This is Cape May, after all, and the summer season is coming up. But are they getting more than usual?" She shrugged again. "I haven't heard that, but who knows."

They passed a couple walking in the other direction, nodding hello. The couple greeted Felicia by name but simply nodded back at Anna.

"Uh-oh," she said. "Am I already being blackballed by the neighborhood? Did my questions about Richard Gormley really turn everyone against me?"

Felicia ran a hand through her cropped hair as she turned her piercing gaze to Anna. Anna felt uncomfortable under her stare, as if Felicia could see everything she'd done wrong.

"No, Anna. They have not. You're a business owner, doing what you need to do to stay afloat. Everyone understands that. But"—she held up a finger as Anna started to respond—"I did find out something that you should know."

Anna nodded with excitement. "Great, thank you! I learned last night that George Hedley was working for a private equity firm at one point. I think he must have done a, what's it called, a hostile takeover—"

She bit her lip when Felicia stopped walking to laugh out loud.

"Oh, honey," Felicia spoke between laughs. "Don't let your imagination run wild on you."

Anna felt her face burn as her embarrassment returned. "Why? What do you mean?"

Felicia grabbed her arm again and resumed their walk. "First of all, a hostile takeover can only happen to a publicly traded company. Richard hadn't gone public. He was a one-man company, just working out deals with local shippers."

"Oh." Anna said. That was an important point she hadn't considered. "But then how did George take over his company?"

"He bought it, pure and simple." Felicia explained, her eyes wide. "No big secret, no big deal."

"But—"

Felicia cut her off yet again. This was getting annoying. "No buts. Richard didn't want to sell, it's true, but it was time. His wife convinced him of that. They were ready to retire, George made a great offer, so Richard was convinced to take it. He might have been grumpy about it"—Felicia shrugged—"not everyone likes growing old gracefully. But it was his choice. He wasn't forced to sell."

"Oh," Anna said again, trying to focus on the beautiful spring day that had entranced and buoyed her only hours earlier. It was hard to do. "So how did you find this out?"

Felicia grinned with a wink. "Gossip, the best type of research there is. It's a small town, everyone knows everyone's business, don't they?"

Anna smiled, picturing Jason in his dress and wig. Did they really, she wondered?

"The Gormleys are friendly with everyone, even though they moved away," Felicia continued. "They still stay in touch. With the parish, with local families. I'm sure everyone in town knows them or knows something of them, and vice versa. A couple of women from the local parish were in the library this morning so I chatted with them."

Anna shuddered. "Oh no, not Mrs. Santiago and Mrs. James?"

"None other. You already know this town so well."

Anna rolled her eyes. "They think I'm crazy. They probably think I killed George."

"Hmm." Felicia wagged her head back and forth with a smile. "They might at that."

"Felicia!" Anna stopped walking. "This isn't funny."

"I'm sorry, honey." Felicia dropped her head. "Of course it's not. I'm sure they don't think you murdered him. No one thinks that."

"But they think something in my house killed him?" Anna asked. "How could they? I mean, what could do that?"

"The gossip is it was something you cooked for him." She offered Anna a sad smile as she took her hand once more. "I'm sorry. I'm being honest with you, Anna, telling you what I heard. I figured it was better for you to hear it from me than someone else."

Felicia was right, it was better to hear it from her. But it would have been best not to have to hear it at all. She needed to prove that nothing in her house had killed George Hedley. She chewed on her lip again, thinking. She needed to prove it to herself, as well.

28

"Stupid flour. Stupid sugar," Anna muttered under her breath as she opened each plastic container, dumping their contents into a black plastic trash bag she'd hooked over a chair. "Stupid baking powder."

She paused as she picked up the container of special spices she'd bought when she first came down here. She'd been so excited to find them: cinnamon, allspice, turmeric, all packaged in adorable little miniature Cape May Victorian houses with removable tops. She'd bought them at the kitchen store in town, convinced it was a sign that her dream was meant to be. She felt tears well up in her eyes as she tossed the whole thing into the bag.

If something in her kitchen was poisoning people, it all had to go. And even if it wasn't, people thought it was. She needed to be able to stand up in public and tell everyone that her kitchen was clean, refreshed and ready to serve.

For the next hour, she moved through her kitchen like an incompetent burglar, tipping jars over, spilling out their contents, dumping everything. Eoin had offered to help, but it took only a few broken jars before she'd thanked him for his assistance and shuttled him back out to the porch with his book and a glass of lemonade.

She kept moving through the kitchen, kept working, knowing that if she stopped, if she thought about what she was doing and how much it would cost to replace, she would break down in tears.

"Are you okay?"

She looked up at Luke's soft voice from the doorway. He laughed when he saw her. She was sitting on the floor in front of two big cabinets, surrounded by empty containers.

"Do you have any idea what you look like right now?" he asked.

She shook her head and raised a hand to stop him, but he ignored it, stepping swiftly into the kitchen and kneeling down next to her. "Anna, what's wrong?" He took both her hands in his. "Let me help."

She felt her resolve weaken as soon as she felt his touch and she pulled her hands away. He leaned back but didn't stand. "What's going on?" he repeated his question.

"I'm sorry, I didn't mean to... I'm just"—she looked around and laughed—"would you believe I'm cleaning out the kitchen?"

"Is that what you call this?" he asked skeptically.

"The police still think George might have been accidentally poisoned. And everyone in town thinks it, too."

"By you?" Luke asked. "That's crazy. No way."

"I know"—Anna looked wildly around the kitchen—"I've gone through everything. There is nothing here. Truly nothing that could have killed him. For goodness sake, I'm a scientist. I think I'd know if I had poison in my kitchen."

"Of course you would know, Anna. Come on."

Luke took her hands again and gently lifted her from the floor, then guided her to one of the tall stools. "Sit here. I'll get you a cup of coffee."

She watched as he moved about the kitchen, grinding the beans, filling the French press with boiling water. The earthy smell of the coffee brought her back to some semblance of calm and she accepted the mug he handed her gratefully.

"You're so good to me, Luke. I know I'm not great about accepting help, but I do appreciate it."

"I sure hope so." he grinned as he perched on the stool next to her. "Now, tell me again what you're doing in here?" His eyes scanned the mess she had created.

"I went through everything." She shrugged. "I thought maybe something had gone bad. Or maybe one of the plastic containers was leaching out BPA. I thought I'd bought everything BPA-free, but you never know. Labels aren't always accurate."

"BPA? I've heard of that. I know it's poisonous, but it wouldn't kill someone, Anna."

"Oh I know." Anna raised her voice as she rolled her head in frustration. "I know that. I know for a fact there is no poison in my kitchen." Now she was yelling and Luke was staring at her.

"Okay." He spoke calmly, gently putting his mug down and taking hers from her shaking hands. "So maybe we should clean this up then?"

She looked at him. So calm, so comforting, so ready to offer to help. What was wrong with her that she wasn't jumping at the chance to accept everything he had to offer? She started laughing, first a giggle, then harder. Suddenly she was crying. Big, sloppy sobs racked her body and she felt her nose running.

Luke leaned forward and pulled her close to him, resting her head on his shoulder as she sobbed, sniffling and coughing as she did so.

"I'm so sorry, Anna. I wish I could do something to help. I really do."

"I know," she mumbled through her sniffles. "I know, I do. And I'm sorry. This is so embarrassing."

He laughed and simply patted her head until she'd calmed down. When her sniffling had subsided, he pulled her away from him and looked her in the eyes. She could only imagine what they looked like, red and swollen for sure.

"I'm going to help you clean this up, okay?" he said.

She nodded and felt herself smile. It was good to have someone to help.

Together, they set to work putting her kitchen back together.

29

The front doorbell jingled just as Anna threw the last dirty dishcloth into the hamper against the wall.

"Saved by the bell?" Luke said with a laugh, looking around the now spotless kitchen.

Anna rolled her eyes at him as she pushed through the door into the lounge, not sure what to expect next. Surprises recently had not been good.

Fortunately, this one was.

Sammy stormed into the lounge from the entrance hall, Eoin's red head poking out from behind her, just as Anna and Luke came in from the kitchen. She triumphantly raised two stuffed shopping bags.

"I brought the ingredients for a Scofflaw!" she crowed. "Since I didn't get to try one the other night." She placed the cloth bags on the coffee table, reaching in to pull out the various items. "Let's see... bourbon, check." She glanced up at Anna and grinned wickedly.

Anna laughed and added, "Obviously."

"Vermouth... orange bitters... grenadine..." Sammy

continued her recital of ingredients as she pulled each item out of the bags. "And of course, fresh lemons." She ended her recitation with a flourish.

Luke walked around the coffee table, examining the ingredients. "That's quite a drink you're planning to make there. Where did you pick up this recipe?"

"Will you join us in a little day drinking?" Sammy asked as she folded the empty shopping bags. "I've heard this is a great drink. It's called a Scofflaw."

"So that's what it is." Luke laughed and joined Anna, who had watched Sammy's performance from where she stood near the door to the kitchen. "That sounds interesting, but I have to decline." He glanced down at Anna. "I still have some more work to do, and alcohol and power tools definitely don't mix."

"I'll try some," Eoin's high pitched voice piped up from behind Sammy.

Sammy ignored him and gave Anna and Luke a sideways look. "What have you two been up to?"

"Just some cleaning." Anna said, moving away from Luke without looking at him. "We went through everything in the kitchen. Just making sure, you know."

"I'm glad you're here to help her relax," Luke said to Sammy. "She was going at that kitchen like a madwoman when I found her."

Anna shrugged and sank onto the couch. "I just had to be sure, that's all."

"Sure of what?" Sammy asked.

Anna glanced back at Luke. "That I didn't poison poor George. By accident," she added quickly as Sammy opened her mouth to complain.

"Of course by accident. But what on earth made you think it might be something from your kitchen that killed him?"

"Well"—Anna looked down at her hands as she explained her reasoning—"the police are looking into the possibility that he was poisoned by something here and everyone in town thinks it was something I made for him. George brought his own toiletries so I know it wasn't one of the little bottles I provide for guests. Plus no one else got sick." She looked up at Sammy. "And George was the only person I served breakfast to that morning."

"Oh, honey." Sammy sat down next to Anna and put an arm around her shoulders. "But what if it wasn't anything here in your house that got him sick?"

"That's what I keep telling her," Luke said, leaning back against the wall next to the kitchen door.

"I know." Anna looked back down at her lap. "I guess I just feel responsible. And the more I get to know about George, the worse I feel. He seems like he was a really lonely guy."

"What the...?" Luke turned suddenly and pushed through the swinging door back into the kitchen.

Anna and Sammy shared a confused glance then jumped up to follow him, Eoin close on their heels.

"I thought I heard something," Luke said, turning toward the women. "Look."

It took Anna a few seconds to identify the thing Luke indicated. It looked like a small mass of dirt. Or a really large dust bunny. Then it sneezed.

Anna and Sammy both jumped. Eoin squeaked.

Luke laughed. "It's that old cat." He looked back at the women. "She's been around for a couple of years now. Just a stray. I think she lived in that old shed out back."

"The shed!" Anna thought with horror of what she had done to the shed. "Oh no, I didn't know there was anything living in there."

She squatted down in front of the shivering animal. "You poor thing, what did I do to you?"

Luke squatted next to her, putting a hand on Anna's back. She felt comfort from his touch, but it didn't change the overwhelming guilt she felt from having destroyed the cat's home. "Why didn't I know about her? I've been here for months."

Luke shrugged. "I guess she prefers to live on her own. I only see her every now and then."

The cat shook again, wood shavings and dust shimmering in the air around her then falling to the ground. Eoin stepped closer and put a small hand out toward the animal. It backed away.

Anna stood, grabbing Luke and bringing him up with her. "Come on, we need to help her."

"How?" Luke glanced back at the cat. "She's been doing okay on her own. She's a pretty tough cookie."

"Tough cookie or not, she needs our help now."

"Will this do?" Sammy asked. She held up a large saucer, part of a set of soup mugs Anna had collected for the B&B.

"Perfect. Grab another one, too." Anna filled the first saucer with water, then held the second one as she looked around the kitchen. "Too bad I don't have any cat food."

"Maybe tuna?" Luke asked helpfully.

Anna shook her head. "I only serve breakfast for the guests. Oh!" She slapped a hand to her head. "I still have some smoked salmon that I was going to serve..." her voice trailed off as her smile faded. She shook her head determinedly. "Anyway, our little tough cookie might like that."

Anna filled both saucers then turned to approach the cat. She stepped softly, making small cooing noises as she moved closer. "It's okay, honey, these are for you."

She placed the saucers within a couple of feet of the filthy cat. "I wish I could help you get cleaned up, too."

"Cats don't clean themselves until after they've eaten," Eoin said, surprising everyone else in the room.

"That's very smart. How do you know that?" Sammy asked him, walking over and draping an arm over his shoulder.

Eoin looked up at her with a gaze of pure adoration. "I read about it. I like to read."

"Yes, I've heard that about you," Sammy responded with a laugh.

Anna heard a quiet ripple of water and looked down to see the cat drinking greedily from the saucer. It then turned its attention to the salmon, tearing off tiny pieces and swallowing them daintily.

"Come on." She grabbed Sammy's arm. "Let's get those ingredients."

30

"How's she doing?" Anna whispered as she leaned over Sammy's shoulder, trying to peer into the kitchen around her.

"Careful... good, look, she's cleaning herself!" Sammy stepped back to let the door swing shut and stomped on Anna's foot.

"Ow," Anna complained, then shushed herself even before Sammy did.

The two women fell back onto the sofa giggling. The cat had eaten all her food and was now busily twisting herself into a pretzel to lick herself clean.

"What do you think, another round?" Sammy asked.

Their empty cocktail glasses stood on the coffee table in front of them. Eoin occupied the chair closest to the doorway, both feet tucked under him, both hands gripping his almost-empty glass of pink lemonade. At least he'd been willing to accept the lemonade as an alternative, despite several attempts to join the women in trying a Scofflaw.

Anna picked her glass up, sucking out the last drops of

her Scofflaw. "Probably not," she replied with regret. "I suspect we've had enough."

The two friends looked at each other and broke out into another round of giggles.

Their laughter broke off as the front door slammed open, the bell swinging madly. It took Anna a second to recognize the man who burst in, his face red and his eyes wide. There was nothing feminine about Jason this afternoon. His sexy dress and blond wig had been replaced by jeans, T-shirt and sneakers. And an expression that could set wet kindling ablaze.

"You set the cops on me? How could you do that?"

Anna and Sammy both jumped up, terrified. Eoin slid of his chair and scuttled behind the sofa.

"What are you talking about?" Anna asked. "We didn't do that."

"Oh yeah?" Jason sneered, moving farther into the room. Anna grabbed Sammy's hand as they both stepped behind the sofa, trying to create space between them and the angry young man without revealing Eoin's presence there.

"I swear," Anna tried to speak calmly. "I never mentioned you to the police."

"Well the cop who talked to me said different." Jason beat his hands together as he talked, one fist banging into the other palm. "He said he'd been tipped off about George coming to the Pink Passion and you're the only person who's come around asking questions about George."

"Oh." Anna swallowed. Should she apologize or defend herself, she wondered. Whichever would most likely calm Jason down, for sure.

"I'm sorry," she said. "I did... I mentioned the club when I talked with the cops. But I didn't mention you, I promise."

Jason threw his hands in the air. "Great. They're cops, get

it? It didn't take them long to figure out I was the only one at the club who spent time with George."

"You told us you'd gone to his office and met his partner," Sammy jumped in. "How do you know the partner didn't mention you to the cops? Maybe it wasn't us at all?"

Sammy's attempt to shift the blame away from them seemed to only make Jason angrier. He spun around, his arms swinging wildly. They made contact with a ceramic vase that stood on a cabinet near the doorway. Anna watched with growing fear as it smashed into the ground, breaking into multiple shards. One large piece skated along the floor toward them, sliding under the sofa and coming to a stop at their feet. She heard a squeak from Eoin, but hopefully Jason hadn't noticed it.

Anna swallowed. "Jason," she tried to sound reasonable. "I'm sorry this happened to you. But I don't understand why you're so mad. The police don't think you killed George, do they?"

Jason shook his head as he sneered at her, but didn't answer.

"Did you want to keep your... pastime a secret?" Anna asked. "I really didn't know that."

Jason blew out an angry breath. "It's not a secret, but it's also not your business telling anyone. Get it? Who I share my story with is my business, and my business only. You need to mind your own business."

He started moving again and his foot fell on one of the pieces of ceramic. He jumped at the cracking sound and looked down as if just noticing the broken vase. Then he looked back at Anna and his smile made her shiver.

"I should break up your home like you've tried to break into mine." He picked up an umbrella from the stand near the door and waved it in the air in front of him. His eyes narrowed. "Where should I start? Hmm?"

Thank God Jason hadn't noticed Luke coming down the stairs behind him and crossing the front hall. As Jason waved the umbrella in the air, Luke jumped at him, grabbing Jason from behind and pinning his arms at his side.

"What are you doing, Jason..." Luke spoke as he struggled with the other man. "You're out of control." Luke took a breath.

Jason twisted against Luke's grip. "Let go of me. What're you doing? This isn't about you, Luke. Let me go."

Anna and Sammy both slumped back against the wall in relief at seeing Luke, but their relief didn't last long. Jason was clearly the stronger man. Anna could see that Luke was losing his grip as Jason struggled against him.

Anna tried again, speaking as calmly as she could. "Jason, I didn't try to break into your life. I'm really sorry if anything I told the police upset you. Please just leave."

"Ladies, can one of you please call the cops?" Luke grunted. "Like now?"

With a final tug, Jason freed himself from Luke's grasp. Luke grabbed at him, trying to wrestle him to the ground, but Jason again pulled free.

"Enough!" He said, jumping out of Luke's reach and heading for the hall. "I'm going. But you"—he pointed a finger at Anna—"stay out of my way, you got it?" He sneered at Luke one more time before storming out. "Not surprised you're with them, you always were a traitor."

Anna and Sammy both sank onto the sofa as the front door slammed shut behind Jason. They had nothing to laugh about now.

Luke came toward them, looking them both over. "You both all right?"

Anna nodded and looked at Sammy, who said, "We are. Thank God you were here, Luke."

"What did you two do to piss off Jason? Everyone knows

he's got a temper he can't control." Luke wiped his hands along his jeans and started rolling up his sleeves, then paused to look at Anna. "I hope I didn't overstep my role again?"

"Luke, you're a life saver. Literally," Anna said.

All three of them started when the door to the kitchen creaked open.

"What the...?" Sammy said.

"Another visit from your ghost?" Luke asked.

Anna smiled widely on seeing the small black and white cat as it slid through the narrow opening. "Not a ghost. Just a real tough cookie."

31

Anna frowned and let out a grumble as the bit of ceramic she'd been holding slipped onto the coffee table.

"You don't have to do that," Sammy told her. "I know it was Aunt Louise's, but seriously, it looks pretty far gone." As Sammy spoke, she reached over and tickled the cat under the chin.

The cat — now black with white and gray patches on her feet and chest — sat proudly on the sofa next to Sammy. Anna sat on the floor facing them and the coffee table, on which she'd placed all the bits and pieces of ceramic she could find from the broken vase.

"I know." She dropped another piece and looked at Sammy. "But I think I can put it back together. As long as this glue holds." She held up the old tube of superglue she'd found in a kitchen drawer, looking at it skeptically.

"So what's bugging you, then. You're not worried Jason's going to come back, are you?"

Anna shook her head. "Probably not, no. But what if he does?" She focused on picking up another broken piece and matching it with the few she'd already glued back together. "What do we do then, if Luke isn't around?"

Sammy grimaced. "I hope we don't find out."

"But don't you see?" Anna knew her frustration was coming out and took a breath to calm herself. The cat turned her head to face her, as if listening closely. "I hate that I can't take care of myself. On my own, you know. And now I have to take care of Eoin, too." Anna thought of the boy, upstairs in his room calling his mother. He hadn't seemed too upset by the encounter, but Anna had no doubt he'd been scared. Who wouldn't be?

"I mean, of course I'm grateful to Luke," she continued.

"We both are." Sammy said sharply. "He totally saved us."

"I know." Anna returned to her ceramic puzzle. "I just don't want to be dependent on a man again. Ever."

"Oh, honey. This is about Steve, isn't it?"

Anna shuddered. "Don't mention him."

"It's okay to let it out. You know, we never really talked about what happened. I mean..." Sammy slid down onto the floor across the table from Anna and pushed a few pieces around, looking for matching ones. "I mean, you told me what happened, but we didn't really talk about it, you know?"

"I know." Anna tried to focus on her work but looked up when she sensed the cat moving. She'd edged closer to the edge of the sofa and was watching Anna closely. "What does she know that I don't?" Anna asked.

"Who, the cat?" Sammy laughed. "Who knows. Maybe she's already on her ninth life. Ooh, maybe she knew Aunt Louise."

The cat opened its mouth into a wide yawn and stretched out its front legs as she lay down on the sofa. Despite her apparently comfortable position, she kept her blinking eyes on Anna.

Anna leaned forward to tickle her behind the ears. "I'm

glad you're a tough cookie. I'm so sorry I destroyed your house. If I'd only known."

Sammy and Anna worked in silence for a minute or two, then Sammy coughed. "You ready to talk yet?" she asked.

Anna didn't look up. "You know I always pictured myself finishing my degree then settling down somewhere in an academic job. Somewhere not too far away, of course."

"Not too far from Steve, right?" Sammy asked.

At least Sammy understood. Once Anna had her degree, she and Steve could finally admit their relationship publicly. Until she had that degree in hand, her relationship with her faculty advisor had to be kept under wraps. Sammy was one of the few people who'd known about it.

"I don't think Steve ever told anyone about me." Anna spoke quietly. "I should have realized that was a problem..." Her voice trailed off.

"Stop it." Sammy chided her. "You didn't know."

Anna bent down to look more closely at two ceramic pieces. "Do these go together?"

She passed them to Sammy, who adjusted one slightly. "Yep, hand me that glue."

The vase was slowly coming into shape as they glued the broken pieces back into their old places. "He was always more concerned about keeping our relationship a secret than I was," Anna continued her thought from before. "I figured that was because he had more to protect — and more to lose."

"Like his job." Sammy raised her eyebrows. "He shouldn't have been in a relationship with a student. There are reasons there are rules against that."

"Well, I figured wrong, didn't I?"

Sammy didn't answer, just worked silently with Anna on the few remaining pieces of ceramic. The cat watched them both through slitted eyes, occasionally yawning or stretching.

When Anna had seen her own original research used as evidence in a series of Steve's academic publications, she knew just how wrong she'd been about him. He'd been stealing her work, claiming it as his own. Her accusation of theft got the far-too-slow wheels of academic justice turning, but it would take months, maybe years, before she got the credit she deserved for her research. And Steve got the reputation he deserved.

"Now I'm just waiting, you know?"

"For what?" Sammy asked.

Anna put down the pieces she'd been holding. The cat lifted its head. "You know what, you're right. For what?"

"Oh." Sammy frowned. "I was just asking."

"No." Anna stood up. "What am I waiting for? For someone else to step up and point at Steve and say 'that man is dishonest.'" Anna pointed at the cat as she spoke. The cat blinked. "Sorry, honey, I don't mean you."

She looked down at the coffee table. "Aha!" She grabbed two more pieces. "These go here..."

Sammy held the larger part as Anna glued the two new pieces into place. Both women leaned back and looked at what they'd created. Then burst out laughing.

"That is not a vase," Sammy said.

"Well it certainly won't hold water," Anna agreed. "Look, this side looks good. As long as I put the hole against the wall..." Her voice trailed off.

This was so typical of her. Whenever she made a decision to do something, she refused to let it go. Refused to give up. Refused to admit when she was in over her head.

"You're not thinking about the vase right now, are you?" Sammy asked softly.

Anna shook her head.

"What have I done, Sammy? What am I doing? Why did I think I could do this?"

"I don't know, I told you not to bother."

Anna gave Sammy a look and she smiled kindly. "I know, I know you're not talking about the vase. Look, the house looks gorgeous, right? And you will get guests again, I promise. You will make this work."

"And George?" Anna asked, watching as the cat jumped from the sofa and made her way to Anna's side. She put a hand out and the cat bumped her forehead against the hand then rubbed her head back and forth, purring. "At least someone here is happy now."

"You'll make this work, Anna," Sammy repeated. "I know you. I know you will."

Anna smiled at the cat then looked up and smiled at Sammy. Sammy did know her. Sammy knew that Anna was stubborn and wouldn't give up. It was going to get her into trouble.

32

Anna stood on the wide front porch watching as Sammy drove away. The late afternoon sun cut through the bare trees leaving long, flickering shadows on the lawn and sidewalk. Anna took a deep breath. She loved this time of day. Actually, come to think of it, before this whole tragedy, she'd loved every time of day in Cape May.

Once Sammy was out of sight, heading back to her bakery to get set up for her early morning tomorrow, Anna found Eoin and bundled him into his light jacket. It was time to take him to his next fun activity. At least, it was supposed to be fun.

He didn't object as he pushed his arms into the sleeves of his jacket, but he didn't help either.

"Eoin, do you not want to go back to the community center? Did you enjoy the last time?"

Eoin shrugged. "I s'pose," he whispered in the little voice he always used around her.

"This time you're going to be learning all about sea creatures, doesn't that sound fun?"

Eoin's eyebrows went up and he nodded. "It does," he answered thoughtfully. "I like learning."

Apparently the creativity lab, the last activity he'd joined, hadn't been particularly thrilling for him. Anna laughed and gave him a quick hug, then took his hand and together they headed toward the center of town.

Once Eoin was safely settled in the right room of the community center, his wide eyes examining the various posters and pictures of sea animals taped to the walls, Anna walked back to Washington Mall. She had some food and kitchen supplies to replace, even if she didn't have any guests.

The streets of Cape May looked completely normal. She passed a few locals who greeted her with cautious smiles, and visitors strolled the streets admiring the colorful wooden exteriors and gingerbread trim of the Victorian houses. She loved the style, too. Her own house had surprising gables and towers popping up in unexpected parts of the house. Aunt Louise's rooms were tucked into the ground level of one of those towers, around the side of the house.

Thoughts of Aunt Louise brought her spirits up a bit. She missed the old lady, for sure. She was going to have to bite the bullet and go through her rooms soon.

With her thoughts focused on Aunt Louise and her house, Anna walked right into Paul Murphy.

"Sorry."

"Excuse me."

They both spoke at once, Paul looking up from the cell phone that had drawn his attention away from his path.

"Oh, Mr. Murphy," Anna said. "How are you?"

"Hmm?" Paul looked at her again. "Right, yes. The B&B owner. Anna is it?"

Paul looked as if he was going to continue on his way so Anna stuck out a hand, obliging him to stop and shake it.

"Yes, that's right. Anna McGregor. How are you doing? With George's death and all, I mean. Are you okay?"

Paul glanced up and down the street, looked down at his phone once more, then slipped the phone into his jacket pocket and smiled politely. "Yes, thank you for asking. I am doing well. As you know, I didn't really know George very well." He frowned, as if realizing that might not have been the most polite response, then added, "unfortunately."

"I understand." Anna smiled comfortingly. "But you really didn't have a chance to, since he worked out of Trenton. I'm curious, had you worked with him long?"

Paul's eyes narrowed. "Why do you ask?"

"It's just that... like I told you before, I met Richard Gormley. It seems like it wasn't that long ago that George bought the business from him. Did you work with him before?"

"I just told you," Paul's voice rose in anger, "I didn't know him well."

Anna raised both hands. "Sorry, of course you did. I'm just... I'm trying to get a better sense of George Hedley, of who he was as a person, you know?"

"You are?" Paul opened his eyes wide in surprise. "Why?"

Anna shrugged. She didn't have a good response to that. Fortunately, Paul continued.

"He was suspicious. That's who he was as a person."

"Suspicious? How?"

Paul straightened his shoulders and shoved his hands into his pockets. "Never mind, it doesn't matter." He looked up and down the street. "I shouldn't have said anything."

"Paul," Anna cautioned him, "George is dead. The police are investigating. If you have suspicions about George, you're going to have to share them. If not with me, then the police."

A cluster of women passed them on the sidewalk. As Anna mentioned the police, two of the women turned to stare at them, their steps slowing. Anna glared back at them and they pretended not to notice, hurrying on down the street.

Paul watched the exchange with a reddening face. Finally, his shoulders slumped. "I might as well tell you, I always assumed George Hedley was somehow connected to the mob."

Another couple approached them from the direction of the main street, so Paul put a hand on Anna's arm to direct her to a bench tucked between two pine trees off the pedestrian path. They sat close to each other, keeping their voices low.

"Why did you think that?" Anna whispered.

"He was a money guy — a great money guy. And really not, I repeat *not* a people person. In fact"—Paul shut his eyes and laughed—"he was terrible with people. They didn't even like being around him."

"But you chose to work with him?" Anna asked, confused. "Why would you do that?"

Paul nodded. "He brought me on board after he'd acquired Varico. He saw its potential, room for expansion. And as usual, he was right. About the business potential. Also right that it wasn't a business he could run on his own."

"So you're like a front man?"

"Ha! You could say that, yes. My job is to run the business and keep George as far away from the clients as possible. Oh, I mean my job was..."

"That's why you didn't like him coming into town so often?" Anna prodded, keeping him on track.

"Absolutely. Plus, I was a little afraid of him. Like I said, I thought he was connected."

"Why would you think that?"

"You met him. He was... I don't know... off."

"That's certainly true. But I think he was just good at numbers and awkward around people."

"I guess so. I just... I just knew the business would run better if I dealt with the customers. So when people came around saying they knew him — like a tough-looking young man once, said George had offered him financial advice. I don't mind telling you, I was scared. I thought he might be a hit man, you know, with the mob?"

"Tough-looking young man?" Anna's brows furrowed, then cleared when she realized he must mean Jason. Her first thought, of Jason in his Brigitte Bardot dress, was immediately replaced by the memory of how fierce he had been earlier that day. "Right, definitely scary. But you don't have to worry about him, he wasn't a hit man. He thought he was a friend of George." Even as she spoke, Anna realized she didn't really know if what she was saying were true. Was George connected to the mob? Was Jason really a hit man? She didn't know either man well enough to answer honestly.

"A friend?" Paul sounded surprised. "Oh. I didn't realize George had friends."

"No, apparently neither did George. But he did, for all the good it did him. So will you be running the business on your own now?"

"Yes, I will." Paul nodded. "Funny. Before George died, I was looking for another job. Working with George, nervous about who he was and who he was connected to... it was getting to be too much for me." He sighed and leaned back against the bench, running a hand through his hair. Then he laughed. "I guess now I'll find out if it was the stress of the business or working with George that's turning my hair prematurely gray."

"What about George's widow? Won't she inherit George's share of the company?"

"No, no." Paul frowned and shook his head rapidly. "We had an agreement. In writing. It's my business now."

"That works out pretty well for you, then," Anna said, trying to keep her face a picture of innocence.

She must have failed.

"You—" Paul stood and cut himself off. He let out a growl but said nothing more, simply turning and dashing away from her.

❧

ANNA HAD TAKEN ONLY A FEW STEPS WHEN HER CELL phone rang. Hoping for a reservation, she answered in a chirpy voice.

"Ah, yes, Ms. McGregor." The voice was familiar, but Anna couldn't immediately place it.

"Yes, may I help you?"

"This is Richard Gormley."

Anna froze where she was on the sidewalk, glanced around, then slipped back onto the bench she'd shared seconds earlier with Paul Murphy.

"Mr. Gormley. Hello. How are you? I hope you and your wife found another place to stay and managed to enjoy the rest of your time in Cape May."

"Indeed. We are still enjoying our time in Cape May."

"Oh, good." Anna was at a loss for how to respond. Why was he calling her?

"Ms. McGregor, I want you to know that I am very sorry about what you must be going through. I can imagine George Hedley's death has not been good for your business."

"Oh." Anna's eyes opened wide. "Yes, thank you. I appreciate that. No, it's not been easy, but I'm sure I'll get by. Climbing Rose Cottage will be available for your next visit to town." Was it appropriate to be pitching her B&B on this call? She had no idea why he was even calling.

"I'm glad to hear it. But I don't think we'll be staying with you again."

Anna slumped back against the bench. "No, of course not," she answered in a quiet voice. "I can't blame you. When someone dies like that..."

There was a pause. Anna was about to repeat herself when she heard Gormley inhale sharply. "I don't think you understand, young lady."

Young lady? Who did this man think he was talking to, his daughter?

"Excuse me?" Anna said, her voice sharper.

"As I said, we are still in town. My wife and I. We are spending time with friends. Good friends. You know by now that I ran a business in town for many years."

Anna nodded, then realizing that was not helpful, simply said, "Mm-hmm."

"We've been hearing stories from our friends, Ms. McGregor."

At least he was back to Ms. McGregor, that was better. Wasn't it?

"It seems you have been spreading rumors about me." Gormley's voice was getting louder, higher pitched.

"Mr. Gormley, please, I didn't spread rumors." She put a hand up as she spoke as if to fend off his angry words.

"Did you not suggest that I had a motive and opportunity to kill George Hedley?"

"Oh... well... yes, I may have said that, but..."

"Enough!" Now Richard was yelling. She heard a woman's voice in the background, sounding soothing, then heard Richard telling her to shush. "I have had enough of this. We may have moved away but we are still part of this community.

I will not have you saying such terrible things about me or my family."

"Mr. Gormley, I'm so sorry."

"Yes, I'm sure you are. Sorry that George died. If you're looking for someone to cast the blame onto, I suggest you look no further than yourself."

"Oh please." She couldn't hide her own anger anymore. "Why would I kill my own guest?"

"How should I know? You were the only person who knew he'd be staying in your house. Do you think I would have booked a room there if I'd known George would be there? He's the last person I want to see on my vacation."

"No, I suppose not." Anna chewed on her lip, her anger receding as her curiosity grew. Richard had just admitted that he still held a grudge against George, hadn't he?

"The first time I saw George Hedley was when he was already dead. In your dining room."

"Mr. Gormley, you are absolutely right. I have been talking out of turn, saying things and asking questions that I now realize could hurt someone. Could hurt you."

Richard sniffed but didn't respond.

"Please accept my apology," Anna continued. "And thank you for calling."

She tapped her phone to disconnect the call before Richard could say anything else. Better to end on that note.

So Richard really did hate George, as she had guessed. Could she believe his claim that he had no idea George Hedley was staying at the Climbing Rose Cottage at the same time? Now that Anna thought about it, they hadn't seen each other at all that first day. George had arrived before the Gormleys and come down to breakfast while the older couple were still in their room.

On the other hand, he was clearly still well connected in town. After all, that's how he heard that she'd been asking questions about him. It would have been easy for him to hear about George's visit through the grapevine. He didn't need to see George to know he was there.

Anna sighed and stood. She'd gathered a lot of information in a short amount of time, so she couldn't complain about a lack of data. But her analysis so far didn't point to any clear relationships of cause and effect. There was no obvious loose thread that, once pulled, would unravel the whole, complex story. She needed more before she could reach any conclusions.

33

Anna inhaled deeply as the shop's door closed behind her with a gentle tinkling of the bell. She loved coming to the kitchen goods store just off Washington Mall. What did she smell today, she wondered as she took another sniff. Cinnamon, for sure. Maybe tarragon?

"Is that lemon grass?" She asked aloud as Wendy Hodgson came in from the back room, alerted no doubt by the doorbell.

"Indeed," Wendy acknowledged Anna in her usual brisk way. "A new blend, just in today." Wendy waved a hand toward a display shelf loaded with jars and small cans of a variety of spices and blends, all produced by a local spice company.

Three small tasting jars sat open on the front of the shelf and Anna walked closer, leaning over the display. She inhaled again, this time focusing on each one individually. The master spice blender who ran the local company knew her stuff, that was for sure.

"The hint of lavender in this one is perfect for spring." She said, then sniffed the next one. "Ooh, I could use this in my scones." She stood up smiling, but the scared look on Wendy's face drove the smile from hers.

"Oh, uh... sorry," Wendy mumbled, unusually tongue-tied.

"It's all right," Anna replied. She would have to get used to the looks of fear, even horror, on her neighbors' faces. At least until they all knew for a fact that her scones did not kill anyone. "You need to know, I didn't poison George Hedley."

"Of course you didn't, sweetheart." Wendy patted Anna on the shoulder. "You would never do such a thing."

"Not even by accident. Do you understand?" Anna looked directly into Wendy's eyes to emphasize her point. "George didn't die from anything he ate in my house. I am one hundred percent sure of that."

Wendy let out a breath and moved back toward her register. "I'm very glad to hear that. I'll make sure others know it, too. You must be aware"—she offered Anna a sympathetic look—"there is some gossip going around that he died eating your baking."

"Oh." Anna shook her head. "No. No. I mean, yes." She threw her hands up. "He died while eating my scone, but not because of my scone. Do you see? In fact, that's kind of why I'm here now. I need to replace a few things in my kitchen."

"Oh?" Wendy raised an eyebrow.

Anna walked around the small store, eyeing the items she would need to replace and mentally adding up the cost. She would have to pick and choose which items to replace first. "I did some housecleaning, obviously. After George died, I mean." She picked up a set of baking pans, then put them down hurriedly when she saw the price marked on the back. "I had to. To make sure, but also to reassure anyone who wants to stay at my place in the future. There is absolutely no connection between my house, my kitchen, and George Hedley's death."

"Ahem." The gentle cough from the front of the store

startled them both. Minister Woodley stood in the doorway, holding the glass front door open. As they turned, he released the door and the bell tinkled gently. "Wendy, Anna." He greeted them. "I see you are discussing the tragedy. Anna"—his face showed true concern as he turned to her—"I am so sorry that you had to be part of this terrible affair. I am pleased that you are confident you were not in any way responsible. That must be a weight off your shoulders."

As he spoke, he reached out and grabbed both her hands in his, crows feet forming around his smiling eyes. His expression offered comfort. And hope. Of course, he knew as well as she did that the weight still hung over her.

"Thank you, Minister Woodley. Of course I feel guilty. How could I not?"

"There is no way." Minister Woodley spoke kindly even though his words could be interpreted as cruel. "But we are all human. We must all deal with tragedy. And guilt."

He dropped her hands and faced Wendy. "I am here for my regular order of sparkling cider."

"Of course." Wendy trotted to the back room to gather the Minister's order. Anna was surprised Minister Woodley purchased his cider from Wendy instead of the grocery store, then remembered that Wendy was also a Methodist. She must be a member of the parish.

"Anna," Minister Woodley broke into her thoughts. "You are welcome to join us at services tomorrow morning."

"Tomorrow?" Anna asked.

Minister Woodley laughed. "It is Sunday tomorrow. Perhaps the tragedy has affected your sense of time."

"Oh, right. No, sorry. Um, thanks for the invitation, but I'm not Methodist."

"That's quite all right, we're happy to welcome our brothers and sisters of other faiths. Aren't we, Wendy?"

Wendy looked up from the dolly she was pushing carefully

out of the back room. It was piled with three cases of sparkling cider. "Of course, yes. Of course." Anna suspected she hadn't been listening and had no idea what she'd just agreed to.

"So I will see you tomorrow?" Minister Woodley asked Anna as he took control of the dolly from Wendy.

"Um... Sure, I guess. I don't really know..." Anna wasn't particularly interested in checking out the Methodist service, but she didn't want to be rude, either. Minister Woodley had always been supportive and kind to her. Maybe it would do her good to get a spiritual lift. "Yes. Okay, I'll be there."

He nodded at them both as he left the store.

"So, we'll see you tomorrow at service?" Wendy asked. "That's a very good idea. And don't worry, I'll be sure to mention to the other members that your baking was not connected to George Hedley's death. Now, what do you need?"

Anna realized she'd been avoiding her neighbors, worried that they would blame her for George's death. But she had been wrong. She needed to embrace her neighbors, build her friendships.

"Thanks Wendy, I appreciate it. I really need some friends right now."

34

Anna awoke on Sunday morning with a sharp pain in her left arm followed by a duller but heavier pain in her chest. Was she having a heart attack? It had been a stressful week, but she was too young, surely.

Her phone lay on the shelf next to her bed. She opened her eyes slowly, planning to reach out to grab the phone, and found herself staring into a pair of bright yellow eyes.

"Cat!" She sat up in bed, throwing the cat onto the covers next to her. "You almost scared me to death. What are you doing in here?"

In response, the cat reached out one paw and tapped her arm, then came closer and used both paws to knead her stomach.

"Ow, your claws are hurting me." She pushed the cat away gently. "Okay, okay, I'm up. I'm guessing you're hungry?"

She wrapped herself in a fuzzy dressing gown and padded down the stairs, the cat close at her heels. She shivered as she passed through the lounge, where the closed shutters kept out the early morning sun. The room seemed sinister somehow. She'd never noticed that before.

She pushed through to the kitchen and turned on all the lights, then screamed.

Eoin looked up from his stool, a book spread open in front of him, a bowl with a few traces of milk in the bottom next to his arm.

"Eoin, good morning." Anna tried to sound cheerful. "Sorry about the scream, I didn't know you were up already."

He flinched when she said his name, but didn't correct her. "I made meself breakfast, Cousin Anna," he said in his quiet voice. Traces of milk along the counter and a few stray cereal flakes on the floor attested to the truth of his statement.

"Good for you," she said as she wiped up the mess. "Now it's my turn."

She started putting on a pot of coffee, but a loud meow from her companion reminded her what her priorities were supposed to be.

"Just give me a minute, will you?" She said, followed by, "Ow!" when the cat responded with a tap from her paw onto Anna's bare leg. "Okay, okay, I need to get this brewing, then it's all you, I promise."

Once she got the coffee brewing, she turned to look down at the cat. The cat looked up at her, blinking its yellow eyes.

"So now I'm feeding you, right? Does this mean you're staying?" Anna smiled at the thought. She'd had a cat once before, when she was a young girl. But her recent lifestyle hadn't allowed her the luxury of a pet. She'd been too focused on her research, her fieldwork and her lab to have that kind of distraction. But that wasn't the case anymore, was it?

"Let's see. You liked that salmon yesterday, didn't you?" Anna spoke out loud as she dug through the fridge. "I have some of that left. I'll go out this afternoon and get some cans of cat food for you. Sound good?"

The cat did not look impressed by the suggestion.

"No, I will not keep feeding you smoked salmon. I'm already struggling with my budget. If I don't get more guests soon, I might be joining you in eating the cat food."

She refreshed the cat's water and placed the saucer with salmon next to it. The cat blinked at her one more time — clearly indicating that she only deigned to eat the food provided as a courtesy to Anna — then leaned forward over the bowls and started eating.

Anna watched her, smiling. "Luke was right about you, wasn't he? You really are one tough cookie. Taking care of yourself one day, then eating out of my saucers the next." She shook her head and laughed. "I wish I could be as strong as you!"

Leaving the cat with Eoin, Anna took a mug of coffee upstairs with her as she showered and dressed for that morning's service. She wasn't really sure what to wear. When she'd gone to Catholic mass as a child, they'd always dressed up a bit for church. She didn't know if Methodists did the same thing, but figured it couldn't hurt. She pulled on a dark blue silk blouse and her nicest black skirt, even suffering through the process of pulling on pantyhose for the occasion.

She had no intention of dragging Eoin along with her. She was pretty sure his parents, good Irish Catholics, wouldn't appreciate her taking their son to a Methodist service. Fortunately, the Catholic church on Washington Mall provided a children's nursery on Sunday mornings. She knew Eoin was too old for that; he'd be the biggest child there, by far. But it was the best option she had.

She still had some time before the service started, so she headed back to the kitchen. She might as well use the time to wash and set up the few pieces of equipment she'd replaced yesterday. She was going to act as if her business were still viable. It was the only way she could think of to move forward.

The cat had finished eating and sat in the middle of the room licking herself. She watched as Anna stacked her new pans and containers in the sink and filled it with warm soapy water. With her focus on the sink and making sure not to get any water on her silk blouse, Anna didn't notice the cat approaching until she felt it rubbing against her leg.

"Hi there," she said with a smile, then frowned when she saw the cluster of hair the cat had attached to her pantyhose. "Oh, fudge."

She dried her hands and started pulling cat hair from her legs. The cat meowed again. And approached her again.

"Oh no, I can't have your hair all over me this morning," Anna said as she backed away. "Eoin, grab your jacket, we need to get going soon." Even as she spoke, she saw that the cat was still coming toward her.

Laughing, Anna stepped through to the lounge, realizing that she was running away from a small cat but not really caring. As she checked her purse to make sure she had everything she needed, the kitchen door creaked open.

Anna watched, wide-eyed, as the cat came toward her.

"Wow, you are really determined aren't you?" She laughed as she said it but still moved away.

When she headed for the front door, thinking to simply leave the house, the cat picked up her pace and circled around to come at her from the front. She found herself being herded away from the front door.

But the cat didn't stop there.

Anna glanced back and knew exactly where the cat was taking her: Aunt Louise's private rooms. The rooms into which Anna had not yet ventured, not ready to face the memories they contained. The reminders of all she had lost when Aunt Louise died.

She stopped and turned her back to the door, facing down the cat.

"I am not going in there. At least, not now. Not today. Why do you care anyway?"

The cat sat. She licked her lips. She meowed.

Without warning, she leapt. Directly at Anna. Her instinct kicking in, Anna caught the cat and held her against her chest before dropping her. Being a cat, the cat didn't fall as much as leap gracefully down, making sure to rub against Anna's black skirt and her legs on the way down.

"Oh fudge!" Anna shouted as she saw the trail of white and black hairs down her shirt, skirt and legs. "You... you cat!"

The cat looked up at her, meowed once more, and sauntered out of the room.

35

Anna slipped into the church, not sure what to expect. It was a small building. Two columns of simple wooden pews filled the main room, leading up to the front altar where Minister Woodley set out the last goblet for the sparkling cider. A cluster of people gathered around him, presumably helping set things up, while more people spread out among the pews.

Anna caught sight of Wendy on the far left of the room and moved toward her, stepping carefully and politely around a family with young children who were sitting on the floor coloring in the back of the room.

Looking up from the playing children, she gasped. Catherine Hedley was the last person she'd expected to see here. She looked around desperately, hoping to avoid having to speak to the woman, but it was too late. Catherine had seen her and was moving in her direction.

"So. You're a Methodist, too?" Catherine's voice held more than a small amount of doubt.

"Well, no. Minister Woodley invited me to join the service today. He thought I might benefit from it," Anna replied, not sure how much information she owed this woman. A woman who had just days before accused her of murder. "Why are you here?"

Catherine's eyes flared. "To practice my faith, of course," she retorted.

"No, I mean why are you still in Cape May? I thought you would have returned home by now."

"Well, you thought wrong." Catherine drew her chin down as she spoke, a gesture redolent of angry school teachers from Anna's youth. "The police asked me to stay in town, but I would have stayed anyway. At least until I can take George home with me."

As she spoke, Catherine's eyes traveled down to Anna's skirt. She glanced down and realized she had failed to remove all of the cat hair. She rubbed at it in embarrassment as Catherine gave her a smug look.

"Um... of course..." Anna mumbled as she pulled at the cat hair. "Again, I'm really sorry for your loss."

Catherine sniffed. "Yes. Thank you."

Thank you? Anna looked up surprised. That was more than she'd expected from the woman.

"I realize now that you didn't do it intentionally," Catherine continued.

Anna straightened to her full height and looked down at Catherine. "What did you say? You still think I killed your husband?"

A few people glanced their way and Anna switched to a whisper. "Mrs. Hedley, we cannot go through this again."

"No, I see no reason to." Catherine also switched to a whisper. "Christ teaches that I must forgive you for what you did, and I do." She sniffed again, suggesting she hadn't completely accepted Christ's teaching. "But whether by accident or not, my husband is dead. Because of his visit to your cheap, unclean residence."

"Cheap? Unclean?" Anna felt her voice rising again but didn't care. "Climbing Rose Cottage is exceptionally clean and well run. And I do not appreciate you spreading rumors about it like this."

"It is not a rumor that my husband died at your establishment. It is not a rumor that you have unfinished rooms in your house, a broken down shed in your yard and... and..." Catherine seemed to be searching for a final cruel insult to hurl at Anna. "And cheap, seagull art in your bedrooms."

Anna bit her lip and her chin jutted out. "You have no right to insult me, Mrs. Hedley. But this is a house of God, so I will let it go. But I will prove that I had nothing to do with George's death."

She felt a light touch on her arm and turned to see Wendy at her side.

"Come on, Anna. We're ready to start. Come sit with me," Wendy said kindly, ignoring Catherine. "Come on." She tugged at Anna's arm, almost dragging her up the aisle toward the pew where she sat.

Anna glared back at Catherine as she walked. That woman had no shame. She simply narrowed her eyes, nodded at Anna, and moved to a seat on the other side of the church.

Anna sat next to Wendy, seething. She hadn't meant to insist that she would find the truth about George's death, it had just come out. But now that she'd said it, she knew she had to do it.

36

Anna followed Wendy down the narrow, carpeted stairs after the service, thoughts of faith and love still echoing in her head. Wendy led her to a white-walled basement room that encompassed about half of the footprint of the church upstairs. Other women were already gathered near the table set against one wall. Anna could see a large silver coffee urn and two boxes of donuts set up next to the coffee supplies. Not a bad way to finish a Sunday morning. She wondered why the men didn't join in.

Smiling and greeting everyone by name, Wendy guided Anna to get their refreshments, then to a low bookshelf across the room where they could rest their cups while they ate.

"You do this every Sunday?" Anna asked after finishing a bite of donut.

"Mm-hmm." Wendy nodded, her mouth still full.

Anna laughed. "Sorry, bad timing."

Wendy swallowed and laughed. "Yes, it helps foster a sense of community among the women. Sometimes we need that, you know?" The look she gave Anna carried a similar message to her words. "Ah, Thea." Wendy turned from Anna to give a quick hug to a woman who approached. "Thea, this is my friend, Anna McGregor."

"Anna." Thea nodded, her hands full of coffee and donuts. "You're Louise Gannet's niece, aren't you? You're running Climbing Rose Cottage now?"

"Yes," Anna responded, surprised but pleased that Thea knew who she was.

"Don't look so surprised." Thea smiled, correctly reading Anna's expression. "This is a small town. We like to know who's moving in and out and doing what."

"Yes, I'm finally beginning to understand that," Anna said, thinking of her call yesterday from Richard Gormley.

More women approached and Wendy introduced Anna around. The talk among the group ranged from comments on the minister's words that morning to weather predictions to good deals at the local supermarket. Anna joined in easily, happy to have a group of women to talk with about something other than secrets and death.

"Front loaders, definitely," Anna said when the topic turned to washing machines and doing laundry. She had plenty of opinions to share on this topic.

"Certainly for me," added a petite brunette, laughing. "You can imagine the trouble I used to have reaching the bottom of the top loader to dig out the last few socks."

Everyone laughed, picturing the short woman hanging over the edge of the washing machine.

"But what about the mustiness?" Another woman chimed in. "Don't they tend to get that musty smell."

Anna nodded. "It's true. You have to clean them regularly. And leave the door ajar when you're not using it."

"Oh."

"Aha."

"Of course."

Anna was surrounded by nods and smiling faces. She realized with surprise she was really enjoying herself. She hadn't expected coffee and donuts after church to be so much fun.

"So you've re-opened Climbing Rose Cottage?" A woman behind her asked.

Anna turned to her, a smile on her face. "That's right. I inherited it from my Great Aunt Louise. I've had to put a bit of work in to get it up and running again, but it's gorgeous now."

The woman scoffed. "I'm sure it took quite a lot of work. I'm Coral, by the way." Coral smirked as she introduced herself, her lips forming a pout that looked like she'd sucked on a few lemons in her day.

"Coral, nice to meet you," Anna replied with hesitation. "What do you mean by that?"

"Oh, just that the house was rather falling apart at the end, wasn't it? Couldn't keep it up, could she? Too busy running around getting involved in other people's lives." Coral put a coffee mug to her lips for a quick sip and it came away with a thick layer of peach lipstick at the rim. Definitely not the right shade for a woman with Coral's mousy hair and pale eyes, but it did match the silk shirt and skirt she wore. She looked like she'd wrapped herself in a papaya.

Anna couldn't decide if she should laugh or be offended. "I beg your pardon?"

"Ah, Coral, I see you've met Anna McGregor, Louise Gannet's niece." Wendy said as she joined their conversation. "Anna, Coral and your Aunt Louise worked together on a number of committees for the township."

She spoke with a smile, but when she reached behind Anna, ostensibly to grab her coffee mug from the shelf behind her, she whispered. "Long story. Fill you in later. Her real name is Carole."

Anna failed to completely smother her laugh and Coral — Carole — glared at her. "That's right, we both served on the Environmental Commission and Shade Tree Commission at various times. Appointed by the mayor." She smirked again, apparently feeling pretty good about her mayoral connections.

"Now, if I recall, Louise also served on the Library Advisory Committee and... what was the other one?" Wendy asked, tapping a finger against her mouth. She gave the perfect appearance of trying to remember something, but when Anna looked at her she winked.

"Yes." Coral frowned, deep lines etching themselves into her lipstick. "You know very well she was part of the Pet Advisory Committee who refused my request."

"Ah yes, your request to have your neighbor put down his dog because it barked too much for your liking."

"That dog was a menace." Coral's eyes narrowed. "And everyone knew it. They just denied the request out of spite. Never mind." She waved a hand and opened her eyes wide. Her copious application of mascara caused some of her top lashes to cling to the bottom lashes and she blinked a few times until they were clear. "It's all over now, isn't it?" She smirked again.

Anna struggled for words to respond that wouldn't be as rude as the words in her head. Then she overheard the last few words of another conversation going on at the side of the group.

"...waiting for her husband's body to be released."

Anna turned toward the women who were speaking in hushed tones. "Are you talking about Mrs. Hedley?" She might be jumping out of the frying pan into the fire, but she had to get away from Carole — that is, Coral — and really did want to know what these other women thought about Catherine Hedley.

Chatter in the room faded away as other faces turned in Anna's direction. She felt herself blushing, but had to know.

"Yes, dear," an older woman answered her. "We met her this morning."

"Interesting woman," another added.

"I'm sure she's distraught over her husband's death," the older woman replied.

"Of course, of course," the first woman replied, but her tone suggested she didn't quite believe it.

"She's not a fan of mine," Anna said, figuring it would be best if she brought it up first.

"Well of course she's not," Wendy said. "But we can't blame her for that. As you said, Mary, she's distraught."

The older woman nodded as Wendy said her name, but then stopped, frowning. "I do think, though, that she's a bit .... well ... stringent in her beliefs?"

A few women giggled, and Anna felt the tension in her shoulders release. She laughed out loud when a woman in a silky dress to her right added. "She's downright puritan. She suggested my dress would be better worn by a high school student. Said it wasn't proper for me to be wearing it."

"She sniffed at my purse because it's a little worn down and inappropriate for church," someone added.

"She scoffed when I tried to show her pictures of my grandchild," someone else responded.

"Ladies," Mary chimed in. "We must not speak ill of her. We all have our own impression, I'm sure. But she is a member of our faith, and we must show her respect. She is a new widow and that must affect her character, at least for a while."

Sufficiently chastened, the women all nodded. But Mary wasn't done.

"That said, Anna, you should know that she tried to say

something to me about you being responsible for her husband's death."

Anna gasped. She wasn't the only one as she heard a few sharp intakes around her.

"That's absurd," Wendy said. "How could she say such a thing? We know it wasn't Anna."

Mary held up a hand. "Of course we do. Anna is our neighbor and our friend." She smiled warmly at Anna and Anna felt tears come to her eyes. "And I told Mrs. Hedley the same thing, in no uncertain terms. We will not speak badly of her and we certainly won't let her speak badly of one of our own."

Anna was at a loss for words, so she simply nodded, then looked around the group smiling.

The sharply dressed woman put a hand on Anna's arm. "We all loved your Aunt Louise, you know. She was an amazing woman."

The petite brunette nodded vigorously. "So active in the community, always willing to chip in and help. Even after she couldn't keep up Climbing Rose Cottage anymore, she was still out and about, doing things for others."

Anna felt the tears return to her eyes and raised a hand to wipe them away. "Thank you, that is so kind. So good to hear. I miss her. I only wish I had spent more time down here with her recently."

"That's always the way, dear," Mary said kindly. "We always wish we'd spent more time with loved ones."

Other women nodded their agreement. All except Coral, who used the opportunity to inspect her fingernails. Anna thought of the dark doorway that led to Great Aunt Louise's rooms. She needed to open those doors, let the light in and enjoy the memories instead of running from them.

"Susan Gormley is doing it the right way, I'm sure," Wendy said.

"Oh yes," Mary replied. "Living with her children but visiting friends here often. That's certainly the best way."

"Susan Gormley? That's Richard's Gormley's wife?" Anna asked.

The women nodded. "Of course," one answered. "They stayed with you, didn't they? Oh—" she cut herself off. "I mean..."

"Yes, that's all right," Anna said. "They stayed at Climbing Rose Cottage the night that George Hedley died."

A redhead who had been fairly quiet up to now spoke up. "I hear you and Richard may have had some words."

"My goodness news does travel in this town, doesn't it?" Anna tried to laugh it off. "Yes, we did. But I believe everything is better now. Unless you know something I don't?"

The woman shook her head, her eyebrows raised. "Not at all. I did hear that he'd said his piece. My nephew saw him and Susan yesterday evening, out for a walk, and they filled him in."

"How is Jason?" Mary asked. "Getting ready for the summer season, I'm sure."

The redhead laughed and launched into a story about Jason and the exercises he and his colleagues had been doing to prepare for their work as lifeguards this summer.

Anna only half listened. It must be the same Jason, mustn't it? Were there many lifeguards in Cape May named Jason?

Listening to the woman talk, the pride evident in her voice as she described his various feats in the boating and swimming competitions the guards all participated in, Anna wondered how well this woman really knew her nephew.

Probably not as well as she thought. It might be a small town; everyone knew everyone else. Yet some people still managed to keep secrets. And one of those secrets must have cost George Hedley his life.

37

Anna jumped up when she heard the car on her driveway. Eoin, who'd been sitting next to her, jumped up when she did. He didn't recognize the car, but as soon as Sammy got out, his eyes lit up.

"Sammy," Anna called to her friend from the front porch. "You got here fast."

"You caught me at a good time. I was just closing shop after the Sunday morning rush."

After her morning of coffee and donuts, Anna better understood what her friend had always said about the Sunday morning rush. Apparently everyone in Wildwood, of all denominations, headed over to the Wild West Bakery after church on Sunday morning. Sammy was usually sold out by 1 p.m. and closed up early.

"Well I'm glad you're here."

"Hi there, Eoin." Sammy said the name tentatively.

"Eoin," he corrected her.

"Right, sorry." She gave him a quick hug, which he seemed to want to prolong. As she pushed him gently away, she looked at Anna. "What are you wearing? A cat-hair skirt? Did that cat attack you or something?"

Anna laughed and swiped at her skirt as she led Sammy into the kitchen. "Oh no, it's not that bad, is it? I was wearing this all morning."

"Right. So you went to church? At the Methodist church?" Sammy asked as she took a seat at the kitchen bar, Eoin hopping up on the stool next to hers. "What's that all about?"

Anna poured out tea for all of them, adding a healthy dollop of milk to Eoin's. "I went because Minister Woodley invited me, and I thought it would be comforting. But it was more than that... it was, I don't know... enlightening?"

Sammy half nodded, half shrugged. "Sure, I've heard religion described like that."

"No, not the religion"—Anna wagged her finger at her friend—"the gossip. With the women after the service."

"Aha, now that could be enlightening." Sammy took a sip of her tea and grabbed a cookie Anna had set out. Eyeballing the cookie, she said. "Almond?" She took a nibble. "With a hint of ginger?"

Eoin mimicked her actions, nibbling on the cookie, then examining it, then taking another bite.

Anna swallowed a laugh. "You know your baking. Yep, that's a new recipe I'm playing around with. I thought I could serve cookies and tea in the afternoons to my guests—" She let out a breath and looked down into her mug.

"Don't worry, honey." Sammy patted her leg. "You'll have guests again, I promise. Now, what did you learn this morning? Anything helpful?"

"No. In fact, the opposite. There are so many secrets," Anna said, hitting the table with her hand.

"Right? And?" Sammy looked confused.

"Look, in this town, everyone seems to know everyone else's business, right? Gossip runs rampant."

"Janet Turner has a new boyfriend." Eoin spoke so quietly, Anna wasn't sure she'd heard him correctly.

"What was that, Eoin?"

He pulled his notebook out of his pocket and flipped through the pages as he explained. "The ladies gossiped in the church where I was, too. I heard them say that Janet Turner has a new boyfriend." He turned another page in his notebook then looked up. "And Alicia Muldoon should be ashamed of herself for the way she behaved on Saturday night."

Sammy and Anna shared an amused look. "We should put you to work, Eoin. You're good at this," Sammy said.

Eoin sat up tall, grinning. "People talk in front of us kids. Sometimes they don't even notice we're about."

"I will definitely keep that in mind," Anna told him. "So Richard Gormley heard immediately when I'd been asking questions about him."

"When you were joining in the gossip, you mean?" Sammy asked dryly.

Anna grimaced at her friend. "Okay, yes, but the thing is, everyone knew about it. Even the Ahavas who run Bric-N-Brac."

"Not the Ahavas!" Sammy said in mock dismay, then laughed. "So, what's your point?"

"Well, everyone thinks they know everything that's going on. But I'd bet dollars to donuts that Jason's aunt has no idea about his... pastime. Remember how angry he got when I told Evan Burley?"

Sammy shivered and put her mug down. "How could I forget. So... there are secrets. Even in a small town."

"Right. And I bet—"

"Please don't say dollars to donuts again," Sammy cut her off.

"Okay, fine, but the point is, everyone has secrets. Even though they think they know everything, they don't."

"Right. And?" Sammy asked, confused.

Anna stared down into her mug again where her tea was slowly growing cold. "How am I supposed to break through that wall? How can I figure out someone's secret when the whole town's gossip system hasn't?"

"Oh, I see." Sammy nodded slowly then downed the rest of her tea. "You think George Hedley found out someone else's secret and that's what got him killed?"

"Murdered, you mean. Sure, why not? Depending what the secret is, someone might kill to keep it." Anna said, thinking about how angry Jason had been.

Sammy stood and walked over to lean against her friend, Eoin's gaze following her every move. "Are you going to keep trying to learn more about George?"

"I don't know." Anna shook her head. "What's the point? If he found out something about someone else, that means I would have to dig into the secrets of everyone in this town. There's no way I can do that." She grabbed Sammy's hand. "Even with your help."

Something rubbed against Anna's leg and she started, shifting suddenly in her chair. She looked down to see the cat sitting below her, staring up at her. Blinking slowly.

"Ah yes, the cat. The one that managed to get all over your clothes this morning," Sammy said.

Anna sighed and tried rubbing her skirt again. It was no use. She'd have to get one of those sticky rollers to get animal hair off her clothes. If she was keeping the cat, that was.

"So, are you keeping it?" Sammy asked, clearly following Anna's train of thought.

Anna shrugged. "I think, more to the point, it's keeping me. She hasn't really left much since we fed her."

"And you did tear down her home," Sammy added.

Anna frowned at her friend. "Please don't remind me. Hey there kitty." Anna leaned forward and dropped her hand toward the ground, rubbing her fingers together to get the cat's attention. When she approached, Anna reached to pick her up.

The cat meowed and jumped back, leaving Anna with nothing more than the feel of her silky tail.

Sammy laughed. "I guess she's not ready for that level of intimacy. Ha! Something else you two have in common."

Anna rolled her eyes, but laughed, too. "That's not good. How can I take care of her if she doesn't trust me?" She got up and walked toward the cat, but the cat walked slowly in the other direction, heading toward the back door. It reminded Anna of their chase this morning, but this time she was chasing the cat instead of the other way around.

She kept stepping slowly toward the cat, her hand low, making cooing sounds. The cat kept walking away, turning back to look at Anna every few steps.

"If I didn't know better, I would say she wants you to follow her," Sammy said, standing to join Anna. Eoin jumped down from his stool and took Sammy's hand.

They watched as the cat slid out through the partially open back door, then followed it quietly. It sat down next to the large garbage bins that Anna kept behind the house.

"Ooh." Sammy waved a hand in front of her nose. "Please tell me the cat doesn't want to live in the garbage."

"I can't believe that." Anna looked around, trying to figure out what the cat was telling her. The cans were almost full. Which wasn't great, since trash day wasn't until Tuesday. Of course, without any new guests checking in, she wouldn't be producing that much more trash. Right now, the bins only held the garbage that had been produced by her ongoing efforts to clean out the house, by her recent guests and the food she'd made for them that morning. The morning George died.

She shuddered at the thought.

"You okay?" Sammy asked.

"Yeah, sure." Anna waved away the question. "Just thinking that I need to be a little more environmentally conscious. There must be more sustainable ways I can run this B&B, without producing that much trash."

Sammy laughed. "So you think the cat brought you out here to tell you that you throw too much stuff away?"

Anna made a face at her friend, then looked back down at the cat. "If I am keeping her, I'll need to name her. I can't keep calling her cat or kitty."

"I don't know." Sammy shrugged and walked back into the kitchen with Eoin to get them each another cookie. "Some people do that. They think it's cute."

"Well I don't," Anna replied. She looked down at the cat one more time. She was only a few feet away, but determinedly ignoring her. "I am glad you decided to stay. It's good to have somewhere to live and someone to take care of you." When the cat ignored her, she added. "Even if you are a real tough cookie."

The cat turned and looked at her. And started purring.

"What do you know?" Sammy spoke from the doorway. "Turns out you have already named her."

Anna approached the cat carefully, once again putting her hand low. This time, the cat rubbed up against her hand, still purring. Anna smiled at the sound. It was comforting, cozy.

"So that's who you are? Tough Cookie."

The cat sat, licked its paw, then walked back into the

kitchen and went directly to the two saucers Anna had left on the floor. One was still full of water, the other empty. The cat put a paw on the empty saucer and looked at Anna.

"Okay, Tough Cookie, I get it. It's time for your lunch. Better eat while I still have food to offer you."

38

Anna tossed the still-cat-hair-covered shirt and skirt into her laundry hamper just as the front doorbell jingled. She checked herself in her mirror quickly to make sure her jeans and sweater carried no traces of cat, then ran down to see who had come. She wasn't expecting any guests, that was for sure.

"Evan." She greeted the police officer from the top of the stairs. "Hi. How are you?"

"Anna. Hi, I'm glad I caught you." He smiled as she ran down the stairs and she was struck once again by the warmth of his expression, the comforting way his smile reached deep into his dark eyes.

"Come into the lounge." Anna gestured as she spoke. "Can I offer you some coffee?" She moved into the lounge then stopped as she thought about what this visit might mean. "Oh. Is this an official visit?" She put a hand out to steady herself against a bookshelf. "Should I sit down?"

Evan smiled again. "No, everything is fine. And yes, I'd love some coffee."

Anna nodded warily and moved back into the kitchen,

Evan close on her heels. She wished Sammy was still there, but her friend had taken Eoin — an absolutely thrilled Eoin — out to the bookshop on Washington Mall.

He watched in silence as she brewed the coffee, then joined her at the tall stools along the counter.

"I actually have good news," he said as he accepted a steaming mug from her and added a spoonful of sugar. "It's not really official yet, but I knew you'd want to know. You're off the hook, at least in terms of the accidental poisoning. The toxicology tests came back positive for poisoning by nicotine. There's no way that could be administered by accident."

"Thank goodness." Anna felt as if a weight had been lifted from her shoulders, then blushed when she saw Evan's expression. "I mean, of course that's terrible."

He shook his head at her as he smiled. "Don't worry, I know what you meant. And it only means you're off the hook for accidentally killing him. You're still on the suspect list."

"Me?" Anna's eyes widened. "Why on earth would I kill my first guest?"

Evan acknowledged the question with a dip of his head as he took a sip of coffee. "I agree, and I'm sure Detective Walsh does, too. But we can't simply write you off. Walsh is a stickler for wrapping up every detail."

"Hmm." Anna considered her options. "So will you be making an announcement or something? About this new find?"

Evan shook his head. "It doesn't work that way. First, this is just based on preliminary toxicology reports. It will take a few more days to get the final report back. We might do a press announcement then, but that's not up to me. Detective Walsh might think it will work in his favor not to make the announcement."

"Not to make the announcement?" Anna stood, her fists

balled at her side. "How could that help? It just means people will keep suspecting me. My guests will keep cancelling."

Evan stood with her. "I know, and I'm sorry. But think about it. There's a cold-blooded killer out there. Doesn't it make it easier to catch him if he thinks we're not looking for him?"

Anna took a breath. It did kind of make sense. But it didn't help her at all. She looked up at Evan, who was watching her closely. "So what can I do? I need to get my business back on track."

Evan slid back onto the stool and picked up his mug. After a second, Anna followed his lead. The two sat in silence for a moment before Anna spoke again. "I need to make sure people aren't afraid to stay here."

"Do you have any guests still booked?"

Anna nodded. "One couple is coming later this week, the others next weekend." She laughed. "I guess they haven't heard the news yet. I keep waiting for them to cancel on me, too."

"Well, at least that's something." Evan spoke with confidence. "You treat them well, make sure they have a good time, and people will start forgetting about... what happened with George."

"And maybe by then you'll have caught the real killer?" Anna asked hopefully.

"We will, I promise." Evan put a hand on her arm. "I will make sure of it."

Anna smiled into his eyes. "Why are you being so good to me?"

Even as she asked the question, Evan started to blush, a deep red that spread up from his neck. "Oh... well..." he spluttered, picked up his coffee mug, then put it down again when he realized it was empty. "Do you mind?" He looked back at her.

She shook her head no. "I guess I don't."

"Come on." He stood and grabbed her hand. "Let's go for a walk."

Anna ran upstairs to get a light sweater, considering what Evan had said. She wasn't a suspect, not really. That was good news. But no one else knew and the police weren't going to announce it. That was bad news. And there was nothing she could do about it.

❧

THE BEAUTIFUL SPRING WEATHER HAD DRAWN PLENTY OF other residents out this Sunday afternoon. Anna and Evan walked down the beach to the water's edge, walking along it and veering away whenever a wave rolled in a little too far. They walked close to each other, their arms occasionally touching. It felt good.

Anna closed her eyes to feel the sun on her face, hear the calls of the gulls, smell the salt of the ocean. She'd always thought she loved the solitude of walking on the beach, but it turned out it could be just as rewarding walking with someone by her side.

She opened her eyes and looked up at Evan, only to see him smiling down at her.

"Do that often?" he asked.

"What?"

"Walk with your eyes closed. You're going to hurt yourself if you keep that up."

She laughed, pushing her hair back behind her ears as it blew out over her face. "Not out here I won't. That's why I love it."

"Hmm," Evan replied, apparently unconvinced.

"I'm glad you're still working on the case, Evan. I've heard you're a good cop."

"You heard?" He sounded surprised. "You've been asking around about me?"

"Oh... well..." She stammered, not sure how to respond. He wasn't going to react the way Richard Gormley had, was he?

He laughed. "It's okay. I'm flattered. So who were you talking to about me?"

"Felicia Keane. When I told her you were part of the investigation, she was relieved. Said that I could be confident you'd get to the right place. Eventually."

"Right. Eventually." Evan looked out over the ocean. "The problem is, we're not there yet."

"You know what killed him. That's a good start."

"Yeah, but we're not just starting, are we? We're five days into the investigation already. I mean, we're moving forward, sure. But way too slow." Evan shook his head and grabbed her hand. "I know how important this is for you. Believe me, I do."

"I know you do, thank you. I trust you to do your job." Anna didn't meet his eyes as she said this, afraid he'd read the truth in them, the fact that she'd thought she could conduct her own investigation into George's death. "So..." she continued, "do you want to bounce a few ideas off me? It can help to talk things through."

Evan took a deep breath, then let it out slowly as he shook his head again. "You know I shouldn't talk about the case with you. Not just with you, with anyone."

"But I'm not just anyone, am I?" She gave his hand a squeeze and he grinned.

"No? I guess you're not." He dropped her hand and wrapped his arm around her waist as they walked on.

After a few minutes of silence, he shared his thoughts. "So we know George was killed. It was intentional. Not an accident. A weird way to kill someone, for sure. I've never heard of murder through nicotine poisoning."

"Hmm." Anna thought about everything she'd ever learned about nicotine. "Do the reports say how it was administered? The poison," she added when he looked confused. "Did he ingest it, touch it, inhale it... that sort of thing."

"Ah. No, not that I saw. I guess they're still working on that."

"If he inhaled it, it could have been a vapor. A lot of vapor, though, to kill him. If it was in liquid form, he could've drunk it. But that's not likely, it would be too hard to mask the flavor... he could have got it on his skin, I know that's a common way nicotine poisoning happens... but it wouldn't be easy to get someone to put that much liquid nicotine on themselves."

"Definitely not." Evan's brows lowered. "So even though we know the poison, we still don't know how it was done."

"I can't tell you that, but I can tell you the stuff acts fast," Anna said, remembering what she knew about the poison from her studies, a poison sometimes used in traditional remedies. Remedies that risked being deadly. "That means it was only a short time before he died. Maybe an hour, maybe less."

"Hmm." This time Evan's tone was more upbeat. "Okay, so that narrows it down. Who might have wanted George dead and been able to poison him that morning?"

Anna chewed on her lip again, then realized Evan was watching her and stopped in embarrassment. "How about his partner, Paul Murphy? I don't know how he could have done it, but he really did *not* like George."

Evan moved his head back and forth as he looked back at the ocean. "Not liking someone doesn't usually lead to killing them."

"It's more than that. He was about to quit. He didn't want to work with George anymore. Now, with George dead, he doesn't need to find a new job. He gets the whole company to himself."

"We knew he inherited sole ownership." He looked sideways at Anna. "Though I'm not sure how you found that out. We are looking into his background"—he held up a hand as Anna started to object—"but he can't be our only suspect. There is a guy we uncovered who had a relationship with George no one knew about."

"Oh?" Anna asked, already worried what Evan was going to say.

He confirmed her worries. "Jason Enright. He's a lifeguard. Turns out he has an... interesting sideline, nights and weekends." Anna realized Evan was blushing and tried not to laugh. "I won't go into it, but he had a social connection with George. And some sort of business connection as well."

"I know Jason." Anna said. When Evan looked at her in surprise, she added, "I met his aunt at church this morning, in fact."

"So what do you know of him? Anything that can help?"

"He has a nasty temper, I can tell you that from personal experience."

Evan stopped walking and turned to her, both hands on her arms. "What happened? Are you okay?"

"Yes, yes, I'm fine. Fortunately, Luke was there."

"Luke? Who's he?"

"Oh right." Now it was Anna's turn to be embarrassed. "You haven't met him, have you? He just does some work for me around the house. He was there when Jason came by. Jason was... angry. And Luke sent him away. That's all."

Evan released Anna and they resumed their walk, turning around to head back toward home. "So Luke is another suspect then. He had access to the house when George died."

"Luke?" Anna gasped. "No way, he wouldn't kill anyone."

Evan looked at her out of the corner of his eye. "I should meet him anyway. Ask him a few questions."

Oh great, Anna thought, that would not go well.

"How about Richard Gormley," she said aloud. "He didn't like George either."

Evan laughed. "You know a lot of people who didn't like George. But I need motive and opportunity, remember."

"Well, Richard certainly had opportunity. He was staying in Climbing Rose Cottage the night before George died. He might have known George would be there as well and booked the room just to get access to him. And he definitely still holds some anger for George."

"Okay, that's true. But because he was there, we did talk to him and his wife. We looked into his background, talked to some of his old neighbors. They don't paint a picture of a man bent on revenge. It seems like he's actually pretty happy in his retirement."

"Hmm." Now it was Anna's turn to think. Evan was batting back all her suggestions. "Mrs. Hedley. Catherine," she said, her eyes narrowing just thinking about the woman. "There's a person who could definitely kill someone."

Evan laughed and looked at her. "Seriously? She's tiny. How would she get him to drink poison or get it on his skin? Plus"—he held up a hand as Anna started to respond—"she has no motive. With her husband dead, she loses his income. We checked, and there's no big life insurance policy or anything like that. Second, she wasn't there. She was in Trenton when he died."

"But you met her." Anna felt her voice rise. "She's creepy."

"Maybe so, but that doesn't make her a killer. And think about it, her first introduction to you and Climbing Rose Cottage was showing up to collect her dead husband's belongings. You can't expect she'd be cheerful and friendly."

Anna stopped walking, a memory jumping into her thoughts. "Is that right? I thought she was there before?"

"No," said Evan, shaking his head. "She was definitely in Trenton that morning, at their home. We have multiple witnesses."

Anna took a deep breath, trying to let the beach work its magic. The feel of the sun on her uplifted face. The sound of gulls calling from over the waves. The scent of sand and seaweed and salt...

"Evan, that's it!"

"What's it," Evan asked cautiously.

"Tough Cookie was right. We need to dig through the trash."

39

"You want to dig through the trash?" Evan eyed the bins in front of them warily. "Why?"

Anna wrinkled her nose but nodded. "Sorry. There's a bag in there from George's room." She lifted the lid of the first of three large cans that stood behind her house. "I'm not sure which bin I threw it in."

"Okay..." Evan opened the lid of another one. "So what am I looking for?"

Anna leaned over her can and poked around in it gingerly. They both wore plastic gloves, but she still didn't enjoy the prospect of digging through the trash. "I guess all the trash bags look the same, don't they?"

Evan laughed. "Yeah. They look like trash bags."

Eoin, on the other hand, looked like he couldn't wait to dive in. "Which one do I get to dig in?" he asked, his eyes wide in anticipation. Anna had offered Sammy the chance to stay and join them, after she brought Eoin back home, but unsurprisingly she declined the offer.

"There's no easy way to do this. I'll take this one. Eoin, you can look through that smaller bin," Anna said, pointing to the gray bin at the end of the row. She really didn't like how much he was enjoying this. She could only imagine what he was going to tell his mother next time he spoke to her — and what kind of earful she'd get from *her* mom in return.

Anna took a breath and started hauling bags out of the bin and dropping them on the ground around her. Evan shrugged and followed her lead, digging into the second bin. Eoin dove headfirst into his bin, his skinny legs dangling briefly before he pushed himself back out, dragging a trash bag after him.

"Well this is clearly from the kitchen." Evan held up one bag. "Are you sure the bag we're looking for is just from George's room?"

Anna nodded, so Evan put the kitchen trash in a separate pile. "One down." He looked around them. "About eleven more to go."

It didn't take long to empty the bins and discard the trash bags that were definitely not what they needed. That left them surrounded by six bags of trash, spread around them on the ground.

Anna gave Evan her most appealing look. "I'm really sorry. But there's a good chance the poison was in that bottle. We need to find it."

Eoin reached for a bag, but Anna put a hand out to stop him. "Sorry, buddy, but we need to be careful with this. We really don't want to miss it. In fact, what I need you to do," she added when she saw Eoin's face drop, "is double check, each of us — two sets of eyes are better than one. And I know you don't miss a thing, do you?"

"It'll be me pleasure," Eoin replied proudly as he moved to the center of the pile where he could easily see what the two adults were pulling out of the bags.

Evan pushed his already rolled up his sleeves farther up and opened the first bag. "Remind me what I'm looking for."

"It's a white, plastic tub. Not labeled. About yay big." She held her hands in a circle to show the diameter of the tub. "It held a cinnamon-scented lotion."

Evan nodded and looked into the bag, poking around with a gloved hand. "There are a few things in here that might fit that description."

Anna stopped her search through the bag she'd torn open. "Pull them all out. I'll need to look at them."

"And why this particular bottle of lotion?" Evan asked.

"It's the smell. You'll see."

They kept digging through the bags, creating a line of white bottles and tubs along the path.

"Cousin Anna, look," Eoin called out in a surprisingly loud voice.

Anna glanced at the bottle Evan held. "Yes! I think that's it."

Evan held up the bottle, turning it in his hands to examine it. He removed the lid and held it a few inches from his face and sniffed. "I smell cinnamon."

"Exactly." Anna stood up excitedly. "That's the one."

She kneeled down next to Evan to get a whiff of the near-empty bottle. "I don't know a whole lot about nicotine, but I heard a story about parents almost killing their teenage son by accident."

"With nicotine?" Evan asked incredulously. "How can you accidentally kill someone with nicotine?"

"They were using what they thought was an herbal remedy. I know," she said, seeing the look of astonishment on Evan's face. "Nicotine does have some positive qualities and there was a time — a lot of years ago — when tobacco leaves were one ingredient used to help with skin rashes, things like that."

"You mean like what George had?"

"Not exactly, no. But anyway, these parents put this

'herbal' cream all over their son, hoping to help him." Anna made air quotes with her hands to make clear her opinion of this particular remedy. "The doctors who ultimately saved the boy's life determined later that if they hadn't put him in the bath right after applying the cream, he wouldn't have been in so much danger."

"But they did," Evan said.

"They did." Anna nodded. "And it turns out that nicotine is most lethal in a warm, humid environment."

"Like when George took a hot shower in the morning," Evan said.

Anna nodded. "But the problem is, when it gets warm it smells kind of fishy. No way anyone would put that on them without noticing it."

"Hence the smelly lotion," Evan finished the thought.

"Was the boy all right?" Eoin asked, his eyebrows raised and his forehead furrowed.

"Oh yes, don't worry, the boy was fine." She smiled brightly, immediately regretting having shared that horrific story in front of Eoin. "The doctors figured out what was wrong and treated him. He was fine. But everyone involved knew what was going on... the parents, the boy. They weren't trying to trick him, so they didn't need to mask the smell of the poison."

Anna looked at the mess around them as she thought through her idea. "If George was used to using this smelly lotion for his eczema, he might not have noticed that it smelled a little off that morning. He said he used it all over. If the killer put enough liquid nicotine in there..." She chewed on her lip. "Typically, it would be hard to get a dose large enough to be lethal. But in the heat of the bathroom, it just might have worked."

She started grabbing the bags, retying them and tossing them back into the bins with Eoin's help.

Evan went into the kitchen and returned with the bottle in a plastic sandwich bag. "I'll take this to the department, see what they can make of whatever's left in there."

Anna turned toward him, a trash bag in one hand, a stray hair blowing across her face, and grinned. "Thank you, Evan. For listening to me, and taking me seriously."

He raised the sandwich bag in a sort of wave and left through the kitchen.

Anna went back to tying and tossing the bags into the bins. Now she knew how George had been poisoned; she just needed to figure out who had done it. And the best way to figure out who, was to figure out why.

40

Anna closed her laptop with a frown. She slipped off the tall stool, grabbing her and Eoin's dirty cereal bowls and dropping them in the dishwasher. She'd hoped a little research would help her pinpoint who might have had access to liquid nicotine, but it was, sadly, too easily available. Even once the police confirmed the lotion as the source of the poison, that still wouldn't prove who had spiked it.

"Come on, Eoin, we're going out."

He slid off his stool and looked up at her. "Eoin. Where are we off to?"

"Eoin," she repeated.

He shook his head.

Anna let out a huff. "We're going to the library." She had intended to say more, to explain why they needed to go, but his squeak of pleasure made any further explanation unnecessary. By the time she was ready to go, he was waiting in the front hall, jacket on and library books in hand.

The short walk to the library gave her a few minutes to

work though her plan of attack, using what she did know to figure out what she was missing.

"Felicia," she greeted the librarian with a whisper as she entered the library. "I'm glad you're here. I could use some help."

"Of course, dear. Hello, Eoin. What do you — oh, hello BethAnne." Felicia cut herself off as she took the pile of books from the girl who'd approached the desk while they were talking. "You all prepared for today?"

BethAnne took a deep breath and let it out. "I'm pretty sure, Ms. Keane. We have a group reading first, then a game based on the book, then lunch, then the art project, then the other game." She counted the activities off on her fingers as she described them, but frowned when she reached the end and wiggled her shoulders to shift the weight of the large backpack she carried. "We may have too much, actually. We might have to skip the last game."

"What's going on?" Anna asked. Eoin had stepped behind the corner of the desk and was peering out at BethAnne, his eyes wide. Anna recognized the look. She'd seen it every time he looked at Sammy.

"BethAnne and some of her classmates run a program for the elementary school students," Felicia explained.

"It helps gets young kids interested in reading, by making it fun," BethAnne added.

"You mean more fun than it already is, right?" Felicia asked with a mock frown.

BethAnne laughed, causing the beads at the end of her braids to bounce around.

Eoin let out a squeak from his hiding place behind the reference desk.

BethAnne leaned down toward him. "Hello, who are you?"

He squeaked again, but this time he reached out to tug on Anna's arm.

"BethAnne, this is my cousin Eoin, from Ireland."

"Eoin," he corrected her in a high-pitched whisper.

"Eoin," Anna repeated, knowing she still wasn't saying it right. She looked back and forth between Eoin and Beth-Anne, the young boy practically blushing as he stared at the high school student smiling down at him. "BethAnne, I don't suppose you have room in your group for one more student, do you?"

Eoin inhaled sharply as she asked, so she looked down at him. "Would you like to join the reading group BethAnne is running?"

Eoin nodded eagerly. "I would, yes, please, thank you."

BethAnne laughed again. "We can find room for him, no problem." She stood on her toes as she looked around the library, then waved at another teenager, who trotted over. "Theo, this is Eoin."

"Eoin," he piped up.

BethAnne frowned. "Oh, sorry. Anyway, Eoin wants to join the group today. Want to show him where everything is?"

"All right, have fun and be careful. Maybe you'll make some friends." Anna tried to give Eoin a hug but he was already pulling away and following Theo to the back of the library.

"You're on the debate team, right?" Anna asked before BethAnne followed them. "That means you spend a lot of time learning various facts?"

BethAnne nodded proudly. "Ask me anything. Go ahead, try it."

"It's true," Felicia said. "As I told you, they have to be prepared to debate whatever topic the moderator chooses, and they don't always know in advance what the topic will be."

"See?" BethAnne struggled with her backpack, finally

pulling out a box of index cards. "With enough data, I can be ready to argue any point."

Anna laughed out loud, then slapped a hand over her mouth, remembering where she was.

"Okay then, what do you know about liquid nicotine?"

BethAnne looked surprised, but thought about it. "Well... I know that nicotine is a poison. It used to be used as an insecticide because it's so poisonous."

Anna nodded, already impressed.

But BethAnne had more to add as she warmed to her subject. "People who work in tobacco plants get poisoned because of their contact with the tobacco leaves. They get Green Tobacco Sickness. And I know that when it's heated up, nicotine decomposes and produces nitrogen oxides, carbon monoxide, and..." she furrowed her brow. "And some other toxic fumes."

"That's right," Anna said. "It's a lot more dangerous when heated. Then it doesn't require as much to kill a person."

BethAnne's eyes lit up. "I remember current guidelines say that as little as six milligrams could be deadly, but recent research has found that it might be a lot more than that."

"BethAnne, I'm impressed," Anna told her with feeling. "You're a walking encyclopedia."

"I can still do more research," BethAnne said. "Resolved"—she held up a finger, intoning the resolution set to be debated—"that nicotine is a lethal poison."

Anna didn't know if she should be impressed by Beth-Anne or horrified that she'd set the girl on to this disturbing topic. Oh well, surely it was something she could use in a future debate about the risks of smoking.

"She's going to be president one day," Felicia said with a smile as the girl returned to her group.

"I suspect you're right. Very impressive."

"So, what are you up to today?" Felicia turned her smile onto Anna.

"Well"—Anna took a breath—"I plan to do a little more poking around in my neighbors' business."

"Anna," Felicia chided her. "I thought you'd learned your lesson about that."

"I know, I did. But this time it's different." She glanced around the library to make sure there was no one else within earshot, then lowered her voice even more. "This time, I know how George was killed."

"You do?" Felicia's eyes narrowed. "How?"

"Someone put poison into George's toiletries."

"They did?" Felicia asked, surprised. "How do you know?"

Anna thought about their adventures in the trash cans the evening before, and the fact that the police hadn't yet confirmed the lotion as the source of the poison. "Never mind that, just listen. George's lotion was poisoned—"

"With liquid nicotine!" Felicia interrupted her.

"Shh." Anna looked around again. "Yes, that's right. So my question is, who had access to his room to put the poison into his lotion?"

"Well, you can cross Paul Murphy off that list," Felicia said as she bent to stack some books under the desk, waiting their turn to be re-shelved.

"What do you mean?"

"I did some snooping of my own." Felicia stood and Anna saw she was grinning widely.

"Felicia, you didn't."

"It just came up in conversation. And maybe I asked a few questions." Felicia didn't make eye contact, returning instead to organizing the books under the counter. "But anyway, the point is, Paul was in Atlantic City the day George Hedley checked into Climbing Rose Cottage."

"Okay, but what about later that night? He could have

sneaked in." Anna pictured the muscular man pulling himself up the side of her house and climbing in a window.

"Really?" Felicia looked up skeptically. "I guess so... but no, actually, he couldn't have. Because he spent the evening with Janet Turner." Felicia widened her eyes as she spoke.

Anna didn't have to pretend to be shocked. She really was. "What?"

Felicia nodded. "They were seen together. Dinner at the Red Taverna then walking hand in hand toward her house. And if I know anything about Janet..." Felicia paused to offer a dramatic voice clearing. "He was there all night."

Anna laughed. "He has an alibi. And someone who can vouch for him. That's great."

"Well, it is for him, anyway."

"So there's no way he could have messed with George's lotion." Anna chewed on her lip. "That still leaves Richard Gormley."

"Anna, we've been through this. I just can't believe that of Richard."

"I know, I know." Anna agreed. "But he was there, it would have been easy for him."

"You'd be better off trying to find someone angry enough to actually commit murder. Richard simply isn't that angry."

"Angry? You're right. I do know someone angry enough."

41

The room smelled of sweat and testosterone. Mostly sweat. The stench attacked Anna's nose as soon as she entered the small gym. Frankly, calling it a gym seemed overblown. It was basically a basement room filled with weights, workout equipment, and a bunch of sweaty, smelly, grunty men. Anna wrinkled her nose and looked around.

Success. Jason had his back to her, holding a weight bar over his shoulders as he did squats. She could see his expression in the mirror in front of him as he squeezed his eyes shut with each repetition, clearly pushing himself to his limit.

She'd checked out two other locations before finding him here, using the few comments his aunt had made on Sunday to develop her short list of where he might be this afternoon. She'd also put off searching for him until after an early lunch at her favorite cafe. She was not eager to confront him again. Or to make him angry.

Fortified with potato leek soup and half a chicken breast sandwich, Anna took a deep breath and walked toward Jason.

His eyes shifted as she approached, watching her. She

gave him a friendly wave in the mirror and pointed to the side of the mat to indicate she'd wait for him. He grunted and did another set of squats. She watched him strain against the weight, pushing himself particularly hard for the last few. His hands shook when he finally dropped the bar back into its stand and turned toward her.

He grabbed a towel off the rack and wiped himself off as he approached her.

"What do you want?" he asked gruffly.

Anna smiled, trying to keep calm. The last thing she wanted to do was make him angry again. "You're pretty good at that," she said. "Impressive." Was she overdoing it?

He glanced in the mirror, flexing his muscles more than seemed strictly necessary just to wipe the sweat off his arms. "I have to be in shape for the season," he said, his eyes still on his reflection. "The beach opens next month."

"Right, makes sense." She looked around the room. "So do all the lifeguards work out here?"

Jason shook his head and shut his eyes for a moment. He let out a breath and opened his eyes. "You didn't find me here to ask about the gym."

"No. Right." Anna shifted onto her other foot and straightened her jacket. "Actually... uh... I need to ask you about Richard Gormley. I understand you know him and his wife?"

"Richard and Susan?" Jason wrinkled his brow in confusion and tossed the towel over one shoulder. "Sure. So?"

"It's just you didn't mention that. I mean, I didn't know you knew them."

Now Jason was looking at her like she was insane. "When would I have mentioned that? While I was chatting you up in the bar? Or when you were tipping off the cops about the club?"

"Right. No." Anna looked down at her hands, clasped tightly in front of her. "Look, I am really sorry about that."

"Sure." Jason took a few steps back toward the mat. "I got a few more sets to do. Is that all?"

"No, it's not. I've heard from other people that you have some... well, to be blunt, some anger management issues. And from what I saw..." She raised both hands in a question.

"Yeah," he mumbled, grabbing the towel again and wringing it between his hands. "So what? I'm working on that. What's that got to do with you."

"You were angry at George, you told me that yourself."

"Are you kidding me?" The redness started from his neck and slowly spread up his face. "Are you serious? You think I killed George?"

Anna took a step back, looking around the room to assure herself that there were plenty of other people there who could come to her aid if necessary. None of them seemed to care about Jason's angry outburst. Maybe they were used to it from him.

"I didn't kill George." He spoke through tight lips, but his voice was relatively calm. "Why would I do that?"

"Because you're a friend of Richard," she answered in a quiet voice. "And I've heard that Richard really didn't like George Hedley."

Jason scoffed. "I know him, sure. But I'd hardly say I'm friends with him and I certainly wouldn't kill for him." He headed back to the mat. "Plus, Richard and Susan are fine. They didn't want George dead."

Anna let out her breath as Jason's color returned to normal. "George's partner, Paul? He thinks you're a hit man. For the mob. And that you worked for George."

Jason turned back to her and laughed loudly. "Seriously? Wow, you are full of fun information today."

Anna joined his laughter. "I know, funny right?" It was funny. Right?

"Look. Anna. Clearly you and I are not going to be friends. So just tell me what you want to know and let me get on with my workout."

"Okay." Anna stepped closer to the mat where Jason was now getting a feel for the amount of weight he had on the bar. "Where were you on Tuesday night, when George checked in?"

He looked her in the eye as he answered. "I was at the club. You know that. I told you I saw George that night."

"Were you there all night?"

Jason shook his head. "I got their later. Earlier, I was at a bar with some friends. Ask your buddy Luke. He can vouch for me."

Anna couldn't hide her surprise at hearing that. "Why were you with Luke?"

Jason gave her an inscrutable look, then shrugged. "I was with a bunch of guys. It's just something we do every Tuesday night."

"We?"

"Yeah. We. All the guys from the football team."

"What team?" Anna asked in frustration, not understanding what he was saying.

Jason dropped the bar back into its holder with a sigh and walked back toward her. "Our high school?" he said, as if speaking to a child. "Over the years, guys who've graduated but are still around, we meet up on Tuesdays. To share stories, talk about the old days, you know."

"You went to high school with Luke?"

"Not at the same time," Jason answered, his focus back on his reflection. He flexed the muscles in his chest, checking himself out. "He graduated a few years before me. But we were both on the football team. He helped me out a bit when I made the team, coached me, that sort of thing."

"So you're friends?"

"Really not." Jason's eyes shifted between his own reflection and the weight bar, clearly losing interest in this conversation. "Turns out your buddy Luke is a liar and a traitor."

"Oh." Anna gulped and felt her hands tighten into fists. She definitely did not want Jason worked up again. She'd find out about Jason's past with Luke some other way. "So then how about Wednesday morning? Where were you then?"

Jason glared at her, his anger returning. "I wasn't anywhere near your B&B before Saturday. Got it?"

"Got it." Anna put both hands up in front of her, acquiescing to his statement without challenging it. "So, does Luke know your secret?"

It was amazing how visibly Jason's anger could rise. Anna watched the redness creep back up from his neck. "He does now," he said in a low voice. "Thanks to you."

"I'm really sorry about that," Anna said, but Jason wasn't listening. He'd returned to the bar and his weights.

Anna tucked her hands in her pockets and left the gym. She could think of an awful lot of reasons why Jason couldn't possibly have killed George. He had so many people who vouched for him and his character. She'd met his aunt herself. Even the fact that he was with Luke the evening George checked in.

But she couldn't shake the thought that he still had one very big reason why he might have done it. Not for Richard Gormley, but for himself. To keep his secret.

42

Anna hooked her jacket over the coatrack by her front door and sighed. Now what? She stared straight ahead where the doorway to Aunt Louise's rooms stood dark. She walked closer, putting a hand against the wall to steady herself, and closed her eyes. She really needed to go into those rooms. This was getting ridiculous.

A soft touch against her leg reminded her that she wasn't alone. She bent down to Tough Cookie, who purred as she walked circles around Anna's ankles. She tickled the cat behind the ears as she picked her up, hugging her close. Tough Cookie relaxed into the embrace, her purrs deepening until her whole body seemed to shudder with them. Anna held her closer, feeling Tough Cookie's vibrations like a massage against her chest. She waited a moment, enjoying the feeling, then loosened her hold.

The cat opened her eyes wide and stared at Anna.

"Oh no, now what?" Anna asked the cat. "What are you trying to tell me now?"

The cat was prevented from answering by a loud crash

from the fourth floor. "Oh good, Luke's here," Anna said as she put Tough Cookie down. "You'll have to tell me later."

She found Luke back in the Royal Room, picking up paint cans that must have somehow gotten knocked over. Empty paint cans, thank goodness.

"Hey Luke," she said to get his attention when he didn't seem to have noticed her. "Do you have a minute?"

"Hey." He glanced over at her. "Give me a sec to clean this up, I'll meet you down in the kitchen."

Anna trotted down to the kitchen to put some tea on and wait for him. She paused as she passed the mirror in the front hall, smoothing her hair and straightening her sweater.

She sat at the kitchen bar, her hands wrapped around a mug of peppermint tea, waiting for Luke. Her feet tapped against the metal bar that ran around the leg of the stool about six inches off the ground. Why was she nervous? She was just waiting to talk to Luke.

Her nervousness dissipated as soon as he entered the room. He came straight over to her and enveloped her in his arms, squeezing her close to his broad chest. She let herself relax against him, taking comfort from his strength.

Finally, he pulled back and looked her in the eye. "Is there any tea for me?"

"Of course." She laughed as she slipped off her stool to get his drink. She felt his eyes on her as she moved around the room, reheating the water, letting his tea steep.

Once back on her stool, two mugs of tea in front of them, she looked up at him.

"How can I help?" he asked.

"Ha!" She let out a laugh that sounded more like a cough. "I really wish you could. But... I don't know." Could she tell him about her investigation? He clearly wanted to help. It would be so easy to tell him everything, let him advise her. Take care of her. "It's about George and his death."

"Of course." He nodded as he took a sip from his mug.

"I found some things out," she started. Then stopped. If she told him about her investigation, told him everything, surely his desire to help her would take over. He'd do whatever he needed to do to keep her safe. And she didn't want him to take over. "I wanted to ask you about Tuesday night," she said instead.

"Tuesday? The night George and the other guests checked in?"

"Jason said you saw him out that night. At a local bar."

"That's right." Luke put his mug down and rested one hand on her leg. It felt good. "I go out with that group every couple of Tuesdays or so. Just to rehash old stories, you know how it is." He grinned and she felt herself smiling back at him.

"Did you see Jason the whole time? I'm trying to figure out if he could've come back here, slipped in and... you know..."

"Poisoned George?" Luke asked with amazement. He shook his head. "Of course I didn't see him the whole time. I wasn't keeping an eye on him or anything. He could have slipped out, come to your house and made it back again without being missed."

"How about Wednesday morning? I don't know where Jason was on Wednesday morning."

Luke shrugged and leaned a little closer to her. "I don't know where he was. He wasn't at the gym, I can tell you that. I was there early. And," he said, grinning again, "lots of people can vouch for me, if you're wondering."

Anna blushed. "I wasn't, I promise." She felt herself leaning in toward him, watching the sexy wrinkles around his eyes as he returned her gaze, the muscles of his shoulder moving under his T-shirt. Whatever he was doing at the gym, it was working.

"Jason seems to think pretty badly of you. What's that about?"

Luke grinned and Anna felt a shiver pass through her. "He's just sour because he didn't make quarterback for the team. Back when he was still in high school, I helped coach him for the tryouts. When he didn't make it, he blamed me. Thinks I told the coach he wasn't good enough."

"And did you?" Anna whispered.

Luke leaned even closer. "I told the coach the truth, what I really thought. I always do."

"Hello?" A voice called out as the doorbell jangled. "Anyone home?"

"Crap." Anna almost fell off her stool as Luke leaned back suddenly.

Detective Walsh pushed through the door from the lounge. "There you are. Oh good, Luke Arnold. Just the man I'm looking for."

Luke stood and the two men faced off, eye to eye. "What can I do for you, detective."

"Just a few questions, if you have some time?" Walsh kept his voice pleasant, but Anna was pretty sure Luke didn't really have a choice about whether or not to answer the questions. "I understand you spend a lot of time here, at this house."

Luke nodded but added nothing more.

Walsh waited a beat, then continued. "So you were here when the guests checked in on Tuesday? When George Hedley checked in?"

"I was here, but not for long. I washed up my tools and left while Anna was getting all her guests settled."

"Uh-huh," Walsh muttered, making a mark in his notebook. "And can you tell me where you were later that evening and the next morning."

Luke threw an amused look at Anna. "I think I can just about remember that."

As Luke filled Detective Walsh in on everything he'd just told Anna, she found her mind wandering. To Patrolman Evan Burley. Why wasn't he here with Detective Walsh? She didn't know if she felt relieved or disappointed. She blinked as she shook her head. She needed to get her mind straight about the men in her life. She couldn't like both of them, could she? Plus, the last thing she needed was another boyfriend.

When she brought her attention back to the kitchen, Detective Walsh had finished questioning Luke. He stuffed his notebook into his pocket and put a hand down on the counter top.

"I appreciate you answering my questions. You've verified what we already knew. And that tells me that you do not have an alibi for the night George checked in. We checked with other men you were out with that night. No one is willing to swear that you were there all evening."

"That's ridiculous." Luke said. "Why would I kill George Hedley?"

"What?" Anna jumped up. "What are you saying? Luke may not have a watertight alibi, but he has no motive."

Walsh shifted his attention to Anna briefly, then addressed Luke. "I'm going to need you to come down to the station with me. We've got a few more questions to ask you."

Luke threw his hand in the air. "Fine. Let me grab my jacket." He slammed out of the kitchen and Anna could hear him stomping toward the coatrack.

She grabbed Detective Walsh before he could leave, holding on to his arm. "What are you doing? Why? Luke didn't kill George. I know it!"

Walsh raised his eyebrows. "You do?"

"Well"—Anna released her grip on the detective—"I can't prove it. But I'm sure of it. He just wouldn't. Plus, he had no reason to."

"That you know of."

Anna took a step back. "What are you saying? Luke didn't even know George."

"Is that what he told you?" Walsh asked sharply. "Did he tell you he didn't know George Hedley?"

Anna's eyes opened wide. "No, he didn't need to tell me. I mean, if he did know George he would've told me that."

Walsh stared down at her, his gaze fierce, his face set in a firm mask. "Luke Arnold may not have known George Hedley. But he knew Paul Murphy. Very well."

"Everyone around here knows everyone else." Anna pointed out.

"But not everyone is related to the one person who benefits the most from George's death. And not everyone had easy access to this house and George's room. And not everyone—"

"Stop!" Anna cut him off. "You're taking the close connections everyone has in this town and twisting them around, making them seem... nefarious. Just because Luke is somehow connected to Paul doesn't make him a killer."

"It's a lead. And I follow every lead." Walsh said. "Which is why we're going to interview him. To get at the truth." He frowned down at Anna. "We will find the truth, don't you worry. And"—he held up a hand—"don't get involved."

43

"I can't tell you how glad I am you're here." Anna hugged Sammy again, for at least the fourth time in the past ten minutes.

As soon as Sammy had heard the panic in Anna's voice over the phone, she'd asked an employee to cover the bakery and had dashed over to be with her friend. They now huddled on the sofa in the lounge, Anna in tears, Sammy doing her best to comfort her.

"I'm glad I'm here, too, honey." Sammy put an arm around her friend's shoulder. "Mark can handle the bakery this afternoon. It's really just a matter of closing and cleaning up at this point. And I could tell you really needed me."

Anna gave her one more hug. "I can't believe they arrested Luke."

"You said he wasn't arrested. Just brought in for questioning," Sammy reminded her.

Anna shrugged and wiped a tear from her eye. "What's the difference? They clearly think he killed George."

Sammy raised an eyebrow. "Are you really sure he didn't?"

"What?" Anna almost screamed the word. "How could you ask that? Of course he didn't."

"Okay, sorry, sorry." Sammy put an arm around Anna once more. "I just... I needed to ask, that's all."

"Well, I'm sure." Anna's eyes narrowed. "I'm not so sure about that beast, Jason, though. You saw how angry he can get. He could do anything in a rage."

"I agree with you there," Sammy answered with conviction. "I hope I never have to see him again."

Anna sniffled and looked over at her friend through lowered lashes. "Are you sure? Cause I was kind of hoping..."

"Hoping what?" Sammy asked, a warning in her voice. "You do not want to go find Jason, do you?"

"Well..." Anna sniffled one last time, then sat up straight. "Why not? He must have told that detective that Luke didn't have an alibi. He's clearly trying to pass the blame on to someone else. And he definitely hates Luke. Doesn't that just scream guilt?"

Sammy bunched her lips up as if about to ask a question, but said nothing.

"And we know he has a secret he wants to keep," Anna added.

"True." Sammy let out a breath. "But that doesn't mean we should talk to him. We should leave that to the police."

Anna stood. "The police who think Luke did it? They're not going to talk to Jason again. They think he's this helpful guy who pointed them in the direction of Luke."

Anna put her hands on her hips and stared down at her friend.

Sammy stared back and didn't move.

"Fine, then I'll go myself." Anna ran to the coatrack and grabbed the field hockey stick she'd left leaning against the wall the other night. "But this time, I'm taking this."

Sammy laughed out loud. "Why? In case he wants to play field hockey?"

Anna narrowed her eyes and glared at her friend. "If I'm going to go confront Jason, I want to have something to defend myself with."

Sammy rolled her eyes, let out a deep breath, and stood. "Fine. I'm coming with you."

❦

ANNA PULLED OPEN THE DOOR TO THE CAPE MAY lifeguard headquarters and stuck her head in. Five men stopped what they were doing and turned to look at her.

"Can I help you?" The oldest man asked, looking up from a desk where he was working.

"Hi, sorry to bother you, I'm looking for Jason Enright."

One of the men whose back was to her spun around in his chair and glared at her.

"Oh, hi Jason." Anna said. "Do you have a minute?"

"No." He answered and spun around again.

"What's going on Jason?" the older man asked.

"Yeah, something you want to tell us?" A younger guy poked Jason with his pen as he wiggled his eyebrows. "What have you been up to?"

The other men, who ranged in age, all laughed. They clearly thought Anna and Jason were having a lover's tiff. Well, that was fine with her, if they got him to talk to her.

"Come on, Jason," she said, pouting. "It'll just take a minute. You know we need to talk about it."

Jason spun around and glared at her again. "Fine. But then this is it, right?"

Anna shrugged and stepped back outside where Sammy waited with their weapons. She handed Anna her hockey stick and held on to her umbrella.

"Really? An umbrella?" Anna shook her head as she took her hockey stick. "What were you thinking?"

"Hey, it's what I grabbed, okay? You headed out pretty fast."

"Fine."

"Fine."

The two women jogged back down the steps to the beach to wait for Jason, holding their weapons inconspicuously at their sides.

Jason came down the steps at a slower rate, taking his time and checking the women out as he walked. He had grabbed a football on his way out of the office and tossed it casually. He seemed less angry today. At least, less red. Anna hoped that was a good thing.

"I'm here. Talk," he ordered.

"You told the cops to talk to Luke. You told them he didn't have an alibi."

"You think I set the cops on Luke?" He laughed. "Well, that's a hoot."

"Why?" Sammy asked, her eyes narrowed.

"Because you're the ones who set the cops on me, remember? Not the other way around."

"And I apologized for that," Anna responded through gritted teeth. "But I'm not sorry anymore." She tightened her grip on her hockey stick and saw Sammy doing the same with her umbrella. They were ready this time. They could defend themselves if they needed to. "I think you did it, Jason. You killed George."

Jason threw up his hands as he tossed the football and laughed again. Loudly. "Why on God's green Earth would I kill George Hedley?"

"So many reasons. To keep your secret? Or because you were doing a favor for Richard?" Anna realized she sounded like she was fishing, so changed tack. "But you definitely set the cops on Luke."

Jason grinned. "Yeah, I did that." He tossed the football in the air a few more times. "So?"

"So, did you kill George? You never said you didn't." Anna pushed.

Jason threw the football up one more time, then shook his head. "I didn't do it."

"Why should we believe you?" Sammy asked.

Jason shrugged. "No reason at all. But I have no idea why you should even care."

"Because it's Climbing Rose Cottage, Jason. Don't you get it? It's my baby." Anna glared at him as she stepped closer, now wielding the hockey stick in front of her. "Your actions have threatened my baby."

"Whoa." Jason put his hands up in surrender. "Mama bear. I get it. But I didn't do it, Anna." He stepped back and dropped his hands, still gripping the football. He looked her in the eye. "I didn't do it."

Anna felt Sammy step next to her. "Should I hit him with the umbrella?" she asked.

Anna grinned at the thought. Then remembered what he'd done to the vase. "No. I guess not. He says he didn't do it. He didn't kill George."

"You believe him?" Sammy asked, wide-eyed, as Jason grinned.

"Of course not." Anna answered, not taking her eyes off of Jason. "We'll come back once we have proof."

Keeping their weapons high, the two women backed away from him, farther down the beach. Anna couldn't help but notice the bemused expression on Jason's face as they left.

"Let me know if I can help," he called out after them.

They shared a look, turned and ran.

They made it back to Climbing Rose Cottage, out of breath and trembling.

Sammy leaned back against the front door and said, "Scofflaw."

"Definitely." Anna agreed, grabbing the ingredients from the kitchen.

"He must have done it, Sammy. I know it wasn't Luke," Anna said a few minutes later, looking at Sammy over her cocktail glass.

"I know, honey. It's ridiculous. As if luscious Luke would ever kill George Hedley. It doesn't make any sense." Sammy sniffed and drained the last of her drink. She threw herself back onto the sofa. "That sure did help."

Anna stood up from the couch and paced around the room. "I don't know what to do, Sammy. I have so many questions."

Sammy raised both hands in an exaggerated gesture. "Did Richard hate George enough to kill him? Do we trust Jason when he says he didn't do it? Did Paul find a way to slip out on Janet Turner, come over here and spike George's lotion?"

"Exactly. And that's just for starters." Anna shook her head. "I'm sure there's something more, some evidence, that we haven't thought of yet. We just need to take a step back from it all."

Anna thought about all the years she'd spent poring over data, trying to figure it out, trying to see the patterns, not just correlations but causes as well. "Whenever I struggled with a thorny problem at school, I'd walk away for a while, you know? Do something completely different. Focus on a different problem or read a book or just do something that redirected me."

"And that helped?"

"Yep." Anna nodded. "It's like if I gave my brain a chance to mull things over, I'd think of things I hadn't before."

"Okay. So we're too close," Sammy concurred and stood to join Anna. "What can we do that will take our minds off it, enough to let us see things clearly? Watch a movie? Go grab a coffee?"

Anna slid her eyes toward the darkened doorway that led to Aunt Louise's rooms. "I know exactly what I need to do."

"Are you sure you're ready for that?" Sammy asked, her eyes following Anna's gaze.

Anna nodded but didn't move. "It's been hanging over me for too long, weighing me down. But I can't do it without you."

Sammy moved closer to Anna. "I'm right here."

Anna squeezed her hand into fists and walked determinedly to the doorway to Great Aunt Louise's rooms.

"Breathe, Anna. You gotta breathe." She heard Sammy's voice behind her in the hallway, but her eyes stayed focused on the closed door in front of her. The door that led to Aunt Louise's bedroom.

With bravery born of a best friend and a classic cocktail, Anna turned the knob and opened the door.

44

The room was neater than she'd expected. The police must have searched here, but unlike in the rest of the house, they seemed to have left things as they found them. Respect for the dead, perhaps? Or at least respect for Louise Gannet.

Anna heard Sammy step into the room behind her as she crossed to the armoire. The doors stuck a bit and she had to pull harder. They opened with a *crack* that made Anna jump.

Inside, Aunt Louise's clothes were neatly hung and folded. Anna picked up on the odor of the cedar planks she must have used to keep the moths at bay. Glancing over the clothes, she saw shades of green and brown, colors she remembered Aunt Louise always wearing, struggling to find clothes that didn't clash with the bright red hair color she shared with her niece. Anna ran a hand along the hanging shirts, feeling the softness of the silk and cotton.

"She had good taste." Sammy said from across the room as she pushed a sash window open. "I remember she always looked beautiful."

Anna nodded and felt a lump growing in her throat. She coughed and closed the doors.

She turned instead to the bookshelf against the next wall, running her eyes along the spines of the books she could see. The shelf wasn't quite as neat as the rest of the room. Some books lay on their sides or propped above other books. She saw books on history, anthropology, archaeology, biology, but also mysteries, romances, classics and others.

"She loved to read." Anna said, remembering Aunt Louise settled into her favorite chair in the lounge, a glass of sherry on the table next to her. "Anything and everything."

Her tears returned, but she didn't bother trying to stop them. She felt drops running down her face, falling onto her sweater and even onto the book she held in her hand. She blinked and returned the book to the shelf. The fresh scents of the garden came in through the open window and she took another deep breath, trying to calm herself.

"I'll need to sort through everything," she said, trying to sound brisk but knowing she sounded more like a little girl. "It would be easier if Luke was here to help." She sniffed.

"You won't be alone," Sammy told her. "I'll be here. I'll pick up some storage tubs and we can label everything."

"Thank you," Anna said. "You really are the best. In the process, I can figure out what to keep and what to give away." Her hand trembled as she reached out to touch a ceramic figurine, one of several that lined a windowsill. Figures of women from the eighteenth century, in fancy dresses and hairstyles, each no more than three inches tall. In a way, they were beautiful. Not something Anna would typically want to have, but did she really want to give them away when they were clearly important to Aunt Louise?

"You don't need to decide right now what to do with things," Sammy said. "There's plenty of time for that."

Anna sat down on the big, soft bed, almost falling into it.

She put her hands behind her to sit up and ran them along the satin bedspread. A group of picture frames huddled together on the nightstand. Anna picked them up, one by one. With each image of herself, her family, her parents, she felt more tears come. She stood and resumed her exploration of the room.

In the low chest she found drawers full of clothes, but also linens and lace doilies, fluffy cotton towels and delicate silk scarves.

These were just things, she told herself, looking back around the room. Things that may have mattered to Aunt Louise but didn't make her who she was. They were remnants of Louise's past. They all looked pristine, unused. As if Aunt Louise had been saving them for a special occasion. A special occasion that never came.

"To be honest, it's all a little spooky, don't you think?" Anna whispered.

"Are you talking about Aunt Louise's things? Or the fact that you're on the trail of a murderer?"

Anna winced. "Probably the latter." She spun around to face Sammy. "It's true. I am scared about the murder. And that makes me mad. Why should I be scared, in my own home?"

Sammy shrugged. "You shouldn't be. But I can see why you are. What's to stop you from being the next victim?"

"Thanks so much for that." Anna grimaced. "But you're right. Evan said Detective Walsh wasn't likely to pay any attention to me or my ideas. They're still interviewing Luke, and meanwhile the real killer's on the loose."

"And visitors are still afraid to stay at Climbing Rose Cottage," Sammy reminded her.

Anna scowled at Sammy. "Yeah, that too. If the police would publicize what they know about the poison — what I found — then at least the rest of the town would know what to watch out for."

"And that your B&B isn't deadly."

"Then again, in the process they'd probably announce that Luke did it, so that wouldn't help."

Anna turned back to the dainty items in the last drawer she'd opened. Doilies, lace tablecloths and napkins. She could picture Aunt Louise talking about her travels through eastern Europe and knew these were items she'd picked up there, where all the lace was handmade and dirt cheap. The sound of gulls broke into her reverie. Such a familiar and comforting sound. But they reminded her of something... what was it?

"Seagulls." She said, turning slowly to look at Sammy.

"Yeah, I hear them, too." Sammy replied, keeping her eyes on the shoes she was sorting through. "There are some good ones in here, you could give some of these away."

"Sammy," Anna said more sharply to get her friend's attention. "She mentioned the seagull. Don't you get it?"

"No." Sammy looked over at her.

"She lied. She lied about being here."

45

Anna tapped her phone to end the conversation and looked over at Sammy.

"That didn't sound great," Sammy said. "At least from what I could hear of your end of the conversation." Sammy had hovered over Anna's shoulder when she'd first placed the call to Evan, but eventually gave up trying to listen in and now was perched on the window seat in the lounge's bay window.

Anna shook her head as she dropped the phone onto the coffee table. "No, not great. I mean, Evan was great, as usual."

"Oh, really?" Sammy raised an eyebrow and Anna felt herself blushing.

"No... I mean... look, Evan listened to my idea, that's all I'm saying."

"Right. And what did he say?"

"He said he'll pass this new idea on to Detective Walsh," Anna answered with a frown.

"Not promising."

"Definitely not." Anna slumped down on the sofa next to

Eoin, who'd been watching them silently. Which, this afternoon, made for a change.

Eoin had come home full of stories about his day. "Then she explained what the book was about. Then we took turns reading it. Then we played a game where we each got to be a character. Then we drew what we thought the characters looked like. Then —"

Eoin finally stopped for a breath and Anna jumped in. "I'm so glad you had fun, Eoin. It sounds like a fabulous day, and you clearly like BethAnne." She laughed, then realized Eoin was staring up at her.

"What?"

He grinned, all of his teeth showing. "You said Eoin."

"I did?"

He nodded. "Say it again."

"Eoin."

Eoin threw his arms around her in a hug, looked up at her, and kept talking. "So after we drew the pictures then she asked the younger kids to read a different part of the book. They were funny. So then we all worked with the younger kids to help them draw their pictures. And then we had lunch and I got to sit next to BethAnne. And then after lunch..."

He'd gone on like that for another half hour. Now she understood what everyone else had been telling her about the boy. He could talk. A lot. But once the conversation had turned to murder, he'd sat back and listened.

Sammy looked out the window for a moment, then turned back to her friend. "Okay. Now what?"

Anna slid down until her head was resting against the back of the sofa, her legs splayed out in front of her. "I don't know. I really don't. I'm sure I'm right."

Sammy came over and slumped down on the other side of Eoin. "I believe you. I do. But you have to admit, it's not exactly firm evidence."

"I guess not." Anna toyed with the fringes of the white cashmere throw that lay over the back of the sofa. "I still don't understand how anyone could commit murder in this town without everyone knowing about it the second it happened."

"Ha!" Sammy laughed. "Don't forget, some people know how to keep secrets. Just look at Jason."

"Ahem," Eoin coughed. He reached into his pocket and pulled out his worn notebook, flipping through the pages. "You could use this," he said, his eyes scanning his pages.

"Use what?" Anna asked.

"I have lots of stories here that I heard people talking about. And when one person talks, then someone else says the same thing later, to someone else."

"Gossip, you mean?" Anna asked, sitting up in surprise. "You've been writing down the gossip you hear in town?"

Eoin nodded. "My mum always says gossip is dangerous because sometimes it's all lies, but sometimes it's true."

"Hmm." Anna slouched down again. "But how can I use gossip?" She cast a suspicious glance at Eoin. "You didn't overhear anyone talking about George's death, did you?"

Eoin shook his head solemnly. "No, Cousin Anna. I was just listening to what you said to Patrolman Evan and thinking about the gossip, and I thought, what if you told people in town about what you found."

Anna's brow furrowed. "Kind of like my own version of a press conference?" She looked down at Eoin. "It could be dangerous, you know."

"What could be dangerous?" Sammy asked. "I'm not following."

Anna grinned at Eoin and the boy smiled shyly back. "Okay then," Anna said. "That's it."

Sammy pushed herself up on the sofa. "What's it? We are not going back to Jason, do you hear me?"

"No, no"—Anna waved her hands and jumped up from the sofa—"I know exactly what to do."

❧

"WENDY!" ANNA CALLED OUT AS SHE, SAMMY AND EOIN entered the kitchen goods store.

Wendy turned from where she was helping another customer, offered a quick wave and held up a finger, then went back to her work.

"Tell me again why buying kitchen supplies is going to help?" Sammy asked quietly, watching the other shoppers warily. "I don't think they sell poison here, do they?"

Anna shook her head as she laughed. She picked up a few items, as if looking them over, then replaced them. "I said I want the police to hold a press conference, but there's something we can do that's even better. Just try to look casual."

"Oh, right." Sammy pushed her hands down into her pockets and started whistling as she wandered the few aisles of the store, Eoin close on her heels.

"Not like that," Anna caught up to them and hissed in Sammy's ear. "Like you're actually shopping, you know?"

"Ooh." Sammy's eyes fell on a retro bowl mixer and she trotted over to it. "I love this color. It would look fabulous in my kitchen."

"There you go, that's better."

"Better what?" Sammy asked, turning a confused expression toward Anna.

"Never mind."

Anna left Sammy and Eoin browsing the aisles and checked out the other shoppers as she pretended to shop. She recognized Carole, aka Coral, from church yesterday. She hadn't expected her to be here, but maybe that made it even better. She didn't recognize the other two women in the store. Perhaps locals she hadn't met yet, perhaps visitors to the town. But it didn't matter, as long as Coral stayed long enough to overhear.

"Sammy, see that woman?" Anna indicated her with her chin. "The really mean-looking one dressed in peach?"

"Sure," Sammy whispered back. "Why?"

"I need you to engage her in conversation. Get her to stay in the store for a little while. It looks like she's ready to check out, but I need her to hear this."

"Got it." Sammy touched her nose with one finger and made her way with Eoin toward their prey.

Anna moved around the store, casually picking up items, waiting for Wendy to be available. Hearing the seagulls while in Aunt Louise's had made her realize that only one person had been in George's room and lied about it. But as both Sammy and Evan had pointed out, she had no way to prove it. This was the only way she could think of exposing the truth.

She'd identified at least five new cooking utensils she couldn't afford but really wanted before Wendy came over and tapped her on the shoulder.

"Hi Anna, how are things?" she said in a low voice, looking around the store before focusing her attention on her. "I'm so glad you were able to join us on Sunday."

"I am too." Anna put a hand on Wendy's arm. "Thank you for taking care of me, I can't tell you how much I appreciate it."

Wendy patted Anna's hand and muttered a few kind words.

Anna stepped back and raised her voice. "Things are great right now, actually."

Wendy took a step toward Anna, keeping her voice low. "I'm glad to hear that. Has something happened?"

Anna kept her voice loud, despite Wendy stepping even closer. "You could say that. I know who killed George."

"Oh." Wendy's eyes opened wide. "How do you know? How did the police figure it out?"

Anna glanced at Coral out of the corner of her eye before replying. As she'd expected, the woman was watching her closely. "They didn't. I did." She cast another glance toward Coral. "It was something she said to me on Sunday, in fact. She said something that proves she was in the house when she shouldn't have been."

Now it was Wendy's turn to take a step backward, but she kept her voice low, speaking in almost a whisper. "What did she say?"

"Oh, just a comment about the condition of my house." Anna replied loudly.

"That seems very vague." Wendy wrinkled her forehead. "Are you really sure?"

"It may seem vague to you, but the police won't think so."

"The police?" Wendy had forgotten to keep her voice down and once again threw her hand up over her mouth as if that could prevent her customers from hearing what she'd already said.

"Oh yes," Anna said and nodded. "I'm going straight to the police from here."

"Are you sure that's wise?" Wendy had recovered her whisper. "You're casting aspersions again, Anna." Everyone else in the store had stopped what they were doing and watched Anna and Wendy with open curiosity. Wendy put a hand on Anna's arm and tried to move her toward the back of the store, but Anna resisted. "Remember what happened with Richard Gormley, Anna. Are you sure you want to do this?"

Anna grinned and raised her voice even more. "Oh yes, I'm sure. And I'm going to tell the police."

One of the other women had moved to stand in front of the register, and now she coughed to get Wendy's attention.

"I'll be right there," Wendy called over to her before leaning toward Anna. "Please be careful, dear."

"I will, I promise," Anna said as Wendy trotted over to the register.

Sammy casually sidled toward Anna and raised her eyebrows. "So, did that accomplish what you hoped?"

Anna glanced around. The other customers, including Coral, had returned to their shopping. "Too soon to say, I guess, but I bet it did. I just don't know if I should be happy about that. Or terrified."

46

"He's angry, isn't he?" Sammy asked.

They were back in Anna's lounge and Anna was back on the phone with Evan while Eoin finished his dinner in the kitchen. "Shh." She waved a hand to push Sammy away.

"Fine, I understand." She said into the phone. "I'll see you tomorrow." She tapped the phone and tossed it onto the coffee table.

Sammy put her head to one side and turned her lips down into an exaggerated frown. "I'm sorry honey, but how did you expect him to react?"

"I expected him to take me seriously," Anna said, fuming. She paced around the room to work off her anger. "I told him the whole plan. I told him I could use his help."

"And he said he'll come over tomorrow, right? I heard that."

Anna glanced sideways at her friend, nodded and kept pacing.

"Well what did you really expect," Sammy was saying. "I

mean, think about it. You told him you went shopping and gossiping in town."

"I know it sounds crazy." Anna threw her hands in the air. "But I'm telling you, Eoin's right. The gossip chain in this town is fast. I'm sure by tomorrow everyone will know what I was saying."

"And if you're right, about who did this to George, she'll be pretty mad," Sammy pointed out. "Are you sure this is wise? You're setting yourself up as bait."

Anna rolled her eyes as she shook her head. "Not really. I mean, what could she do?"

"Oh, I don't know, kill again?" Sammy slid back onto the window seat and stared out the window.

Anna walked over a put a hand on her shoulder. The setting sun cast long shadows across the yard. Fingers of darkness approached the house, slowly covering the grass and the pile of rubble that used to be the shed, approaching the wide porch.

"And what if it wasn't her?" Sammy asked. "What if Jason really did kill George?"

Anna shook her head and tightened her grip on Sammy's shoulder. "First of all, it was her. I'm sure of it. But if I'm wrong, then nothing. I mean, she'll be annoyed that I'm spreading rumors about her, but that's it."

Sammy turned in her seat to look up at Anna. "Or?" She raised her eyebrows.

"Or what?"

"Or, Jason follows through on his threat." She leaned forward in her seat, warming to her theory. "Think about it. The police already have Luke in their sights and thanks to us, everyone will know you suspect someone else. He could kill you now, too, and walk away with everyone else taking the blame except him."

"Oh." Anna dropped her hand from Sammy's shoulder and resumed her pacing. "I guess I didn't think of that."

"Mm-hmm." Sammy narrowed her eyes as she watched Anna pace. "All right, enough of that. Let's do something. Do you want another drink?" Sammy gestured toward the bottle of bourbon on the sideboard. "We have enough to make more Scofflaws."

Anna chewed on her lip as she shook her head. "I'm not in the mood."

"Okay." Sammy walked across the room and grabbed the TV remote, flicking through the options available at a streaming movie site. "How about some popcorn and a movie."

Anna stood next to her, watching the titles scroll by. "I guess. But, oh no"—she gave an exaggerated shudder and pointed at one of the titles—"nothing scary, please."

Sammy laughed and the two friends scrolled until they found a romantic comedy they could both enjoy.

With some difficulty, Anna managed to get Eoin into bed. Not asleep, but at least he was tucked in with a book and a flashlight. She knew he'd drop off soon, after the excitement of the day. Then she ducked into the kitchen to produce two bowls of popcorn, water for her and a soda for Sammy. She dimmed the lights then joined Sammy under the cashmere throw to enjoy their movie.

As the opening credits finished, the front doorbell jingled.

47

"Tell me you locked the door," Sammy whispered, grabbing the remote control to pause the movie.

Anna shook her head. "I ... I don't remember."

"That's kind of an important detail." Sammy's whisper sounded frantic now.

The two women grabbed the blanket and pulled it higher up to their chins.

They watched, wide-eyed, as a shadow moved across the doorway that led to the front hall, shrinking as the figure moved closer. They heard a light step, then a creak from the floorboards, then the figure stood in full view.

"Mrs. Hedley. What are you doing here?" Anna asked, the blanket still tucked up around her chin.

"Hello, girls. Nice evening?" Catherine grinned. Anna preferred her sour face.

Sammy looked at Anna, then pushed the blanket away and stood up. "Catherine Hedley, I assume? I'm Sammy Shields. And I'm here to help Anna."

"How nice for you." Catherine's puckered face had returned and she glanced around the room as she spoke. "I'm here, to... uh..." She focused her gaze on Anna, who remained sitting on the sofa. "I'm looking for something that should have been in George's suitcase. But it wasn't there. I'm sure that was just an oversight on your part."

Anna stood slowly, keeping her gaze firmly on Catherine. She knew how surprising, and how strong, the woman could be. "There's nothing here that belonged to George, Catherine. I put everything in that suitcase." She paused, then allowed herself a small smile. "Or gave it to the police."

Catherine's eyebrows shot up and she spoke through narrow lips. "You did what?"

Anna's courage rose with her anger. "You accused me of murder, Catherine." She took a small step closer to the woman. "You told other people that I killed your husband. You made me feel guilty." She balled her hands up into tight fists at her side as she spoke. "I felt *bad* for you."

Catherine took a step back and tightened her grip on her ever-present triangular purse. "Don't you come close to me."

Sammy took a step closer as well. "Why, what will you do? There are two of us." She glanced at Anna. "You were right about the gossip channel. Works even better than a press conference."

Anna took a breath, wanting to stay in control and not let her anger get away from her. "Absolutely." She took another step closer to Catherine.

"Stop right there," Catherine hissed.

Anna and Sammy froze where they were, both staring at the tiny gun Catherine had pulled from her purse.

"You have a gun?" Anna asked, her voice breaking.

"Are you serious?" Sammy asked.

Catherine grinned again and waved the gun at them. "Now, back down on the sofa. Both of you."

Neither of them moved.

"Don't think I won't use this. As you seem to know, it

won't be the first time I've killed someone." She looked back and forth between the two women. "I didn't expect two of you, but that's no problem. I have plenty of bullets."

Anna held her hands up in front of her, thinking frantically. She hadn't counted on the gun. She slid her eyes toward Sammy, but Sammy looked as scared as she was. She looked back at Catherine.

"You can't be planning to just shoot us. Not after you took so much care to make George's death look like an accident."

Catherine took a step closer. Anna and Sammy both took a step back toward the sofa. Don't sit, Anna thought, hoping Sammy could read her mind. We're better off standing, then at least we'll have a fighting chance.

"George was my husband," Catherine said in a calm voice. "I had to be more careful with him. You are nobody to me. No one will connect me to a random break-in at your house." She let her eyes roam around the room. "Too bad you tried to stop the thief yourself. I've heard that you like to pretend to be a cop."

Anna tensed when Catherine's gaze moved off her, but Catherine must have sensed her plans and swung the gun back to her.

"You must know the police will link the shooting to your gun," Sammy pointed out. "I mean, you had to register it, right? So they'll know it's yours."

The gun wagged as Catherine shrugged and offered another tight grin. "I'll simply tell them the truth. George brought it with him. He always carries it when he travels down here. Never know what kind of trouble you might encounter."

"But I know he didn't. It wasn't with his things." Anna said.

Catherine laughed, only her mouth moving while her eyes stayed focused on Anna, the gun still pointed directly at her.

"But you'll be dead, sweetheart. You won't be able to tell anyone that. Obviously, you stole it instead of packing it away with his things when I came to get them. You had it in the house, tried to use it to defend yourself when someone broke in, and ended up getting shot with your own gun. It's a common enough story." She looked around the room again. "It will be easy to make this look like a break-in, though I can't see what you have in here that anyone might want to steal."

"That's a pretty good story," Sammy whispered to Anna, who grimaced in response.

Anna kept her hands in the air and shifted her weight, moving one foot closer to Catherine. Sammy saw her movement and replicated it, moving to the side.

"That won't work," Anna said calmly. "The police searched George's things after he died. If he'd had a gun with him, they would have found it. They'll know you're lying."

Sammy opened her mouth to say something, then shut it again at a look from Catherine.

"It won't work," Anna repeated, shifting her weight once more, sliding a little closer to Catherine. *Just keep talking,* she thought. *Keep her distracted.* "You'll have to come up with another plan."

Sammy screwed her face up and glared at Anna. "Please don't help her."

Catherine looked worried now. Tenser. That was good. "So I won't shoot you, then. I'll find another way to kill you."

A black streak moved through the hall behind Catherine, then rubbed up against the doorframe. Tough Cookie! Anna tried not to look at her, tried to keep her gaze focused on the gun pointing at her and Sammy. She shifted her weight one more time and saw Sammy do the same thing.

They weren't going down without a fight.

48

"Anna? Are you in here?" Evan's voice rang out from the front hall as the doorbell jingled.

Everyone moved at once.

Catherine spun around to point the gun at Evan.

Tough Cookie rubbed around her ankles, causing her to miss her step.

Sammy and Anna both lunged at Catherine, jumping on her and throwing her to the ground.

Evan lunged at the same time, grabbing the gun and wresting it from Catherine's now loosened grip.

Evan stood, looking down at the three women on the floor as he popped the magazine out of the gun, removed the bullets and dropped them into his pocket. Catherine lay flat on her stomach. Sammy had landed on Catherine's legs, Anna covered her body. "What's going on here, ladies?" he asked.

Anna twisted her head back to look up at him and started laughing. Then crying.

Catherine shifted as Anna's grip loosened, struggling to free herself.

"All right, come on." Evan grabbed Catherine's arms and

lifted her up as Anna and Sammy both stood. He spun her around and clipped his handcuffs on her wrists.

She looked so tiny standing up against the tall officer. How could such a tiny person generate so much fear?

Anna rubbed a hand across her eyes and turned to Sammy. Both women broke into tears and fell into each other's arms. They hobbled in an awkward embrace back to the sofa.

Anna heard Evan talking into his radio, heard him calling for backup, explaining the situation. She opened her eyes enough to see him gently nudge Catherine into a wooden Queen Anne chair and adjust the cuffs through the back so she couldn't get up then read her Miranda rights to her.

Anna pulled herself away from Sammy and leaned back against the sofa, rubbing her eyes again.

"Evan. I... I don't know what to say."

"I do," Sammy said. She jumped up and threw herself at Evan, wrapping her arms around him. "Thank you. Thank you. Thank you."

Evan laughed, gave Sammy a quick hug, then held her back at arms' distance. "I'm glad I came by tonight."

Glancing at Catherine, who simply sniffed in disgust, Evan moved toward the sofa and perched next to Anna, holding her hands in his. "Your plan sounded too dangerous. Setting yourself up as bait like that. I came to try to talk you out of it, to find a way to change it." He glanced back at Catherine, but she had simply closed her eyes, pretending to ignore everyone. Or perhaps fallen asleep, Anna couldn't be sure.

"I'm glad you came, too," Anna said. "I'm so grateful you're here."

Evan looked down at her hands, squeezed them tightly, then let her go and stood up. His voice took on an official tone. "We tested the container you found. You were right, it contained high levels of liquid nicotine. The smell of the lotion must have masked the nicotine and George just rubbed it all over himself."

Catherine opened her eyes and scoffed. "Is that your evidence? Ha! That's nothing. If you knew anything about nicotine, you'd know that it takes more than just a little liquid nicotine to kill a healthy adult."

Anna's shoulders tightened and she narrowed her eyes, staring at the woman who had just tried to kill her. "I know enough about how the poison works. And apparently so do you. You knew George always put that lotion on right out of the shower. In a hot, humid bathroom. The heat would cause the nicotine to decompose, making it even deadlier than usual. The way George suffered from his eczema, he must have slathered that cream all over himself. Makes sense that when he came down to breakfast half an hour later, he was almost dead already."

"I guess there's no point asking you why you did it," Evan said to Catherine. "I know most murders are committed by spouses and partners. Maybe there's no understanding marital anger."

Catherine didn't respond, but Anna could see the silent gloat in her eyes.

"You think you're so clever," Anna said. "But I know why you killed him. It was the Pink Passion, wasn't it?"

"The what?" Evan asked, clearly confused.

Catherine did not look confused. "Of course it was the Pink Passion." She spat out the words, glaring at Anna. "I found out about the club and was mortified. I'd rather have a dead husband that one who frequents transvestite bars."

"But why do it here?" Sammy asked, throwing both hands in the air. "You could've killed him any time at home."

Catherine's face grew even more bitter. "I needed him to die here. Far away from me, from our home. But the stupid man took the wrong bottle, didn't he? After all my planning, he took the wrong lotion. Stupid man couldn't even do that right."

"Good to know you had a motive." Everyone turned to see Detective Walsh standing in the doorway.

"You really need to get in the habit of locking your door," Sammy whispered.

"Sorry to startle you, the front door was wide open," Walsh said, looking around the room. He looked carefully at Catherine, cuffed to the chair, then turned to Evan. "Good job, Patrolman Burley. Well done. We'll take it from here," he added as another uniformed officer followed him into the lounge. "You coming with us, Burley? We'll need your statement."

"I'll be there in a minute, Detective." He glanced at Anna. "I need to make sure things are safe and calm here."

Walsh eyed the two women. "I'll need your statements, too. Once you're ready to give them."

"Of course," Sammy said.

"Absolutely," Anna said.

Evan approached her once more, taking her hands and gently sliding onto the sofa next to her. "Are you sure you're okay? Both of you?" he added, looking at Sammy.

Anna nodded. "We are now. Just..."

"Terrified." Sammy finished her sentence.

"Terrified." Anna repeated. "But safe now." She let out a shuddering breath and felt more tears coming.

Evan raised a hand and wiped a tear from her cheek. "You did good, Anna. You showed incredible bravery tonight. You, too, Sammy."

"I know." Sammy sighed and slid onto the window seat, leaning back against the wall and closing her eyes.

Anna let her eyes close, too, as she lay back against Evan. He felt warm and safe.

⁂ 49 ⁂

"To us." Sammy held her cocktail glass high. Anna, Luke and Eoin clinked their glasses with hers and they all took a sip. Sammy grimaced. "It's stronger than I remember."

Eoin mimicked Sammy's expression, but then licked his lips. "It's sweet, I like it."

"That's because it's only just noon," Luke said to Sammy, laughing. "You two better eat something with these."

"Ugh, I couldn't eat another bite." Anna held a hand over her stomach.

Sammy had spent the night at Anna's, neither woman eager to be alone after their encounter with Catherine Hedley. After a late start and a brunch of french toast, maple syrup, fresh strawberries and crispy bacon, they had settled down to digest when Luke came over.

Clearly, it was time to celebrate.

"I still can't believe what you two ladies went through yesterday," Luke said, leaning back against the sofa, one arm draped causally across the back toward Anna, who sat next to him. "I'm just sorry I wasn't here to help. Once the cops finished questioning me, I went home and crashed."

Sammy settled into the window seat. "Don't be silly. We know you couldn't be here because of those ridiculous cops."

"Ridiculous cops?" Evan spoke from the doorway. He wore jeans and a windbreaker, his aviator glasses hanging from the V-neck of his black T-shirt. His hair looked mussed from the wind and he ran a hand through it to straighten it out as he spoke.

Anna jumped up from the sofa and Luke frowned, first at Evan then at Anna.

"Evan, we didn't hear you come in."

"You seem to be a little distracted," he replied, looking around the room, his eyes pausing briefly on Eoin, seated crosslegged on the floor, both hands grasping a glass full of a similarly colored pink beverage. "Got one of those to spare?"

"You betcha," Sammy said as she stood. "And don't worry, Eoin's is pink lemonade. I'll be right back with the real thing for you." She pushed her way through the kitchen door.

Anna stood in the middle of the room, first smiling at Evan, who had stopped in the doorway, then at Luke, who was sitting up on the sofa. "I don't think you two have met yet."

"Oh, we met." Luke said. "At the station."

"Right. No hard feelings, I hope. You understand we were just doing our jobs." Evan shuffled his feet as he spoke but kept his gaze firmly on Luke. "Murder investigations aren't easy."

"Sure." Luke raised his glass in a sort of toast to Evan before taking another sip.

Sammy barged into the room waving Evan's glass around. "A fresh Scofflaw for the officer of the law." She passed the glass to Evan then settled back onto the window seat. Evan followed Anna as she returned to the sofa, sliding into the chair that only last evening had held Catherine Hedley. He shifted a little in the chair and raised his glass. "Cheers."

"To you," Anna said. "For being here and saving us."

Luke's lips narrowed, but he took a small sip. "So tell me again how you figured it out."

"It was the seagulls," Anna explained.

"Yeah, I don't get that either," Evan said, shaking his head. "What seagulls?"

"When I talked to Catherine at church on Sunday, she criticized my cheap seagull art. But I took that picture down right after George checked in."

"So if she didn't get down here until after George died," Sammy chimed in, "there's no way she could have seen the painting."

"Exactly," Anna took up the tale again. "At the time, it struck me as odd that she'd seen it, but I figured maybe she had come down earlier. To help George unpack or something."

"Right, but she said she didn't." Evan jumped in. "We confirmed she was in Trenton that morning, and never checked her alibi for the evening before."

Anna nodded. "And when you told me that morning was her first time in my house, I should have made the connection immediately. It wasn't until I had stepped away from the investigation—"

"Going through Aunt Louise's room," Sammy interrupted her.

"Then you figured it out," Evan finished her thought. "Genius."

"But I still don't see why George would put the poison all over himself," Luke said.

Sammy raised her eyebrows and took another drink. Evan looked at Anna expectantly.

She shrugged. "She probably just handed him the lotion,

told him it would make him feel better, and he used it. Why wouldn't he trust her? Then she left and we never knew she was here."

"Ah, the ghost." Luke held up a finger. "You thought someone had snuck in, but didn't see anyone."

Anna put her glass down on the coffee table, linked her hands behind her head and sat back, closing her eyes. "I just feel bad," she said.

"You do? Why?" Luke asked.

She opened her eyes. "I wish I had recognized the symptoms of poisoning when I saw George that morning. I was so focused on my breakfast. My stupid scones. Maybe I could have saved him."

Evan leaned forward in his seat and put a hand on her leg. "It's not your fault, Anna. We don't know if there's anything you could have done. And I have to admit, you did help catch his killer."

Anna turned her head to look at him. "Would Detective Walsh admit that?"

"Ha, of course not." Evan leaned back. "I told him you were the one who produced the vial and suggested we test it, but he didn't take that too well."

"He didn't want my help?" Anna raised her eyebrows.

"He didn't want to hear that he hadn't singled out the critical piece of evidence faster. We took samples of all of George's toiletries, of course, but we were still waiting for the test results. It was only thanks to you that we were able to identify the specific sample to focus on and prioritize that test."

"Maybe he needs to do a better job of detecting next time." Luke mumbled the words into his glass, but everyone heard them.

Evan frowned. Sammy laughed out loud.

Anna felt laughter bubbling up from inside her and let it

out, enjoying the feeling of happiness and safety, surrounded by friends and family. She and Sammy laughed until they cried, tears running down their faces.

She did feel better for having helped catch George's killer. For getting Luke off the hook. And for getting to know George a little bit better in the process. A lonely, unhappy man, awkward around people, looking for a way to relax and enjoy himself.

When she finally regained control, she wiped her eyes with her sleeve and looked around the room. Things would be okay. She had new guests coming tomorrow, and even more booked for the following week. After a start like this, things could only get better. Right?

THE SCOFFLAW

Curious about the cocktail? The term "scofflaw" was coined as the result of a competition in 1924. A wealthy prohibitionist wanted a word that would refer to lawless drinkers. He sponsored a contest and two participants came up with the same term: scofflaw.

Scofflaw the drink was also created in 1924, in the midst of prohibition. But it was created at Harry's Bar in Paris, not in the United States, the name clearly a barb aimed at those poor American tipplers who would be breaking the law if they drank it!

Ingredients:

2 oz. Bourbon or rye whiskey
1 oz. dry vermouth
3/4 oz. fresh lemon juice
1/2 oz. grenadine
2 dashes orange bitters

Combine ingredients in a cocktail shaker, add ice and shake. Serve in a cocktail glass. As with all cocktails, modify quantities to suit your taste!

CAPE MAY

The entire Jersey Shore town of Cape May is a National Historic Landmark, due in no small part to the gorgeous Victorian mansions that dominate the town center — all the colorful gingerbread trim, gables and turrets. How did Cape May, a town that was already a beach destination in 1766, end up with this particular style, you ask?

After its start with rustic lodges and small cabins, the island by the early nineteenth century was attracting well-to-do tourists and boasted a variety of boarding houses, private homes and large hotels. But a devastating fire in 1878 destroyed over thirty acres of the city.

Refusing to be cowed by the disaster, residents of Cape May joined together to rebuild their town. They did so in the style of the time. They rebuilt on a smaller scale, no longer trying to become the biggest seaside resort in New Jersey — simply the best. The homes and businesses that were rebuilt after the great fire remain as perfect examples of late nineteenth-century architecture and design. You can see buildings in Queen Anne, Gothic and, of course, Victorian styles.

While the fire was no doubt a catastrophe, it's the reason why Cape May is so attractive today.

AUTHOR'S NOTE

I hope you enjoyed reading Scones and Scofflaws as much as I enjoyed writing it! If you liked the story, please leave a review on the website of the store where you purchased your copy. I can't tell you how important reviews are to authors! You can find out more about upcoming books in the series on my website, janegorman.com, where you can also sign up for my newsletter and follow me on Facebook.

I've been dreaming of writing my Cape May Cozy Mystery Series for years. Anna is based (loosely) on my beautiful niece, who inspires me with her creativity, energy, drive and ambition. I have no doubt the real Anna will go far!

Cape May is an inspiration for me as well. Only a little over an hour away from my home, Cape May has been the site of too many vacations and weekend jaunts to count, not least of which was my own wedding in the historic beach town. I hope my writing has captured the beauty, joy and peacefulness that the town offers visitors. And the unique nature of each of the many B&Bs there!

While writing a book requires sitting alone at a computer for long stretches, it is not a solitary activity. I would like to thank my early readers and my general writing support group, Jane Kelly, Matty Dalrymple, Lisa Regan and James McCrone. Where would I be without Table 25? I also want to thank Terry Grundy for his accurate and insightful edits and the fabulous Daniela with Stunning Book Covers for this beautiful cover design. I owe a debt of gratitude to Janet Chrzan for her review of my medical anthropology details. I am a cultural anthropologist by training, so I may have taken some liberties with the specifics about medical anthropology – for that, I apologize and take full responsibility!

Finally, I want to thank you, my readers. I write books that I love to read, and if you're a fan of cozy mysteries, then I know we have much in common! Please reach out with any thoughts, comments, ideas or questions. You can contact me through my website, janegorman.com, or my Facebook page. I hope you enjoyed this book and are looking forward to the next book in the series!

Made in the USA
Middletown, DE
09 September 2022